Irma Vep
and the Giant Brain
of Mars

BY THE SAME AUTHOR

The Quest of Frankenstein
The Triumph of Frankenstein
Napoleon's Vampire Hunters
The Devil Plague of Naples

Irma Vep
and the Giant Brain
of Mars

by
Frank Schildiner

A Black Coat Press Book

ISBN 978-1-61227-845-2. First Printing: February 2019. Published by Black Coat Press, an imprint of Hollywood Comics.com, LLC, P.O. Box 17270, Encino, CA 91416. All rights
reserved.
The stories and
characters depicted in this novel are entirely fictional. Printed
in the United States of America.

Prologue

"Just as ripples spread out when a single pebble
is dropped into water, the actions of individuals
can have far-reaching effects."
Tenzin Gyatso, the 14th Dalai Lama

A giant was dying on Mars. Not a human-shaped construct like those of myths and fairy tales—those beings were merely the reflection of the inner desires of humanity to be greater than their fellows—nor was this a metaphoric giant, such as the great leaders of humanity's short existence in the ancient cosmos—such figures were no more than specks of dust compared to this titanic leviathan, who had once ruled over the red planet.

The dying leviathan's death throes shook the very surface of Mars. The races of Mars retreated, knowing the Great Brain's life leaked away daily. The name, "Great Brain," was not an allegorical title, but a simple description of this monstrous horror that had once called all of the red planet its fiefdom.

The Great Brain was a Brobdingnagian organ, a brain whose vastness hid beneath Olympus Mons, the largest mountain on Mars. The titanic structure of stone and sward barely contained the immense tissues and electrical impulses that empowered this dying deity.

The mountain home of the titan shook each day as its power weakened and caused segments of the vast mind to fail and harden. The Great Brain convulsed, seeking a means of preventing its imminent demise—an end that was mere days away. The monstrous mind shrieked as each cell failed, feeling death for the first time in millennia. No longer could it feed on the inhabitants of Mars, or use the bestial "vampires" as its dreaded aerial hunting hounds. Death, formerly a philosophical state that only others faced, finally existed as a reality for the Great Brain.

As more cells and neurons expired, the Great Brain screamed in defiance, disregarding the universe's edict, determined to live another million years. And there was only one place this terrible, vampiric creature wished to rule: Earth. Had it not been the Earthling, Robert Darvel, that had caused the natives to revolt against their living God? That world deserved subjugation beneath its will—a true enslavement, not the distant method that had reduced the inhabitants of Mars to savagery.

Its decision taken, the Great Brain detached a shard of itself and, summonsing what little power it had left, hurled that splinter into the ethereal void.

A lightning bolt sailed from Olympus Mons, traveling towards the blue-green star that appeared only as a distant speck to the inhabitants of the red planet. The thirty-four-million-mile distance was traversed in a mere instant, thwarting the laws of physics through a method known only to the dying god of the red planet.

The bolt struck the Earth, enveloping the closest human near it. At once, the human's mind, once a barely used object, filled with the thoughts, memories, and, for lack of a better term, soul of the Great Brain of Mars.

The human collapsed under the weight of the experience, unable to control the immense energy as it exploded outward.

Then, a secondary explosion rocked the street where the human stood. Fire leaped from a nearby building and the screams of many victims filled the air as the building collapsed.

Ignoring the conflagration, the Great Brain, existing now in the weak, miniscule body of a young human, dusted off his inexpensive clothes and headed into the night. There was much work to do—a new world to enslave…

And so, the Great Brain had tossed its first pebble in the pool that is time and space, transforming the Earth forever.

By appearing on one random street in the city of Saraje-vo, its energy had ignited a bomb in a nearby apartment. The explosion caused the death of a man named Danilo Ilić and his followers—a terrorist cell known as the Black Hand.

Thus, on the next day, 28 June 1914, Archduke Franz Ferdinand and his wife Sophie, passed through the city unmo-lested. The remaining members of the Black Hand, most nota-bly the Chief of Serbian Military Intelligence, Dragutin Dimitrijević, found themselves discredited, and later outlawed. The Austro-Hungarian Empire never declared war upon Ser-bia, never triggering the various alliances of European powers to begin the terrible conflict known to us as the Great War— World War I.

Millions of lives, once lost to that war, survived, shaking the very fabric of the universe. The ripples spread, becoming a tidal wave, transforming the Earth and starting the world anew...

CHAPTER I

Adam Blanc ran down the pedway, pushing aside the swing shift men and ignoring their cries of anger at his rudeness and violation of the basic rules of conduct. One did not walk or run down red pedways; they were for up passage only! You used green for down or waited for one of the public lifts to take you to another level. To do otherwise was a violation of public order. A few citizens vowed to contact the gendarmes upon reaching the distant walkway.

Marseilles level three, western zone, was normally a placid location despite the dozens of taverns, red lotus dream dens, and dance parlors. The authorities received multiple complaint calls. Six separate pedway violations by the same man who had also forced twenty people out of a public lift with a large, silver pistol.

But Adam Blanc arrived at the safe house three steps ahead of his brother, Noël, and their cousin, Abel. He spotted the wild look in their eyes, the blood on their shoes, and waved them inside.

Locking the door and placing a chair under the doorknob, Adam led them to the rear of the house and repeated the procedure. Then, pouring himself a stiff tumbler of American whisky, he downed the smoky liquid in one pull.

"Take one to steady your nerves," he whispered, eyes hard. "I need you both calm."

Noël and Abel complied. Abel's hands were shaking badly as he tried to bring the glass to his lips. Noël downed his drink exactly like his older brother, frowning slightly at the flavor.

They were known to the Marseilles underworld as the Blanc Brothers—a nickname they encouraged, despite the fact that Abel was only second cousin. They looked alike—squat men with straw-colored hair and the battered faces of former pit fighters. They were tough, brutal, dangerous—killers with a reputation for efficiency.

"Noël, you first. What happened?" Adam demanded, opening a cabinet and pulling out an old, gray shotgun.

Noël grunted and looked down at his favorite revolver. Opening the chamber, he loaded the gun with eight new rounds and snapped the cylinder in place. He was the sharpshooter of the three, having been trained in rifles and handguns by the Legion. He still proudly bore the scars from his battles against the Sultanate. Called "Sergeant" by the members of their gang and their enemies, people walked softly around the middle Blanc brother.

Noël finally spoke, his voice a light tenor.

"I was checking on the red lotus shipment. Then Ali and Hector, who stood at the door, began screaming like they were being ripped apart. I ran out with Anais and all we found were their heads. The bodies were gone. Then knives appeared in Anais' and George's skulls and I heard the rest from inside the warehouse. I ran screaming. I didn't have a choice."

Noël looked at his older brother, waiting to hear the swear words that usually followed any act of cowardice or mercy. But they never came. Adam turned his watery brown eyes onto to that of Abel. Abel was the weakest and cruelest of the three, a poisoner, a knife-lover, with a skill for figures. The underworld denizens knew better than to underestimate the youngest Blanc brother, calling him the "Hyena" for his skill at attacking enemies at their weakest point.

"I was leading the count before bringing the scripts and coins to Leon, when the door exploded," Abel whispered. "Someone in black came in and tore through all the counters and the guards. I couldn't get close enough to attack him. I ran when blood starting splashing over the walls."

Abel looked over at the whisky longingly.

"No," Adam said to his brother's unasked questioned. "You won't find your manhood in a bottle. I need you awake You're the mind here."

Abel nodded and straightened his back slightly. He put down his glass and drew a thin stiletto from his sleeve, showing his willingness to fight.

Nodding, Adam chucked his cousin's shoulder in friendly acceptance. Though not as skilled as Noël, or as intelligent as Abel, he was still the leader. He knew the best means of defeating enemies, of finding markets for their loot, and most importantly, who to trust.

"My story is the same as Abel's," Adam explained as he loaded the shotgun. "I was in my office at the club when blood started to leak under my door. Every one of my men, including Lisette the waitress, lay dead. All I saw was someone in black throwing Amir's headless body in my direction. I slammed the door and escaped through the basement."

"Throwing Amir? But he weighs three hundred pounds!" Noël exclaimed, his hand tightening on his revolver.

Adam nodded. "Precisely why I ran. We need to…"

He never completed his statement. They heard the front door locks snap open. There was a creaking sound as the door caught on the chair—though the splintering sound that followed indicated that seat had just been shattered under a terrific force.

Adam stepped away from the door, raising his shotgun and taking a position behind the desk. Abel moved to the side of the door, prepared to spring and attack when the killer stepped through it. Noël kneeled to Adam's left, taking his pistol in a two-handed grip. Silence hung over the Blanc Brothers, an oppressive hush that caused all three to sweat as they watched the door.

A loud explosion of noise caused the door to shake and all three brothers to start in fear. Adam unloaded both barrels into the wood. A pair of huge holes appeared in the center of the door. Adam opened the shotgun and expelled the shells, reloading and grinning at his brother. Noël, never looking in his direction, frowned and shook his head.

Adam was about to ask Noël about his concerns, when a pair of black-gloved hands exploded through the wall. One of the monstrous fists grabbed Abel by the chin, while the other raked his throat. A shower of blood sprayed across the room as the crimson fluid escaped from the Hyena's ravaged neck. The hands vanished a moment later, allowing Abel to tumble to the floor, gagging and grasping his torn neck with rapidly weakening hands.

"*Bordel de merde!*" Adam screamed.

He discharged both barrels into the wall. He glanced in Noël's direction just in time to see a massive cleaver cut his brother's head nearly in twain.

Noël dropped to the ground, his finger unconsciously tightening on the trigger of his gun in his death throes.

Recognizing the danger, Adam overturned the desk and pulled the televisor unit down to his prone position. He entered a series of codes and watched as the picture tube wavered and changed from black to light green.

With infinite slowness an image appeared: a round face with a pouting mouth and heavy bulldog-shaped jowls. A frizzy, curly head of hair that appeared disarrayed, visible even as the picture wavered and attempted to resolve.

"What do you want, frog?" Margery Maggs barked, her voice the harsh, grating cough of a heavy smoker of tobacco or black dust. "It's three o'clock in the Goddamned morning here!"

"Shut up, woman! Tell the Director that we are under attack! Tell him that we…"

Adam's screaming voice cut off as someone yanked him out of the camera's sight.

Margery Maggs flinched as a shriek of agony exploded from the tiny speaker in her televisor. The sound cut off seconds later, followed by the meaty thud of a body striking the ground. Margery caught a sideways glimpse of a black-gloved hand before the screen cut off.

"Bugger," she muttered.

She tried to dial back in the connection, but without success. This was not good…

CHAPTER II

Margery "Mama Maggs" Maggs cursed long and loud, surprised and frightened by the turn of events. Three attempts to return the connection failed, with the same result each time—the party on the other end was not picking up.

This was what she always feared might be her downfall—the need to make a unilateral decision. Her superiors did not allow mid-level managers like Mama Maggs to make decision more important than the day-to-day running of their small area of business.

Mama Maggs frowned, knowing that it made her second and third chin crease and caused a fourth to appear. But she did not care, disinterested in how she looked to others even on her best days. At a moment such as this one, what the Director had once referred to as a "dire event" often resulted in the deaths of everyone involved. The last thing Mama Maggs wanted was to be "cleansed" by the Director's special employees.

A giant woman, Margery Maggs was an institution in the Brooklyn underworld. The daughter of gang boss, Jim "The Zeppelin" Maggs, she'd been the only family member present when Fabrizio Fanucci had gunned him down in a barber chair. In retaliation, Mamma Maggs, already as tall as her father, and stronger than most of his gang, had led the attack that had killed Fanucci and all of his Black Hand members.

Having made her "bones" over the body of a feared killer and his followers, Mama Maggs had made a move that had surprised the entire New York underworld—she'd given away most of the gang's business ventures. Some had viewed this move as weakness, but they were sadly mistaken in the massive woman's motives. Mama Maggs had a plan, one that would mean her continued fortune and longevity.

Unknown to most gangsters, Margery Maggs was a thinker, a planner, and most especially, a businesswoman *par excellence*. She had grown up in the household of her mighty father, watching as he struggled daily with rivals, old and new. The stressor that had controlled his daily life were killing Jim "The Zeppelin" Maggs, causing him to take foolish risks and ignore even the most basic protection rituals. He had known that Fanucci was seeking a means of expanding into Brooklyn, taking over the protection business as well as the other rackets. But instead of keeping Arturo, his best bodyguard, nearby, her stupid Papa had decided to walk about like a baron, surveying his land. His death had been unsurprising. Every Thursday, he got a haircut and shave at precisely nine o'clock in the morning. Even a fool like Fabrizio Fanucci was smart enough to wait until the shave started and then gun his enemy down with a shotgun.

Fanucci had paid for that murder, dying screaming for mercy at the hands of Mama Maggs. After his death, Mama Maggs had only kept two businesses, both of which the New York Mob did not object to her owning and controlling.

The first were a series of bars and restaurants sprinkled throughout the New York/New Jersey area. The food and drink in each of these places were acceptable, even bordering on excellent. The true purpose of these places was to launder money, with gangsters paying in illegal capital and receiving it back, with a percentage kept by Mama Maggs. She currently had arrangements with four different banks, the Prizzi family, the Barzini family, Leo O'Bannon and his organization, and a dozen or so smaller groups sprinkled about the area.

The second was a fencing operation, operating through the Gold Ball Pawn shop business she owned, and a few antique shops. This operation was popular with every thief in the area. The deal was simple: you got a fair, if low-ball, payment in coin, script, or credit, to one of the red lotus parlors in the area. Nobody would claim the gold necklace you stole was fake, unless it really was a forgery.

This honesty in the criminal world was refreshing, and had enabled Mama Maggs to hold a virtual monopoly over the markets. She had also earned extra favor when she had personally cut off the hands of an employee named Ringo who was lying to customers and stealing their goods.

Mama Maggs had a simple philosophy: honesty in all dealings with customers or she would cut off your hand—or worse…

With the explosion of growth over the last few years, Mama's business had flourished, so much so that she needed a partner. Too much money was flowing—it would be simplicity itself for a high-flying gangster to move in and take away all her heard-earned profits. Her arrangements with New York Mob held because of on her ability to self-police and control her two areas of expertise. If the Barzini, Prizzi, or any other group, sensed weakness, they would pounce on her with the ferocity of a shark on a wounded seal.

The Red Hand, an organization of enormous and growing power, seemed to know her dilemma prior to extending an offer. This was frightening, but also reassuring—if Mama Maggs had to live as an employee, best to be one for the biggest fish in the criminal sea. Nobody was bigger than the Red Hand; no group was as insidious and capable in battle. They had managed to intimidate all the five New York families, the small gangs, and apparently much of the east coast of America.

The plainly stated offer had come from a Chicago gangster named Bandello, a brutal little man with tiny eyes, a growling voice, and a willingness to kill anyone in his path. He'd burst in on her one night, slapping aside her pair of lovers with astonishing brutality.

"This is how it's going to be, you see," Rico Bandello had snarled, "Sixty forty. Sixty for the Red Hand, forty for you. You won't lose no money; you might even make more because the Red Hand will take care of you. Got me? Got me?"

"And if I don't say yes?" Mama Maggs had not moved, staring down at the little man with angry eyes.

Rico had smiled, an ugly sight that lacked even a trace of humor. It was the feral grin of a wild dog, one about to be un-leashed to tear apart a soft, weak animal.

"Then my guns will speak and all that'll be left of you is a stain on the wall. I'm telling you the law, skirt. You do what the Red Hand wants, or I take you for a ride. See?"

The gleam in the short gangster's eyes had frightened Mama Maggs, sending her a clear signal. So, of course, she had agreed, immediately seeing a spike in her revenue as the Red Hand's people added to her business.

Bandello had told the truth; the dead had not cost her a cent. In fact, she possessed greater wealth than ever.

Her only other duty was to act as go-between with cer-tain men in Europe. She was only their emergency contact, receiving a small stipend each month for agreeing to keep a televisor set by her bed at all times.

Two years of easy money—until this night.

Her first call had been one that people above her needed to hear about immediately. The question was how? She could not simply call her bosses—they kept her as a very distant block at the bottom of their organizational pyramid. But to not inform them of this attack on their businesses in Marseilles was just as dangerous.

Best to take things in hand and hope everything went well, she thought. Pulling out her journal, she turned to a number and dialed it quickly.

The screen shimmered and shook for a few seconds, be-fore a dark face appeared on the screen.

"*Oui?*" Pierre Gérard asked.

Mama Maggs did not know a thing about this man, only that he lived in the same frog city as the Blanc Brothers.

"Send men to the Blanc Brothers safe house near the harbor. Report in whatever you find in one hour," Maggs or-dered.

Then she cut the connection before the Frenchman could question her orders.

Pulling on her robe, Mama Maggs ran into her office and sat in her high-backed wooden chair. The office was simple, a rarely used area of her house. The room consisted of a large wooden and metal desk, her executive chair, copied from one she had once saw in a bank, and a large framed portrait of her late father on the wall.

Sighing, Mama Maggs picked up a shiny metal microphone from the desk's surface.

"East Union telegram," she ordered.

The desk shuddered and a metallic clicking sound emerged from beneath the surface. A moment later, a red light appeared on the microphone.

Mama Maggs did not know how this device worked, marveling at the machine's ability to create realistic documents. The Red Hand had placed it in her home, though a warning had accompanied the gift.

"Use this here gizmo for anything but Red Hand business and you'll wish you was dead," Rico had rasped her way, accepting a light from his underling.

The giant man at his side was a murderous monster named Brasi, one whose eyes only held death in their depths. Mama Maggs always needed a drink when that man was nearby.

"Louis the Fourteenth chair damaged in shipment, stop. Insurance men sent to investigate, stop. They will report in one hour, stop." She dictated,

She watched as the top drawer slid open. An Eastern Union telegram lay within, which she snatched up and read twice to ensure accuracy. Then, sealing it in an envelope, Mama yelled:

"Scott! Get in here! And bring your delivery man uniform!"

Mama Maggs sat back in her chair and waited as her lover/assistant retrieved one of his costumes. She said a quick prayer to God or the Devil that she'd made the right choices this night.

"Bugger," she whispered again.

CHAPTER III

Pierre Gérard adjusted his cap as he, Anton, and Robert stepped out of his steamer. He grinned at his two compatriots, hoping that the arrogant Blanc Brothers were finally on their way out of the business. The Marseilles underworld did not need another trio of swaggering, poorly dressed, ill-spoken Apaches wandering about the streets, behaving like cartoon killers. The Blancs' behavior had always annoyed Pierre, who indulged in higher, stronger methods of enriching the *Main Rouge* syndicate.

The Gérard gang, as it was known to the few who comprehended their power, was an organization devoted to two distinct areas of criminality: smuggling and bribery. The importation of Red Lotus, diamonds from the Zulu Kingdom, and spices from the east, earned Pierre Gérard and his cohorts five to six times the profit all the brothels, thefts, and other activities the Blanc Brothers engaged in with half the personnel.

As to the bribery, that enhanced the *Main Rouge*'s position for the future. Fully two-thirds of the gendarmes, most of the judges, and almost every politician in Marseilles, received a weekly stipend from Gérard. In return, they obeyed the rare orders sent down from the shadowy man known only as "*Le Directeur.*"

This was modern crime, but one still retaining the savage fury of the past. Pierre Gérard was the perfect example of this new breed. The son of a local smuggler and a Moroccan mother, he had been a street tough who had killed his first man before he'd hit his teens. Someone, possibly even the Director himself, had recognized that a keen mind lay hidden beneath the brutal exterior. They had arranged for Pierre to learn new skills, such as accounting, political science, tax and criminal law, and leadership.

The results of their investment was a gangster perfectly at home in either a corporate boardroom or stabbing a man in the chest for attempting to cheat the *Main Rouge*. They even assisted him by suggesting that his mother, a former barmaid from Casablanca, possessed royal blood. Since Empress Salma was the daughter of the current Sultan of that satellite kingdom, the bankers and business people of Marseilles now treated Pierre with careful respect.

The only unfortunate aspect of his life was the need for occasional contact with men like the Blanc Brothers. Pierre Gérard had kept the Blancs at the proverbial arm's length, sending only the occasional order or suggestion through third parties. Despite that, an emergency such as this one required a personal response.

Dressed in the flat caps and heavy jackets associated with stevedores, Pierre Gérard led his two best men to the Blanc safe house. These two had first stood at his side when they had battled other gangs for power in Marseilles. Between them, they had cowed all the small groups and political organizations within two years, and had received impressive rewards for their effort.

Anton Morin, normally Pierre's chauffeur, possessed a wide, crooked grin that provided a brief glimpse into his inner madness. A handsome man of medium height, dark hair, and a rakishly broken nose, Anton resembled a dissolute playboy who spent his days sleeping and his nights gambling, wenching, and experimenting with the latest narcotics.

Anyone who might come to this conclusion would be completely correct in every aspect. The second son of a wealthy noble, Anton Morin was the embodiment of the spoiled, sociopathic rich kid. Growing up, he had been a terror to every nanny and boarding school, and had devoted himself to committing pranks guaranteed to injure his victims. Pierre had recruited him after watching Anton cut the brake lines of a car.

"Not a clever move, Morin," Pierre had said that night.

He had stepped from the shadows while lighting an American Red Apple cigarette. "If this car is in an accident tonight, the gendarmes will see the knife slices."

"They never did in the past!" Anton Morin had snarled back, waving his thin knife menacingly through the air.

Pierre Gérard had exhaled a quick puff of smoke and nodded at the blade.

"Put that toy away and use some sense. You just argued with that Scotsman, Bond, over his lovely wife. If they die or are injured in an accident, who do you believe everyone will name as their enemy?"

Morin had frowned, and then nodded.

"Sadly, the job is already done. I'd better disable their vehicle to prevent such an occurrence."

Pierre had smiled, glad that the younger man was capable of listening.

"No, I shall have one of my men steal the automobile and drive it into the water. None shall learn of your involvement."

Morin had stared, his eyes narrowing with suspicion.

"Why should you do this for me?"

Pulling out a gold and diamond cigarette case, Pierre Gérard had extracted a small card.

"Call me. I like what I see of you, Morin. You have talents I can use…"

Now, years later, Anton Morin, known as a former race boat driver, served as the personal chauffeur and advisor to the wealthy shipping magnate, Pierre Gérard. His true duties were arranging lessons to enemies or individuals who thought of rebelling against the rules of the *Main Rouge*. Anton possessed a positive talent, born from decades of pranking friends and enemies, at determining the best method of psychologically wounding anyone. Moreover, since he did not possess a drop of empathy in his body, there were no limits as to what he would do for Pierre Gérard.

Robert Ménard, Pierre's valet, looked the part for the position he ostensibly held in Gérard's service. Tall, heavily built, with a fleshy pale face, a precisely trimmed mustache, and a dour expression, few mistook him for anything other than a well-paid manservant. Possessing a dry, biting, sarcastic wit, wealthy men and women often complimented Pierre for having discovered the perfect valet. This clearly demonstrated the lack of awareness that most men and women possess regarding danger.

A perfect manservant in every way, Robert Ménard had spent the majority of his life as a professional killer for the French Republic. Known to a spare few in Paris as the Tinamou, his duties were the execution of terrorists, both foreign and domestic. After the fall of the anti-monarchists, Robert had wisely destroyed his file in the "Black Archives" of the Secret Bureau and vanished under the cover he had played so many times and so well in the past: that of a butler to the wealthy.

The Director, through means still unknown to Pierre Gérard, had discovered the truth of the former Tinamou's identity and had assisted Pierre in recruiting him.

"How do you kill people?" Pierre had asked as Robert stood before him and a lounging Anton.

"By whatever means necessary, Monsieur. I prefer knives to firearms. They're so much quieter and more gentlemanly."

His tone was a phlegmatic monotone, as if he was speaking about the weather.

"A knife over a gun?" Anton had sneered, rising and circling the manservant. "Are you mad or just a liar? It takes really courage to knife a man. Even more to a woman or child. A gun is quicker and less messy."

Robert had languidly raised his left hand, as if he had been about to shrug. Suddenly, without warning, the hand was filled with a long, wide blade, the edge of which lingered an inch from Anton's neck.

"If you say so, Monsieur," Robert had replied, his tone still calm and neutral.

Anton stared at the blade for a moment, his face creasing with fury. Then he smiled, laughing and shaking his head.

"It appears I am the fool today. I withdraw my words. You may be the exception to the rule."

Robert had glanced in Pierre's direction and, upon seeing the nod, withdrew the knife.

"Yes, Monsieur," he said.

Pierre had hired Robert Ménard on the spot, prizing the man's unnatural calm as well as his skills with proper clothing, grooming, and the best societal fashions. Though they occasionally clashed regarding household matters, in the end, the manservant appeared to know best. This freed his employer from one area of concern—a rarity for most men among the wealthy class of Marseilles.

"If these idiots contacted America for foolish reasons, we shall make them regret wasting my time," Pierre said, as the safe house came into view. "No deaths, but a bit of maiming should provide an excellent lesson, no?"

Suddenly, he frowned, not liking the sight before his eyes. The door to the home was a shattered ruin, torn apart by a massive, terrible force. One hinge dangled by a single screw in the frame. There were only few scraps of wood and metal visible.

"Arm yourselves," Pierre Gérard ordered, pulling out his personally-made Apache revolver.

These weapons, legendary in the criminal world, usually consisted of a weak, unsighted firearm placed on a set of knuckledusters, with an attached flick knife. Despising such sloppiness, Pierre Gérard had hired an American gun manufacturer to redesign this French weapon into something impressive and useful.

The result was an Apache revolver capable of defeating any type of enemy. The gun portion fired a .45 caliber hollow point bullet with the accuracy of a modern firearm. The knuckle duster made up the handle and, with the push of a button, extended lethal steel spikes. Finally, a knife emerged from the top with the push of another button. The blade, a thin steel stiletto, could cut a throat, slice open a belly, or remove an eye. A perfect weapon for Pierre Gérard.

Robert Ménard's right hand flicked out and a twelve-inch knife appeared in his hand. The razor edge glimmered in the electric light, casting odd shimmers across his pale face.

A few steps behind the tall valet slouched Anton Morin, a pair of shining silver Marley revolvers in hand. A fan of the western tales of the United States, he practiced daily at quick draw firing and other typical Western gunslinger activities. He wasn't exactly accurate, but his steady rate of fire scared most enemies into fast compliance.

Pierre Gérard stepped to the side of the door and quickly peaked inside. He spotted the destroyed wall as well as the wide-open door next to the shattered wall. He thought he caught a glimpse of a figure in the shadows far from where they stood.

Signaling to his men, he stepped forward. Part of the *Main Rouge* training was spending time with a former professional cat burglar. The man, a retired former soldier named Arthur, had taken the job and imparted his skills for a tidy sum of money. His best lessons were shadowing and moving silently, skills Pierre used to his advantage to help his businesses flourish. After all, if one knew a competitor's secret shipments, it was simplicity itself to rob or destroy the contents and weaken said rival.

Creeping forward with a light, almost painfully slow, stride, Pierre approached the open door. Robert stayed a step behind him, ready to stab or slice anyone attempting to approach his master. Anton moved to the right, his guns raised, aiming for the holes in the wall.

The room before them possessed a thin electric light from a single, naked bulb hanging from the end of a heavy wire. An overturned desk and a shattered wooden chair appeared in their view, as did the legs of a fallen man.

A few steps closer allowed all three to see the arm of a second man behind, the limb reaching like an overturned arachnid towards the ceiling while lying in a thick pool of drying blood.

The shadows surrounding the remainder of the bloody massacre hung like an impenetrable blanket over the small space. Pierre and his men tensed, unable to discern the details as a wave of scents struck them, causing their eyes to tear and their throat to burn from a rising wave of bile. The metallic scent of spilled blood hit them first, a smell they had often experienced in the past. It was the next odors that followed, the true aroma they knew surrounded violent death: the smells of urine and excrement, the contents of the human bowels spilled out at the sudden end of life. The gangsters still felt revulsion at this bizarre function of the human body; an inner fear that came from the deepest recesses of the human mind.

A twitch in the darkest corner of the room revealed the location of the person Pierre had first spotted.

Someone swathed entirely in black straightened, appearing to have his back to the three gangsters. The indistinct shadowy image gave the impression of great height and width, though this could merely be a trick of the eyes.

"Raise your hands and turn around, slowly," Pierre Gérard said.

He nodded to Anton, who dutifully pulled back his gun's hammers with distinct, loud clicks. That was one of their favorite intimidation exercises, a means of frightening even the heartiest crooks in Marseilles.

The figure in black slowly turned, hands held at head level. The sight revealed before their unbelieving eyes caused all three gangsters to stare in open shock.

"*Bon sang!*" Anton exploded. "What in Hell is that?"

CHAPTER IV

"Professor," the Great Brain said, seating himself in his lesser throne.

Touching a button on armrest, he closed the doors and windows and activated the sound shields.

"Report upon your latest test," he added.

The Professor was a man with a wide, oval face, red cheeks that appeared rouged or sun-burned, bulging eyes that denoted great intelligence as well as a touch of hidden madness, and pale colorless hair that looked uncombed. His black clothes stank of machine oil, grease, and a body that hadn't bathed in weeks. A genius in several esoteric areas of human science, the Professor appeared disdainful of even the most basic functions of life. He wouldn't eat, were it not for the Great Brain's insistence that he always operated with prime efficiency.

"Test M six stroke A twelve performed the task with eighty-six percent efficiency," the Professor explained, "There was some incidental damage to the scaphoid bone, which will be corrected through the removal of such inefficiencies. I now have a new alloy made from a metal I created that possesses a tensile strength that exponentially exceeds that of the human anatomy."

He handed his master a gold metal sheet that appeared tissue-thin, yet remained ridged. A series of computations shimmered on the face of the document, almost appearing to dance before the eyes of the former mastermind of Mars.

The Great Brain silently cursed his now-human eyesight, feeling weakened by the simple act of using ocular tissues. The cornea and sclera were outdated objects used by those unevolved creatures. This meaty confinement was a trial he had to undergo, but he was working on a way to start the transformation into something closer to his original self.

"Agreed," the alien mastermind replied, handing back the flimsy sheet. "Have you found a means of preventing rejection and ensured continuation of the cellular entity?"

"Sadly, no," replied the Professor, shaking his head. "My area of expertise is robotics and metallurgy. I find work on biological issues to be… distasteful. However, I did record the cellular degeneration as it occurred in subject M six stroke A twelve. It appears that the longer under the control, the faster the breakdown. The organs weaken and fail at an exponential rate. I believe the heart fails first, and the unit expires."

The Great Brain thought for a moment and asked:

"Could you replace the heart and four of the five vital organs? The brain must remain, yet the other viscera are unimportant."

The Professor's gloved hand ran through his wild hair, further adding to the insane impression he exuded.

"I believe so, but that returns to the original source of concern. We will require a biological agent to prevent rejection."

"That is in hand. I arranged for a brief exchange of technology with a biological expert. Have you heard of Oxus?"

The Professor rolled his eyes, an elaborate gesture that appeared alien on his bizarre countenance. His expression looked as if he was imitating an action he did not fully comprehend, attempting to appear human.

"I am a scientist. I leave such distasteful biological functions to lesser functionaries."

The Great Brain ignored the jibe towards those devoted to the biological sciences. He knew his underling was dysfunctional, but had a brilliant mind—for a human. However, he was limited by his small area of expertise. Human geniuses were like insect royalty, important in their small function, but overall, only important in a microscopic sense.

"Once Oxus provides me with the reagent, you must have replacements for the heart, lungs and other areas of the human body. Start with the replacement of the bones you requested and move to the vital organs. The one area that must remain intact must be the brain. Oxus's chemicals shall prevent neurological collapse in that tissue."

The Professor's eyes widened, then he smiled, his sparkling white teeth appearing false and too large for his thin-lipped mouth.

"My dream comes to fruition," he said gleefully. "But this shall cost a great deal of money to ensure the best means of preventing system failure. The Nimrod shall not agree to an increase in our operating budget."

"I am ensuring a secondary means of income to ensure that the Nimrod's paltry demands are no longer essential to my plans."

"That is something of a shock, sir" said the Professor. "Few are willing to question the demands of the Nimrod. Unless…you plan on supplanting… no, that is too great a risk for any man…"

The Great Brain waved a hand, disliking the use of gestures as a means of communication. Unfortunately, this primitive method sometimes conveyed more information to this unevolved cretinous creatures than speech.

"You leave such machinations to me, Professor. Assemble the items you require and a cost list. I shall utilize our resources, even if it means all will expire after their operations."

The Great Brain turned his throne back to his workbench. Placing a jeweler's loupe in his eye, he picked up the etching tools and returned to his work.

CHAPTER V

Fritz Kramm resisted the urge to berate Mama Maggs, knowing the woman acted in the best interest of the Red Hand. The difficulty was that her actions possessed little insight into the deeper affairs of the organization. Like all criminals, she showed little foresight when confronting situations outside her limited area of expertise.

For example, this situation. She'd done correctly by sending Pierre Gérard and his men to investigate the fearful televisor call from the Blanc Brothers. She should have waited until receiving a full report, but instead she had sent a clumsy dispatch, forcing him to get involved personally. At least, she did not know his brother's identity.

Fritz Kramm was a tall, corpulent man with a jovial face, an oversized jowly jaw, and hard gray eyes that rarely blinked. His massive hands possessed short fingers and appeared capable of great feats of strength—an impression that was quite correct, and one of his characteristics that few men realized. Fritz possessed an outwardly congenial manner that caused those who met him to be charmed by his apparently open behavior. As always, he dressed in understated, well-tailored clothes that added to his air of trustworthiness.

To normal society, Fritz Kramm was one of the most reputable and reliable art dealers in the business. A known patron of the arts, he was an enviable man in the eyes of those who spent time in his company. This was a perfect example of the unreliability of first impressions, for Fritz Kramm was a dangerous man, responsible for more evil on Earth than many of the worst dictators. The second in command of the Red Hand, his primary job was to keep that worldwide crime cartel operating and growing larger each day. If someone needed to be eliminated or recruited, it was his job to ensure either. Failures and disasters, such as the one in Marseilles, were also his responsibility. His brother expressed only a passing interest in such trivial matters.

There was an effective relationship, a symbiotic arrangement, between Doctor Cornelius Kramm, the world-famous plastic surgeon and mastermind behind the Red Hand, and his brother, Fritz, who ran the operational side. The difficulty lay in keeping the majority of those involved unaware of either men's presence. Hence, the reason why Mama Maggs' dispatch represented a potential difficulty.

Fritz considered having the woman eliminated after the current crisis. But the difficulty in that was that he would also have to kill her assistant and reclaim the mechanical desk. Better to have Rico and Lupo show up and give her another scare to keep things nice and quiet.

Fritz pulled a small metal box and a tool kit from an inside pocket and approached the televisor. After a few twists with a screwdriver, he opened up the back panel.

Reaching inside the web-like mass of cables, wires, and tubes, Fritz extracted a pair of loose wires. Stripping the rubber covering and exposing the metal, he slowly laced the thick strands into the small metal box's openings. He then began manipulating unseen parts in the televisor, muttering to himself as he extracted tool after tool from the kit.

Twenty minutes later, Fritz straightened and closed the televisor. Removing a gold and diamond inlayed watch from his vest, he returned the toolbox to his coat and sat down behind the desk.

"What now?" Mama Maggs asked, wringing her hands as she sat in the visitor's seat.

"Now, we wait," Fritz explained. "In eighteen minutes, the Director shall link up with this machine and then we shall attempt to speak to our agents in Marseilles. Until that time, we shall sit quietly."

Usually he was a gregarious man, willing to speak to anyone on any subject. The early hour, combined with the need for secrecy, made him feel disgruntled and determined to make this woman suffer.

Mama Maggs nodded quickly and sat back in her chair. The clock on the wall seemed to be moving even slower than normal. This would be a long wait...

CHAPTER VI

"Bon sang!" Anton exploded. "What in Hell is that?"

The man standing before them, his body hidden in the deep gloom, could be tall or short, wide or slender, obese or emaciated. None of them knew, nor could any recall when asked later. Only one facet of this odd individual remained in their minds, burned irrevocably in their memories for all time.

The face, or more accurately, the mask, enshrouding all features. A pale beak-shaped nose, nearly a foot in length, hid the features and shocked all three gangsters. The beak pointed downward at the tip, resembling that of some terrible raptor. A pair of eyeholes protruded like jeweled portholes at the top of the mask, reflecting a scintilla of colors as the light struck the glass opening.

Pierre Gérard straightened first, raising his Apache revolver and snarled:

"Take off that mask, buffoon!"

The masked man reached with one hand towards the edge of his mask, his movements slow and methodical.

Pierre smiled, knowing that the Director would appreciate his zeal in capturing this crazed murderer with such apparent ease.

Just as he was about to relax, the masked man's black-gloved hands slashed through the air in a blur of motion.

Pierre cried out as something hard and metallic struck his shoulder, causing his gun hand to go numb. The Apache revolver tumbled from his nerveless fingers, clattering to the ground and out-of-sight.

At the same time Pierre yelped in pain and shock, Anton moaned and fell backwards, striking the stained wooden floor with a dull thud.

Robert, unlike the other two, snarled wordlessly and threw one of his knives at the bird-masked man. The attack was merely a ploy, a means of causing his enemy to be off-balance as the former intelligence agent closed the distance between them.

Robert Ménard had used this tactic in the past to great effect against foreign agents, criminals, landlords who asked for their rent, and anyone else who tried to make a demand upon him for money. Thrown knives were poor killing tools, but they were excellent distractions. Cause a man to duck, run a few feet forward, and stab him in one of the guaranteed killing locations. An excellent means of killing an enemy…

At least, in theory.

Instead of flinching or ducking, the bird-masked man slapped aside the flying blade and sped towards Robert. He grabbed the butler's extended knife hand by the wrist and seemed to fall backwards. His legs extended as he fell and propelled Robert forward, his massive body flipping as it struck the distant wall.

The masked man sprang back to his feet and, with a single bound, was at Pierre Gérard's side. A black-gloved hand hammered into the reeling gangster's solar plexus, dropping Gérard to his knees in an instant.

Anton, still on his hands and knees, groped for his guns, looking up as the black-clad masked man ran out the ruined door. Stopping under the flickering electric light of the street, the masked man stopped. Looking upward, he leaped into the air and vanished from sight.

Anton, having located one of his revolvers, stumbled outside and looked up. Nobody was in sight, nothing stirred on the tenement roofs, nor the nearby larger apartment complexes. The only sounds were that of a baby wailing in the distance and a steamer heading down an unseen street, vanishing in the distance.

"Merde!" Anton muttered, trying to shake his head free of the dizziness that threatened to make him ill.

With plodding steps, he returned to the destroyed safe house to check on his boss and co-worker.

CHAPTER VII

"You are trying to tell me," Fritz Kramm drawled, amused and annoyed at the same time, "that a single man murdered the Blanc Brothers, destroyed the safe house, and then beat you three fools without receiving so much as a scratch?"

"Nevertheless," Pierre Gérard snarled back into the blank screen of the televisor, "it is the truth."

The Lord of the Red Hand never appeared on screen and that irritated him mightily. Also, their voices were odd, like those coming out of a poorly working loudspeaker in one of the new factory complexes.

"How? That is the detail you are failing to explain," Fritz replied, his voice dripping with condescension. "By your own admission, you had your odd firearm aimed in his direction as did your two underlings. Yet, all you can tell me is that he wore a bird mask. This is very disappointing."

"Monsieur," Anton said, stepping into the televisor's view, "I found some paper and a pencil and, with Robert's assistance, I sketched what this bizarre creature looked like."

He raised up a quick, yet precisely drawn, sketch of the long bird mask, front and side view. No other details other than the rough outline of a human body appeared on the page.

"If I may?" Robert added, stepping to Anton's side. "I believe the wearer of this mask also wore a round hat. That is a point over which Anton and I are in disagreement."

"How very odd..." Fritz said, recognizing the mask immediately.

Under his guise as an art dealer, he had attended Carnival in Naples and even engaged in some of the festivities. The costumes had impressed him, and he had used the opportunity to disguise his assassins and execute several individuals who stood in the way of the Red Hand.

"*Il Medico della Peste*," he added after a moment, clearly remembering the mask.

Pierre Gérard mentally translated the words from Italian and looked confused as he asked:

"The Plague Doctor? You believe a medical man was our attacker?"

Fritz rolled his eyes, wishing he was visible to his subordinate. Pierre Gérard was excellent at his duties, but the man thought far too much of himself. A sneer or three from a superior would improve him.

"No, not at all," he stated, leaning closer to the screen. "The Plague Doctor is a costume from the *commedia dell'arte* often worn at the Carnival of Venice. It is a famous outfit. However, the presence of such garb is outlandish, to say the least."

"If I may interrupt?" suddenly said Doctor Cornelius Kramm, in a harsh voice, with a lecturing tone. "We shall return to the ridiculous clothing the attacker wore in the near future. I require a closer examination of the bodies as well as the rest of the room. Monsieur Ménard, please pick up the televisor unit and slowly scan the room. You will stop and move as I instruct."

"Yes, Monsieur," Robert replied, picking up the box and slowly beginning to scan the room from left to right.

"Stop!" the man known by his superrich clientele simply as the legendary "Doctor Cornelius" or the "sculptor of human flesh," said as the mutilated form of Noël Blanc appeared on his screen. "Approach the head and bring me within two feet. Good... Now, move several inches to the right." No sounds emerged from the televisor unit for a full minute. "Continue scanning. Stop. Move closer to those holes in the wall... How very anomalistic. Gérard? You stated that you and your minions received blows from thrown objects. Please show me that which struck you and the locations of the attack on your body."

Pierre Gérard smiled inwardly, grateful he had retrieved both objects prior to speaking to the Director. He raised a long throwing knife with a white handle and an odd crest etched on the surface. The second item was a metal spike, a heavy object probably used for constructing pedways, or the new box-like houses that factory workers received as part of their pay.

"The white one struck me in the shoulder. Fortunately, only the handle hit me and caused a bruise," Pierre Gérard explained with a supercilious smile. "The iron nail creased Anton's skull and nearly knocked him unconscious. Our attacker was messy and very lucky."

"Incorrect," Doctor Cornelius said, his metallic voice rasping. "Every single supposition you uttered demonstrates your ignorance of every facet of this affair."

The gangsters winced at the sound, sensing the Director's cold rage.

"My apologies. Please explain, sir," Pierre replied, hiding his embarrassment under a guise of polite behavior.

"I do not have time to provide all the details, but I will explain this much. Your Plague Doctor attacker did not kill the Blanc Brothers. Nor was he inexpert in his attacks upon you three. The fact that you are still alive indicates that that individual's presence here was purely in an investigatory capacity."

"But sir... he missed us both, and we..." Pierre interjected, but found himself cut off by Cornelius' voice.

"The attacker did no such thing. He chose to strike you precisely in a nerve cluster that disarmed you instantly. Then he threw an odd metal piece he found on the premises and creased your minion's skull just enough to injure him, but not enough to cause permanent damage. Do you realize that, had that nail struck your man in the forehead or temple, you would have a fourth corpse in this chamber? It's a real quandary. Keep the weapons in a safe location."

Then Cornelius disconnected from the line.

Fritz, seeing his brother's signal vanishing, said:

"Clean up the scene thoroughly. We shall contact you forthwith by normal channels."

Not waiting for Pierre Gérard's response. Fritz Kramm cut the signal.

He quickly returned the televisor to its normal functions and turned to Mama Maggs.

"You performed your job precisely as required," he said. "You will receive a bonus payment."

Fritz Kramm waved the large woman into silence, not wishing to hear her whiny voice any further. He fully planned on sending Rico and Lupo to deliver the money. This way, Mama Maggs' fear of the Red Hand would remain in place for the future.

More importantly, Fritz wanted to know what had disturbed his normally imperturbable brother. Cornelius rarely demonstrated any form of emotion while dealing with employees. Yet, this time, while speaking to Pierre Gérard, the Lord of the Red Hand had shown irritation, anger, and even, just possibly, a trace of concern. This was unprecedented for so phlegmatic a man...

A face-to-face discussion. That's the only way to ensure security and find out what there was about that scene that disturbed him to such a mighty degree, Fritz Kramm thought as he left his office.

CHAPTER VIII

The masked man climbed through a narrow skylight and dropped to the floor ten feet below. He alighted with nearly no sound, a shadowy figure standing in a gloomy attic. Indistinct shapes and figures cast a peculiar spectral ambiance into the small room, only heightened by the presence of a man dressed as a plague doctor, attired in black garments.

A yellow light rose a moment later, a soft gas glow that illuminated a small area of the room while adding deeper shadows to other locations. The spacious attic was rectangular in shape, with unpainted wood plank walls and a matching floor. Several large trunks lay stacked along one wall, creating an almost claustrophobic feeling.

"You look ridiculous," Irma Vep said, chuckling as she looked up at the masked man.

She covered her mouth with a long slim finger hand and pretended to suppress a giggle. A throaty laugh emerged from between her unpainted fingernails, and her large eyes appeared to dance.

"Thank you," the masked man said, not hiding his annoyance.

He removed the round, wide-brimmed back cap and tossed it onto a nearby trunk. With a few motions, he unbuckled the mask, revealing a tan face with a livid gray scar over one eye. His hair was dark, so much in fact that it seemed to merge with the dark in which he stood.

"Can you tell me why you would go out dressed in that comical outfit without leaving a word?" Irma asked, crossing her long legs as she spoke.

She appeared to vacillate between amusement and annoyance as she stared his direction.

"I needed to ensure that I was not recognized" the man replied. "The choices were plague doctor or one of the spare clown costumes. I chose the former. A clown running about the rooftops and fighting gangsters could send an odd message."

He removed the long black coat, dropping the vestment next to the mask.

"Don't be so sure" said Irma. "An American burglarizes the homes of wealthy criminals while dressed as a clown. That country does appear to attract a theatrical element to their criminals." She shook her head. "You are attempting to distract me. So I'll ask again: why did you head into the night dressed as a plague doctor?"

"Igor heard from an admirer that the Blanc Brothers were fleeing for their lives," the man said, dropping into a small wooden chair. "Their red lotus parlors and other concerns ended up filled with corpses. I tracked them down, but they were already dead. You would recognize the wounds and the destruction. They split open the head of one of the brothers in one blow..."

"What of the doors and walls?" Irma inquired, uncrossing her legs and leaning forward.

"Shattered. They looked as if fists punched through each. Just like the fort. Everything was the same. But I did find something..."

The man reached over to the wall and, with a flick of a latch, unfolded a small writing desk. Pulling out a pen and paper, he drew a crude image and handed it to Irma. The drawing was that of a leering devil, with a protruding forked tongue and narrow eyes, filled with flames.

Irma frowned and grabbed a pencil and a second piece of paper. She sketched for twenty minutes, humming lightly to herself as her trained hand etched out an image with simple, clean lines. Then, sliding the paper his direction, she asked:

"Is this what you sensed?"

The image was that of a leering demonic face, narrow and skull-shaped, with a lolling forked tongue and sharp, pointed teeth. The eyes looked like those of a cat, with fire in each pupil and tiny faces within the flames, screaming in agony.

"Exactly," said the man, nodding. "Is that the symbol of a devil cult?"

"Only in the barest sense," Irma replied, shrugging. "The group called itself the *Amants du Diable*—the Devil's Lovers. They were a group of well-bred academics and their wives who dressed in costumes, held silly ceremonies, and traded wives and lovers for sexual naughtiness. None of them actually believed in any of that rot; it was just an excuse to pretend to be wicked and experiment sexually. I burgled a few, stealing money and any jewelry they possessed for their meetings."

"You said they were a group—past tense?" the man asked, folding the table back into the wall and ripping apart both drawings.

"Yes," Irma replied. "They held most of their functions aboard a yacht, traveling out where nobody could view their idiocy. One day, it sailed away and vanished—never a trace found again. Tales of pirates from Crete, or even the Ottomans, floated about for a time, but nothing came of investigations. Then the Russians moved troops into Poland and everyone was afraid of war until, quite happily, the Czar agreed to a peace treaty with the Prussians. The Devil's Lovers became just another odd tale."

"Given the evidence I discovered, the destruction and similar deaths, I surmise that there is a distinct possibility that the same folks who destroyed the Vampires' gang, did so to those idiots."

Irma rolled her eyes, again looking amused and annoyed.

"We never should have sent you to train with that English detective."

"He was not a detective," the other said. "He was a criminal mastermind. And his training helped teach me control. Something I didn't have until then."

"It also made you very strange—always looking for clues and tiny pieces of non-existent puzzles," said Irma, standing up. "On the other hand, in this case, I believe you are correct. What shall we do next?"

"Only one thread to pull—the man I met this night, the man replied, reaching down to tug off the short boots covering his feet. "His face was familiar. Ask Madame Kezia if I can see her newspaper files. I would like to find out who he is and what his connection to the Blanc Brothers was. Then, possibly, we can find out if he is linked to the other disappearances and deaths. One step at a time."

"Then we are staying in Marseilles?" Irma asked, a smile curling across her narrow, sculpted face. "That is acceptable. We will need to work a schedule of shows out and have Milena make posters by tomorrow afternoon. I will be back, but, Victor…"

"Yes?" Victor Sicarius asked, pausing as he reached for his other boot.

"Pack away the bird mask. Besides looking ridiculous, every criminal in the city probably believes you murdered the Blanc Brothers."

Victor Sicarius smiled for the first time since returning.

"I sincerely hope you are right. I lingered long enough to make my presence known."

Irma Vep rolled her eyes, shook her head and left the room.

Victor heard her shouting to the rest of the troupe, ordering the roustabouts to start unpacking the tents. Pulling off his other boot, he moved mechanically, attempting to determine his next move in this metaphorical chess game.

I hope I can find the other player this time…, he thought as he undressed.

CHAPTER IX

Three hours had passed since Doctor Cornelius Kramm had ended his televisor call when Fritz presented himself to his surgery.

The temptation to rush to his brother's side had proved easy to manage. The Lord of the Red Hand always operated on his free patients in the early morning. Most of these were children with correctable deformities, all from families unable to pay for even basic medical care. By providing his services without charge, Doctor Cornelius enhanced his reputations as one of the great healers in the world.

At first, upon learning of his brother's intention to help the poor with his vaunted surgical skills, Fritz had been skeptical. Men and women around the world paid high prices for the legendary "sculptor of human flesh." His publically acknowledged clients included top bankers, politicians, wealthy heiresses, and heads of state. Secretly, he earned three to four times more income from criminals seeking to escape the authorities under a new flesh mask.

"Why would you waste your time, and money, helping some burn victim that can't pay you a dime?" Fritz had demanded right after the free surgeries had begun.

"Not that I must explain it to you, Fritz, but I shall," had replied his brother. "Consider my reputation. The public and the medical community view me as the greatest in my field, an unassailable genius. The daughter of the King of Naples personally begged for my help in narrowing her nose before her wedding to that Austrian Archduke. I'm unimpeachable and even somewhat intimidating."

The two brothers had been watching a low-end gangster named Manliss receive a beating for attempting to steal from one of their gambling house.

"Yes," Fritz had agreed, leaning against the reflective glass they hid behind whenever visiting the business. "The

41

perfect identity to hide behind when running our other... concerns..."

Cornelius raised one long finger up and shook his head.

"Incorrect. Such a reputation comes with a certain degree of fear. Should there be any hint of impropriety, even a mere suggestion, my label would soon change to that of a dangerous madman with a scalpel. Therefore, I decided to bolster my reputation. I take difficult cases, the nearly hopeless ones amongst the poorest in the community. That work enables me to test my skills against that of nature, as well as earn the respect of a grateful world. Should anyone hint that I may be more than I seem, they would discover great resistance. My patients, their families, the newspapers, and the medical community at large, would fight off such attacks and mention all my good works. I am not untouchable. Even the Caliph or the Pope cannot claim such a position. Yet, I added an extra layer of protection should difficulties arise."

Fritz had accepted the explanation, knowing Cornelius possessed remarkable instincts in such areas. Still, it was such a mighty waste of time and money.

Arriving at his brother's surgery, Fritz had allowed himself to be ushered into the private back office where they often met to discuss business. Accepting a Turkish style coffee from Arturo, Cornelius's personal valet/butler/bodyguard, he had waved the man out and chose to sit in silence in the tiny workspace. The room was simplicity personified—a desk, three chairs, one table, and a brass pen and inkwell. The desk contained a few sheets of blank paper and a box of blank envelopes. No adornments covered the walls, nor were there any windows. It was the perfect space to meet and discuss terrible deeds.

Doctor Cornelius Kramm breezed into the room an hour later, his bald head glistening with a thin layer of perspiration. This was the only means of determining that he had been doing more than meeting with potential patients.

He stood a head shorter than his brother, and there were few similarities between the two. Cornelius was thin, with a triangular shaped face, an aquiline nose and a morose expression. Even when he was content, he rarely ever appeared "happy;" there was always a bitter morose quality to the man, offset only by his uncanny skills with surgical steel.

Locking the heavy wood and steel door, Cornelius settled behind the desk.

"Surgery on the Johnson child went well," he said. "I can give you fifteen minutes before my next patient. A lovely woman, mauled by a gorilla. She's been a seductress and a poisoner in the past, and people believe her dead. She shall do so again to pay us back once I make Madame Haynes look lovely again."

"Very well," Fritz replied, glad to talk business. "Shall we discuss the situation in Marseilles? Your reaction to the murder of our people, frankly, alarmed me. Gérard and his followers do not know you as I do. They accepted your rebukes and reactions without concern. But I know you better and realized your reactions were far from usual."

Cornelius steepled his fingers and asked:

"Do you know how much pressure is required to fracture a human skull?"

"No," said Fritz shaking his head. "I have seen it happen a time or two. Usually with a lead pipe or a baseball bat."

"The answer," Cornelius continued, as if he had not heard the reply, "is eleven hundred pounds. This translates to twenty-three hundred Newtons of force. The human hand is capable of such feats of strength for only infinitesimally brief periods. Even your Cossack friend could not generate such power for the time required to destroy a skull."

"That split skull was done by a cleaver. You could see it still stuck inside the head," Fritz said, his face creasing with confusion.

"That is precisely my point." Cornelius slapped the desktop with his palm. "The blade that sliced Noël Blanc's head in twain was thrown, not swung. The force required for such an attack is far beyond the strength of even the mightiest man."

"How do you know it wasn't swung by a strong arm?" Fritz leaned forward, wondering if his brother had a point.

"The floor," Cornelius said, waving a hand languidly. "There were no bloody footprints near the body. Additionally, arterial blood spray would bathe the attacker from head to foot. Do you believe Gérard and his minions would have missed such a detail on the man whom they thought had performed the assault? Then, there is the wall…"

"Yes, yes," Fritz said, nodding his head. "You saw the holes in the wall. Large and irregularly shaped—probably by a pair of fists. What of it? I have seen Sven do worse when we subdued those gangsters in the Midwest."

"You did not," Cornelius pronounced with a slow headshake. "Those walls were at least six-inches thick, based on the dust and the few bullet holes. The speed and power required to perform such an act is easy to calculate, but impossible for any human limb."

"What about a club or a ram?" Fritz asked.

"Would it be capable of such an act? Yes, of course. But the difficulty now lies in the placement of the holes, as well as the guns present in the chamber. Both holes must be created at the same moment, since the Blanc Brothers could have rained down gun fire upon their attacker in the time required to use a ram or a maul. The short distance between each gap rules out a assaults from two individuals. No, Fritz, a single person shattered that wall with their fists and killed one of the Blanc Brothers in the process. Normally, such a feat would reduce a human hand to a mass of splinters and blood. Yet, somehow, some way, the attacker retained the strength to throw a cleaver across the room and nearly decapitate Noël Blanc. This is why you saw me disturbed when I viewed the scene. We are confronting a power beyond that of modern science. This profoundly concerns me since its motives are still completely unascertained."

Fritz frowned, then nodded once.

"I will book the next available seat to France. I believe Acme Air has a flight tomorrow. I could be in Marseilles in two days."

Cornelius shook his head.

"No. This requires a lethality beyond your skill level."

Fritz's eyes widened and he sat back in his chair.

"You can't mean… using… her?"

Cornelius nodded slowly.

"Yes. Send word we shall double her normal fee if she leaves by morning. If she agrees, contact Gérard and inform him that she is to be in full command and acts as my supernumerary."

Fritz pulled out a red silk handkerchief and mopped his now damp brow.

"I am not convinced this is the best idea," he muttered.

Cornelius stood, removing his watch and checking the time.

"Noted and overruled. Do as I say, then send word to our accountants to perform a random check on the Rooney gang's numbers. Tell them nobody is a suspect, but I think the son has been living a little too well over the last six months."

"Understood," Fritz said, standing up and heading out.

He shuddered at the thought of the forthcoming meeting.

CHAPTER X

Lisandru Matarese laughed as the French pig wept and begged for his life. There was nothing more satisfying in this world than watching a formerly powerful man grovel and beg for his life. Simon Bonheur, once one of the feared men of the Blanc Brothers' gang, knelt on the dirt floor, a sodden wreck of his former self. That was both amusing and alarming at the same time—Bonheur was a respected man in Marseilles. Now he was little more than a shell of his formerly savage self.

"Padrone, please, please," Bonheur wailed as tears streamed down his face. "I will give you whatever you wish! Information… I can tell you all of the Blanc Brother's holdings. Killing? I will execute anyone you name in public if you ask. Only please, please, please get me out of the city! Somewhere far away! Please!"

Everyone in the city knew of Simon Bonheur, known to all as "Le Cratère," the Crater, thanks to his heavily pockmarked face. The son of a street cleaner and a maid, Simon Bonheur had nearly died from the terrible outbreak of Palombian Pox. The disease, which had killed thousands throughout Europe, including his parents, had also cost him any chances of growing up to be a handsome man. Forced to live in one of the many poorly-run state orphanages, Simon Bonheur had run away at fourteen and joined a gang led by another pox survivor named Achille Marteau. Within two years, Simon Bonheur had taken over the gang, after having executed Achille over a fifty franc gambling debt. Afterwards he had served a term in prison for a series of robberies, but the authorities had not been able to prove his role in his many killings, Le Cratère had returned to Marseilles, a hardened criminal, willing to work for anyone and do anything for a sou.

The Blanc Brothers had been his longest employers, having bid for his services early and made him into one of their top agents in the diamond smuggling business. Simon Bonheur had been perfect for the role, loyal to those who paid him well, and willing to kill friend or foe if they broke the gang's rules. During his time in charge of that concern, theft from the couriers had dropped to nearly zero, an unprecedented success.

"First you shall tell me," Lisandru Matarese drawled, pulling out a thing knife and slowly cleaning his fingernails, "why you are so afraid of this new gang. You fought well against the Bonnot Gang, and in the small war against the Ottoman spies of the Sublime Portal when they tried to take over the Fos harbor. Have you lost your nerve for bloodshed, Le Cratère?"

Simon Bonheur shuddered, looking up from the floor and smiling slightly. A hint of his previous character leaked out from behind the shattered man's face who groveled before the Corsican gang leader.

Matarese saw a man who once lived on the razor's edge between life and death. This killer feared nobody—he was capable of any act necessary. Yes, this once daring crook was now little more than a weak, simpering, pathetic wretch, but Lisandru Matarese admired whoever performed this act—the duplicity on Le Cratère's face demonstrated true art on a human level.

This skill set Matarese apart from most criminals. His motives were, in his mind at least, higher than that of your average crook. Most gang members possessed a simplistic agenda... money, easily supplied sexual releases, and power. None of these interested the leader of the Union Corse section in the city of Marseilles. He knew these were mere toys, cheap baubles that vanished as easily as one could obtain them in this world. If he needed money, that was easily available. If he wanted sex, the money bought him anything he wanted. As for the rest, big estates, a new electric Hirondel automobile, who needed such luxury? After a time, those items ended up owning you. The cost of maintaining even a cheap steamer or an alcohol-powered vehicle had forced many criminals to take stupid chances and perform crimes that brought about their downfall.

Lisandru Matarese needed no such trappings of wealth. A child of the Corsican hills, he had learned the ways of life and death from the terrible master of the Union Corse, Angelo Draco. Appointed to this elevated position by the Colonel-Who-Never-Died, Draco had unified the myriad of large and small native gangs into the Union Corse syndicate. He had carefully chosen Matarese, along with his son Marc-Ange Draco, to run things on the Continent. The latter had been placed in charge of the Toulon territory, while Lisandru had been granted control over Marseilles. His slow approach, slowly working his way into areas with minimal violence, had proved successful. Within a year or two, a battle with the Blanc Brothers would have been inevitable. However, those plans now appeared to have been spoiled.

"A day or so ago," Simon Bonheur said, his voice an echo of his formerly snarling tone, "I would have killed you for such an insult. Now… after what I saw… I will take your sneers and scorn. I don't care. Just get me out, fast and hidden… They might follow me if I am seen again…"

Lisandru Matarese leaned forward, stabbing his blade into the wooden desktop. A high-pitched screech from the shattered wood caused the kneeling criminal to whimper.

"Not until you provide me with information about what turned you into a whipped dog smelling of blood and urine. Do so quickly or I will not even bother to kill you. I will simply toss you into the street and make sure this is known by everyone in the city. Do you understand me? Speak now! Your whining and flinching irritate my innards."

Bonheur looked down staring at his shaking hands.

"I was seated in the back office that I used to meet with the diamond cutters. The front of the building is the counting house set up by the Blancs to hide the money earned with each shipment. We had a small package arrive two days ago from Russia. That was when I first heard the screams… the worst sound in the world. I've killed men, women, even children. I am not afraid of death, or having blood on my hands yet...."

"Continue," Lisandru Matarese said, interested despite himself.

Simon Bonheur never looked up, speaking in the same monotone voice:

"The sound was like someone was being torn apart. The accountants started shooting, but the screaming grew louder with each second. I grabbed the rifle I kept behind my desk and opened the door a crack to look outside. The door was..."

That was when the door to the small Union Corse hideout exploded inward.

Simon Bonheur swiveled his head and looked over his shoulder. His eyes widened, and he let out a high-pitched shriek of terror that was cut off a moment later.

Lisandru Matarese's wails of agony lasted only a short few seconds, though the agony he experienced was profound and terrible.

CHAPTER XI

"We go in tonight," Victor Sicarius said as Irma Vep stepped onto his shoulders.

Irma rolled her eyes and exhaled loudly.

"You said that already. I still believe it is a mistake."

Victor stepped forward, feeling Irma's weight shift with each motion.

"I know. You believe this is too easy. I still want you to explain what that even means."

"Concentrate on what we are doing, if you please," Irma said.

She bent her knees, leaped up and somersaulted through the air one and a half times.

Victor raised his hands and caught her, causing their hands to slap together. Then he held her high above his head in a hand stand. They walked two steps in this position, his steps deliberate, her body stiff and unwavering. The oohs and aahs of the watching crowd drifted their direction, though neither responded. They had performed together since they were children, though as members of this circus only in the last few years.

"I can do more than one thing at the same time," he said. "What does too easy even mean?"

He threw Irma into the air. She flipped again, and he caught her legs, throwing her up and stepping forward as she spun over and over, only held from falling by his hands.

"Can we finish this before we debate the merits of burglarizing the Gérard mansion?" Irma hissed back. "Final position, on three... one... two... three!"

Victor bent his arms and threw Irma a little higher. He then back-flipped and landed in a handstand. Irma's feet landed on his and she opened her arms wide, smiling down at the hushed audience.

The crowd erupted into applause and yells of delight. The cheers grew in volume as Victor turned slowly, allowing Irma a chance to bow deeply to the four stands that filled the tent.

Victor's legs bent and threw Irma up once again, allowing him time to spring to his feet and catch her in his arms. She whipped the blindfold off his eyes and they smiled down together at the crowds, forty feet beneath their feet.

Their high-wire act, never announced, occurred randomly daily. It always amazed and impressed the circus patrons. Though aerial acts appeared periodically in circuses that travelled through the region, Irma and Victor's always managed to stun the crowds. Their routine changed each time they appeared, sometimes involving other areas of the circus, allowing other performers to join and benefit from the applause.

"*Mes amis*," Léon Leo, the ringmaster and nominal owner of the circus called out, "Irma and Victor—the defiers of death! You will never know when they grace us again with a performance!"

Bowing again, they climbed down and returned to their trailer, locking the doors tight. Irma whipped off her blond wig, shaking out her naturally red hair and dropped into a seat. She accepted the hot tea Victor handed her and drank deeply.

"Excellent," she said. "I particularly liked the last catch. You did that because of the large number of families?"

She poured herself a second cup.

"Yes," he replied. "The romantic façade causes the mothers and stiff-necked fathers to view us with kind indulgence. The factory workers will receive a different show. Now, can we return to our previous discussion? What does 'too easy' mean? It sounds like a line of dialogue from one of those American Woltz pictures you enjoy."

Irma rolled her eyes and started unlacing her shoes.

"You need to give the cinema another chance, Victor. As to your question, the phrase is simple enough to comprehend. This burglary is meant to be an entry into a millionaire's home. The security is minimal, despite the dogs wandering about the lawns. The walls are moderate height with shards of glass embedded at the top. A burglar with a *soupçon* of brains could navigate that wall with ease. *Mon amour*, this man is a wealthier shipper who's worked with the now-deceased Blanc Brothers. He probably imports half the red lotus in Marseilles alone. Why does such a man not employ a full contingent of guards? Given his high position in the city, he could also call upon the gendarmes as protection. Yet none are in evidence."

"Hidden?" Victor asked, pulling off his shoes and dropping them on top of a trunk.

"None" said Irma, shaking her head quickly. "I searched in earnest. Two theories therefore emerge from this scenario. The first is that this Pierre Gérard, despite being a hidden master of the black markets, is an utter fool. For only a supreme idiot could trust his two bodyguards as his only protection against the rest of the criminal world."

"No, he is no fool," said Victor. "Based on his style of dress and actions in the Blanc safe house, Gérard is a suspicious, dangerous, methodical killer."

"Bravo, you came to the correct conclusion" replied Irma, silently clapping her hands. "I did wonder if you would get there. Then we come to our second, simpler, and quite probably correct, theory: Gérard wishes you to enter because he has something unpleasant waiting for you within the stone walls of his home. In other words, I believe this is a trap. Hence, my statement: 'this is too easy.' We must find another way of investigating this man."

"On the contrary," Victor said, smiling for the first time. "Your deductions only prove my point. We will enter tonight at four a.m. and make sure we perform a particularly memorable act for the third-shift workers that come in for the eight a.m. show."

Irma sighed and ran a hand through her curly scarlet locks.

"When you say such things, I know I will not like your plan. Very well. Pull down the bed and tell me your strategy..."

CHAPTER XII

"Hail to thee, great Mardon. Hail, hail!" the elderly man wheezed as he limped into the Great Brain's audience chamber.

The man, known as "the Lamane," possessed hard, unyielding dark eyes that never appeared to move. He was tall and gaunt with a long, heavy beard that appeared too large for his narrow head. He wore a heavy, shiny white robe and carried a long ash wood staff that looked too heavy for his claw-shaped hand. A thin slash of a mouth peeked out from under his heavy whiskers.

"Greetings, Lamane," the Great Brain replied, not bothering to hide his boredom with the ridiculous rituals.

The Lamane waited for the sacramental responses, staring without expression as the Great Brain stared back without interest. They remained in that pose for ten minutes, neither willing to yield, waiting for the other to break. The Great Brain appeared amused by the contest while the Lamane's anger grew with each passing moment.

A newcomer who stood a few steps behind the Lamane asked angrily:

"Is this the reason you interrupted my work? Am I here to watch you and a man with a well-groomed beard stare at each for hours? If so, may I have a chair and a book?"

He was a tall man with broad shoulders and a barrel chest that appeared to be turning to fat. He had a square-shaped head, a broad, bulging forehead, narrow slits for eyes, and a wide down-turned mouth.

The interruption allowed the Great Brain and the Lamane a chance to break eye contact. They looked at the man. He stared back at both, unmoved by their gimlet gazes and seemingly waiting for an answer.

"Who are you?" the Great Brain asked, interested in this man far more than the Lamane.

"He is a butcher who indulges in alchemy and, I surmise, casting spells, and other such nonsense," the Professor said, stepping away from behind the Great Brain.

The broad-faced man's lip curled up and he stepped forward.

"What is this that I smell? Machine oil and lubricants? I assume a steamer mechanic must be present."

The Professor stopped less than a foot away from the newcomer and spat back:

"You can smell something other than the viscera fluids of human innards? How surprising!"

"Tinkerer!" the broad-faced man snarled.

"Vivisectionist!" the Professor yelled back.

Then they were hugging each other and noisily patting each other on the back. Both men laughed as they spoke, their words indistinguishable to the Great Brain and the Lamane.

"Master," the Professor finally said, stepping aside while keeping an arm across the newcomer's shoulders, "this is my oldest friend and scientific colleague, Jakob ten Brinken. He wastes his life upon medical research and biological scientists, yet he has a worthwhile mind."

"And this is Claus Ad Rotwang," ten Brinken added, looking at the older man, "who prefers tinkering with metals and toys than people. Nonetheless, he is a genius in his limited field."

The Great Brain nodded, studying ten Brinken with deep attention. His reverie may have continued had not the Lamane spoken up once again.

"You work with metal and devices? Why would you choose to spread such abominations upon the Earth? The Children of Giphantie are only dedicated to the arts and sciences of the world! Abomination!" the Lamane repeated the last word as a whisper, a hushed sibilant hiss.

"I do not answer to petty functionaries," the Great Brain shot back. "You may hold the title of a king, sir, but we know you are little more than an advisor with no true power in our circle."

"I represent the Nimrod. You are under review, Mardon," the Lamane croaked, unmoved by the heated words.

"Cease caterwauling that silly title. All here call me by my current name—Master. I accept nothing less, for now," the Great Brain replied, his voice casual.

He languidly turned his attention back to Jakob ten Brinken and Professor Rotwang, a smile briefly crossing his face.

"There is only one master of the Children of Giphantie and they are called the Nimrod. You are not the Nimrod—and based on your flouting of the rules, you shall not remain the Mardon. The title you hold is an honor, second only to our leader!" the Lamane said, tapping his staff on the stone floor in emphasis.

"And the title you hold," the Great Brain replied, still not looking the old man's direction, "was adopted by the Kings of Serer until they joined that kingdom in West Africa. You do not look like a native of that region. Based on your speech, you sound like an Ottoman subject."

The Lamane struck his staff on the floor three times, his face turning purple with rage.

"Abomination!" he thundered. "The law of the Children of Giphantie is that we give up all ties to the earthly realm upon swearing allegiance! You reject our ways, Mardon! The Nimrod was right to send me here. I shall tour your facilities and examine your plans to discover the full weight of your perfidy!"

The old man stomped out of the room, the tapping sound from his staff echoing as he vanished into the distance. A sneer threatened to cross the Great Brain's face and he covered his mouth with a hand. Turning back to the scientists, his eyes narrowed.

"Why are you here, Doctor ten Brinken?" he asked, leaning back in his throne. "I presume that is the correct title of address. If not, I apologize."

"It is correct, sir. The Lamane demanded my presence as an advisor on scientific matters. I protested, yet my words fell on deaf ears. This trek forced me to suspend my new researches on several promising areas of ethnopharmacology using the Mandrake and Datura plants."

"That is quite unacceptable. Perhaps we can supply you with a small distraction. Professor?" the Great Brain asked, looking to Rotwang.

"Yes, master?" the Professor inquired, smiling as he realized the direction of the Great Brain's thoughts.

"The reagent Oxus provided us with is in the medical wing of the facility. Please take Doctor ten Brinken to the laboratory and allow him to read the pages. You will find them in the green cabinet. Perhaps he shall discover details or variants of the chemical formulas that escaped our attention."

The Great Brain removed the hand from his face and smiled brightly down at his new servant, Jakob ten Brinken. This was the method he had used to subvert Rotwang—the medical mastermind would follow soon enough.

"Oxus?" ten Brinken declared. "That madman who, while somewhat intelligent, is weakened by his lack of systemic applications and theoretical comprehension? Like Moreau before him, he is slipshod in his approach to his work and fails to follow proper experimental procedures."

The Great Brain nodded, realizing he had his much-needed biological expert. His friendship, or at least friendly rivalry, with Rotwang, ensured they would toil to outdo each other.

"Precisely, Doctor," the Great Brain said. "While Oxus's aid may prove helpful, I doubt he fully tested the substance of his work. Could you lend us your insight?"

"Or at least, as much insight as a biologist is capable of providing at any one time," Rotwang added.

Ten Brinken snorted and rolled his tiny eyes.

"Go back to your clockwork toys, Claus. I must return to the only true science—that of life. Not your cold facsimile of the highest functions of existence!"

The Great Brain listened as the pair sniped at each other during their walk down the corridor. Pulling on his jeweler's loupe, he turned back to his worktable and returned to shaping the gem.

Perhaps this was the final element. Confinement in this animalistic form caused him to crave for the days when he, the Great Brain of Mars, was one of the mightiest beings in the universe.

CHAPTER XIII

Victor vaulted the wall, landing in a low crouch. Only the slightest whisper of sound emerged from the well-manicured lawn as his hands and feet struck. Beneath his plague doctor's mask, he silently cursed. Unless a human stood within three feet of his location, they would not have heard a sound. To guard dogs and other animals, however, his entry was as noisy as a brass band in a parade.

Reaching into his jacket, he pulled out three black egg-shaped objects. Remaining low, he tossed the obsidian ovals into the dark-left, right and center. Each shattered upon contact with the grass, propelling large globules of a viscous yellow/red fluid about the ground. The fluid splashed across the ground, vanishing from sight seconds later.

Still remaining low, Victor watched as two guard dogs charged towards his direction. These were massive animals, Irish wolfhounds bred for size, power and ferocity. These canines once served as wolf hunters; they were terrifying beasts even for those who loved such animals. Victor gave some grudging respect to Pierre Gérard. The man did choose his guards well enough.

Suddenly, the dogs soundlessly stopped, sniffing the air and dipping their heads with naked, unhidden, fear. With a low whimper, the two massive animals turned and fled back in the direction whence they'd come, their heads low, their tails tucked between their legs.

Victor waited, watching the dogs as they retreated, remembering his conversation with Madame Defarge.

"What do you do with dogs when you enter homes?" she had asked him two years ago as she sat by his side.

She was a stout, powerful woman, with man-shaped hands and a strong face that garnered second looks from both men and women. The mistress of the circus's animal act, she had three lovers, five children and a patient, if dangerous, disposition.

"Avoid them," Victor had answered, earning a laughed from Defarge and her eldest daughter Anais.

The latter was a younger replica of her mother and already the best cook in the company.

"Feed them and run," Irma had added, adding to the laughter.

Once the laughter had died down, Madame Defarge put aside her knitting and smiled their direction.

"Good. Had you spoken of drugging the poor, innocent animals, or killing them, I would no longer consider you family. Animals are innocent, beings of purity. Humanity is tainted and few deserve anything more than contempt. A murderer of poor dogs is my enemy for life. We, Defarges, are quite capable of holding grudges for long periods. Remind me to tell you about one of my ancestors one day... However, since you are like one of my children, I shall provide you with something that shall serve you well..."

The solution to dogs? Wolf urine!

Madame Defarge kept a small pack of massive Siberian wolves as part of her troupe of animals. They were not performers, but occasionally, she allowed the public a chance to witness the mighty creatures from a distance.

"All dogs," Madame Defarge had explained, "even ones raised in a city, fear wolves. They instinctively know that and flee at the scent. Throw this onto the ground and you will keep them from you for days."

Watching the Irish wolfhounds as they ran across the lawn away from his position, Victor Sicarius mentally thanked Madame Defarge. Neither he nor Irma ever wished to injure an animal on their duties. They had been around circuses since the destruction of their organization, and viewed animals as more than lesser creatures. Each possessed individual personalities, strengths, weaknesses, hopes, and fears. As such, they sympathized with dogs, cats, and other creatures, often more so than with the rest of humanity.

Victor silently padded across the lawn, spotting a light in a distant window. The chamber was located on the west side of the house, a perfect vista to view the nearby sea. Victor believed that this was Pierre Gérard's bedroom, the largest of seven in the mansion.

That fit his estimation of the man's character, that of an individual in need of proving his self-worth through visible demonstrations of power. Why else would a wealthy shipping magnate personally lead a team of killers to check on three gangsters? Gérard's ego caused him to take foolish risks.

Reaching the wall of the house, Victor quickly scaled it. His powerful fingers and nimble feet discovering miniscule handholds, ones that even professional burglars would have found daunting.

Climbing above the window level, he scurried along, resembling a massive black insect as he seemed to defy gravity.

Seconds later, he arrived at an unlit window down the hall from his intended destination. Lowering his head, he peeked over the top of the ledge, viewing a dark, well-furnished bedroom.

The bed, a four-poster lacking sheets and coverlets, appeared empty, and looked unused—for months if not years.

Reaching into his belt, Victor retrieved a piece of wire, which he slowly edged against the window. With a slight popping sound, the metal slid between the twin glass panes and entered the chamber. Victor slid the wire down a few inches and unlocked the window.

A moment later, he dropped inside, landing in a low crouch. He did not move for several minutes, listening to the house, awaiting a signal.

Approximately two minutes later, a low *chirp* drifted into the room. The sound was that of a Bonelli Eagle, a large predator native to the seaside. Beneath his mask, Victor smiled and suppressed his desire to snicker. He then stood up straight and made a show of moving across the room and into the corridor with less stealth.

The hallway was long—the full length of the mansion—and sumptuously designed. Rococo motifs covered the walls, and full-figured naked maidens cavorting with chubby cherubs adorned the ceiling. Gilded plaster with sweeping curves painted in gold was everywhere the eye could see. The intent appeared to be elegance and royal grace—an exhibition of naked wealth using the styles of the past. But the result was, in fact, gaudy, ridiculous, demonstrating only the owner's lack of breeding or taste.

Gérard believed that this spectacle of wealth placed him among the great families of Europe, unaware that he lacked the knowledge they had of when to use a degree of moderation. Some, like the Bonapartes or some of the American billionaires, had learned this—for lack of a better term—grace. But men like Pierre Gérard never realized such concepts even existed.

Spotting a light emerging from one room, Victor walked quietly to the location. Examining the door, he realized that it was locked from within. No matter. In fact, it was better that way.

Pulling out a skeleton key set, Victor quietly unlocked the door and stepped inside.

Pierre Gérard sat in a small wooden chair reading a leather-bound book. He wore a long, red satin dressing gown with an ascot tie, complete with a ruby stickpin. A small silver revolver lay on the table by his elbow; yet, he did not move to pick up the weapon. Instead, he smiled, looking quite satisfied with the results of the evening.

"At last!" he said. "I despaired you would ever return. Please, do come in Monsieur Plague Doctor. We waited for you three nights. Oh, and do not attempt to flee."

Languidly, he marked the page in his book. Anton extended a hand from behind the door and jammed the barrel of his revolver against Victor's neck.

"I hope you do make a move, *connard*." He said. "I owe you for our last meeting."

Finally, filling the doorway stood Robert Ménard, his bulk nearly blocking out the illumination from the hallway. His hand flashed and a long, heavy silver blade appeared in his wide, outstretched palm.

"You are quite trapped, Monsieur," he intoned.

His face exhibited no emotions and he watched the scene with the dispassionate gaze of a gardener about to prune an annoying weed.

"Yes," Pierre Gérard drawled, his smile transforming into an enraged sneer. "I lured you in, knowing you could not resist trying to murder me. Now, let us find out who lays beneath that ridiculous bird mask..."

CHAPTER XIV

"Is that a Rukh oscilloscope? I thought that he refused to release the machine." Jakob ten Brinken asked, peering down at a large machine encased in unpainted gray metal.

Rotwang shook his head, snorting with derision and looking slightly offended.

"That is my design, sir! The Master presented me with notes from a scientist from China or one of those countries. A fellow called Fen-Chu, who possessed a few kernels of cleverness. His ideas ran parallel to mine, yet he discovered a means of synthesizing certain elements to which I had no access. My research now moves in leaps and bounds! I imagine a thing, and it is so!"

Ten Brinken's tiny eyes transformed into mere gashes in his face, minuscule chips of gray ice that subtly reflected the mad genius beneath the surface. He pursed his lips and said in a hissing tone:

"The Children of Giphantie abhor work such as yours. How can you justify tinkering with metal and processed fluids in the face of their ways?"

"Children of what?" Rotwang asked, his face darkening. "That is the second time you've invoked such a nonsensical name. Have you joined a cult, Jakob?"

"Religion? *Verdammt! Was zur Hölle?*" ten Brinken snarled. "Have you taken leave of your senses, mechanic? Science is the only God of humanity! The Children of Giphantie are the group who pay for your shiny equipment and food!"

His face went pale, though he did not appear frightened. In fact, ten Brinken was one of those rare individuals whose face transformed into an insipid white rather than a florid scarlet. An odd quirk of biology that caused many enemies to underestimate this mad doctor.

Rotwang giggled and slowly raised one gloved hand up in a triumphant pose.

"The only allegiance I have is to the Master. He makes a few requests and my work commences at an exponential rate. Payment? What do I care about such dross?"

"Then how does he afford to indulge your metallurgical whims, eh?" ten Brinken said, slamming a fist into an open palm with a dry slap. "The funding must come from somewhere!"

"Ask him! I have all I require and need nothing more today. What was it Herr Blucher used to say at the Gymnasium? Ah yes! He who chases two rabbits at once will catch none. The rabbit I chase is science—the pure art without concerns of economics or ethics. Your Children of Giants, or whatever you call them, are like the fools I confronted in Heidelberg! My work is an abomination? An abomination?" Rotwang thundered.

The insanity, which always ran beneath the surface of his lined face, caused it to take on a demoniacal cast. People that viewed the monster within this man often fled at the sight of the fanatical monster that ruled his psyche. But not so with Jakob ten Brinken. His wide, flat countenance appeared to transform into the harsh, unyielding stone of the ancient statue of a warrior saint. He appeared unmoved by his friend's fury, allowing the rage to sweep over him without reaction.

"The Children of Giphantie are an ancient order, whose origins go back to the legendary Garden of Eden. According to them, their ancestors were the guardians of the ancient plants, and raised humanity from the thoughtless beasts to the thinking creatures of the present day. The original guardians transformed into higher beings, leaving behind their servants to carry on their legacy. The current organization is devoted to similar aims, raising humanity to a higher level of consciousness—with themselves in command, of course. My work attempts to find means of pacifying the wilder impulses, the atavistic aspect of humanity."

Rotwang, did not reply, but led his friend from the robotics lab down a small concrete corridor. Stopping before a metal door, he inserted a bronze color rod in a gap just above the handle, and removed it after a loud series of clicks.

The door swung open and lights rose from hidden sockets in the concrete ceiling. The room was rectangular in shape, about forty feet by twenty. A series of low chrome metal tables filled the far end, like a full surgical theater. Nearest to the two men was an advanced chemical and biological laboratory, complete with equipment that would have earned the envy of the finest institutions in the world.

"*Was zur Hölle?*" ten Brinken breathed, "How? How did you get such wealth? It cannot be wasted on a mechanic such as you!"

Rotwang grinned condescendingly and shrugged.

"Who else? I have no interest in such obsolete vivisectionist tools. However, I am all the Master possesses at the moment."

"Such wealth… and he allows you to pursue your own projects?" ten Brinken asked, passing the Professor and gazing upon equipment he did even knew existed.

"Of course! Nothing less than that would keep me in his service. But his requests always match my pursuits. Thus, we share a symbiotic relationship. That should appeal to a student of the outdated concepts of life such as yourself."

Rotwang reached a small steel countertop. Opening a drawer, he pulled out a series of gold flimsies.

"What is that?" ten Brinken asked.

His narrowed eyes almost vanished beneath his heavy lids as his attention turned to the items Rotwang produced.

"Oxus' formulas. The Master instructed me to present them to you earlier. I think it is all utter nonsense, but perhaps your training in such matters will divine the truth behind that lunatic's theories. The prepared reagent is in ampoules in the electronic cold locker on your left. If you require the results of the clinical tests, you will find them on the third page. Oxus appears to have tested his chemical concoctions upon a series of drunkards and wandering gypsies."

Rotwang watched his friend closely as ten Brinken read each page with the greed of a miser staring at his gold.

A brief silence passed, then ten Brinken looked up. His face looked confused for a moment and he blinked slowly.

"Forgive me, er, Claus... I mean, Rotwang. I was engaged in these equations. You were saying... oh, what did he mean by that... ah... fascinating..."

Seeing his friend's eyes returning to the document, Rotwang turned and left the lab. He had his own work to pursue.

CHAPTER XV

Anton's free hand yanked off Victor's hat and tossed the object on the floor. He pressed the gun harder while remaining at an arm's length.

"I do not see how to remove his mask," he said, his voice sounding aggrieved "There are no buckles in the back."

Still, Anton did not move any closer.

Victor grudgingly recognized these three were not complete fools. Had the one holding the gun approached any closer, he would have lost his weapon. Still, he was not worried—in fact he found the matter was quite amusing.

"Remove your mask," Pierre growled. "Otherwise we will make this very painful for you."

He stood up, balling his hands into tight fists.

Victor rolled his eyes beneath his mask, amused by this sad, little lie. Obviously, Pierre Gérard and his minions intended to torture and kill him in a slow manner. Their collective egos had received a thorough bruising a few nights earlier. To save face and regain some of their confidence, they intended to make the process as nasty as possible.

"Do it yourself," Victor replied, his voice an echoing purr.

He deliberately spoke in a higher register and used an Alsatian accent to add a little confusion to the current situation.

Gérard's teeth clicked together as he gritted them with fury. He was not used to anyone defying his will with such an open lack of fear, or respect. The time when Pierre Gérard was mocked for his half-Arab origin was long past. Yet, he still received the rebuke with the same stinging embarrassment he had felt as a child on the streets of Marseilles.

He reached for his gun, when a loud explosion caused him to step back in surprise. His head swiveled left and right. He saw that Anton was also confused by the noise. Robert, as was his custom, appeared unmoved and merely gazed slowly about the chamber.

The stranger in the plague doctor mask had not moved, but that was understandable. After all, there was a revolver pressed against the back of his skull.

Gérard opened his mouth to ask what just occurred, when more explosions shattered the night. The sounds were not especially loud, more like a series of low-pitched pops.

Beneath his mask, Victor Sicarius blew Irma a metaphorical kiss and spun in place.

He kicked the door into Anton's head and arm, knocking the gun off. Through an involuntary muscle movement, Anton pulled the trigger, sending a bullet across the room, shattering a pane of glass.

With a hard wrench, Victor tore the gun from Anton's grasp and threw the weapon at Pierre Gérard's gun sitting on the table. The firearms struck and, with a metallic clatter, flew off and ended up under the nearby bed.

Robert Ménard stepped forward, raising his blade, only to fall back as the door, kicked by Victor again, struck him squarely in the face. His knife fell from his fingers, bounced across the wooden floor before coming to rest under a chair.

Grabbing the stunned Anton by his lapels, Victor flipped the gangster over and sent him crashing into Pierre Gérard. Both men fell in a tangle, a light moan emerging from one of them. Suppressing a chuckle, Victor kicked the door again, knocking down the rising Robert, before moving to the window.

Placing a foot on the sill, he turned his masked head in their direction and called out in the same accent:

"*Adieu, pathétiques imbéciles!*"

Then he leaped out the window and into the night, vanishing from view instantly.

The three gangsters scrambled to their feet, despite their injuries, and rushed towards the large open window.

"Get away from me, *connard*!" Pierre Gérard yelped, pushing Anton aside.

Robert's face appeared bruised and battered, his nose a swollen, bloody, ruin.

All three men arrived at the window at the same moment. Anton handed Pierre one of the fallen revolvers and they raised their weapons, ready to shoot.

"*Mon Dieu!*" Pierre Gérard exploded, almost dropping his gun.

"*Bordel de merde!*" Anton breathed, stepping back and almost bumping into the enormous Robert.

"*Oui, Monsieur,*" Robert said, as unemotional as ever.

The sight before their unbelieving eyes made their exhalations of astonishment understandable.

Fifty meters away, they spied the high wall that surrounded the property.

There, a figure in black pulled itself onto the top of the wall and vanished from sight a heartbeat later.

Silence reigned over the lands surrounding Pierre Gérard's mansion. Even the birds did not chirp in the distant trees.

"That is not possible!" Anton bellowed.

CHAPTER XVI

Gabin Masson hated his life. He knew he was not the most clever man, nor the most handsome, yet he did possess some of each virtue. Pretty girls did not exactly flock in his direction, but he rarely spent a weekend alone. They were not the astonishing beauties that visited the grand casinos or magnificent beaches near his home in Nice. Such perfect ladies never lowered their gaze his direction. One needed to be muscled and possessing Apollo-style splendor like Yves Bachère the bellhop to garner such interest. Yves received invitations from widows, young women on a last fling before marriage, and the like. Gabin's incitements arrived from waitresses, maids, and the occasional kitchen staff.

Still, he dreamed of joining their ranks and being viewed as one of society's elite. One observation he had made about men in that world cheered him daily—once they joined that microcosm, they need not possess the exquisiteness of a man like Yves Bachère. Take that group of English millionaires and titled idiots who just sailed from the hotel last night. None were particularly bright, other than that Fink-Nottle chap. He was an odd, fish-faced creature whom the others, especially a pair of twins named Wooster, treated as strange.

Gabin knew he had the ability to be as vacuous and unimportant as those men. The trouble was, he had no entry into society. All he was, the only area he excelled in, was driving. It did not matter the size of the vehicle, steamer, electric, or even one of those weird Russian autos that ran on foul smelling petrol. Place Gabin Masson behind the wheel or steering sticks and he piloted the vehicle as if he had done so since childhood.

Unfortunately, the only job that paid anything close to a living wage was that of chauffeur at the Hotel Negresco. Every day, he arrived at work, ferried men, women and children about the city and beyond, and occasionally received a gratuity in response. The rest of the time, Gabin spent maintaining the vehicles, cleaning them, and checking the schedule for his daily driving duties. To call this work dull was an understatement.

Today was one of those rare special duties, when he received an assignment from management. Those were never pleasant, usually involving driving an ailing noble or a wealthy foreigner to some distant location. Past trips had involved transporting his charge to the middle of nowhere to look at ruins or at an elderly mansion once owned by the passenger's family. He had even traveled across the border to Clerville and watched as a family wandered around a tumbled down bunch of stones.

This trip was particularly odd—driving a female passenger from the hotel to a mansion in Marseilles. Why? He had no idea. There was a railway service that would have gotten the silly woman there in a mere three hours. Instead this wealthy fool preferred a six-hour trip by car. And the trip had not gone well so far.

"Miss?" Gabin had asked as he drove the Austin Electric Fox out of the hotel's parking garage. "The vehicle is equipped with an electric music system as well as a bar."

The woman, who hid her face beneath an oversized hat and an open copy of the English newspaper, the *Daily Yell*, said:

"*Merci*. Close the slide."

The newspaper never lowered, and the voice was deep, almost masculine in tone. Gabin, who had experienced such rudeness in the past, raised the slide and sighed. *Six hours of silence and another six back. And I doubt she will tip.*

However, he did respect the demands of his passenger, which, unbeknownst to him, saved his life.

He dropped her off at her destination and headed back towards Nice, *sans* gratuity

CHAPTER XVII

"That is not possible!" Anton bellowed.

He looked ready to raise his revolver and fire, despite knowing he could not hit the distant wall, let alone the vanished figure in black.

In fact, Anton's supposition was entirely true. As gifted as Victor Sicarius was physically, no man or beast could have covered such a distance in mere seconds. Instead, he had jumped out the window and pulled himself onto the roof above Gérard's bedroom. The remote person in black was, of course, Irma Vep! This had been the crux of their plan, the aspect of it they had fought over repeatedly until agreeing this was, in final analysis, the best method.

"I still do not like this plan," Irma had stated as they were leaving the circus "You are trusting that your ridiculous costume will keep them focused on your face, and that they won't shoot you in the knees in anger.".

"I agreed to wear an extra layer of protection," Victor had replied, ending the debate.

An hour earlier, Irma Vep had climbed over the wall, dropping on the other side, and dashed towards the house. The massive dogs had appeared at the corner and she had stopped, allowing their fast lopes towards her position. Pursing her plump lips, she had whistled a high-pitched note, a blast that grew in pitch until it was nearly inaudible to her ears.

The dogs, three shaggy, titanic canines, had stopped running and trotted her direction. They had dropped into seated poses and dipped their heads in submission.

Smiling, Irma had stroked all three of the unshorn skulls and then, had waved the animals aside. They had run off, resuming their patrols as if she did not exist.

Crossing to the east side of the mansion, Irma had pulled out a small sliver of metal and unlatched the servant's entrance door. The gloomy corridor, unlike the rest of the house, did not possess a hint of the overwhelmingly grandiose architecture. The walls, green in color, did not even have a trace of artwork or a religious image like a crucifix. A series of stairs had taken her to an oversized kitchen.

Irma knew such places, having burglarized dozens since childhood as a member of the infamous Vampires gang. As a young girl, the older criminals had taught her to enter homes through small gaps and windows too small for an adult. Later, after the leader, known then as the "Great Vampire," had kidnapped Victor, they had operated together as a highly successful criminal team.

The trick was to use careful, correct movements, not too fast, not too slow. Closing her eyes, Irma had counted to twenty and opened her lips slowly; her night vision was now fully engaged. Irma had then walked forward, her step a light, almost balletic stride. Her feet appeared to almost float above the wooden floor, her soft shoes never causing so much whispering noise.

Arriving at the kitchen door, she had examined the visible hinges. The brass metal on the top one looked clean and operational. The lower one possessed a thin layer of rust near the edges. This was normal—people often forgot to fully care for such areas. They accepted a light creaking sound as unimportant, a normal facet of life in a household.

Pulling out a small can, Irma had lightly oiled the hinges, top and bottom. This was her habit, an inner compulsion. If she felt the need to oil a single hinge, she had to do the same to the second one. Though this was unnecessary, some inner feeling of incompletion nagged her if she failed to act in this manner.

"Why do you always do both? It wastes time and liquid?" Victor had asked one day after they completed a difficult theft.

A member of the Prussian King's court had possessed and had been planning to sell military documents to the Russians. They had stolen them along with all his money, several diamonds, and a list of Russian contacts. A very profitable job.

"I need to," Irma had answered. "I just need to. Stop asking me."

That had ended the conversation, but Irma still felt a troubled sensation when she acted this way. Still, not doing so would bother her far worse. She just accepted this was one of her quirks, just like her need to always eat with forks with rounded edges. Victor never seemed to be prey to such compulsions, and at last he had learned to stop commenting on hers.

Opening the kitchen door, she had smiled beneath her heavy makeup as the hinges neither squeaked, nor squealed. Walking in the same aerial manner, she had insured that her body never moved within a foot of the counters, stove or icebox. The easy way to cause a clatter in a house was to knock over a pot or a stray jar sitting near the edge.

Soon, she had exited the kitchen and, after striding down an over-decorated hall with a black marble floor, had discovered Pierre Gérard's private office.

The room had been locked, though her skeleton keys had it opened and relocked in less than thirty seconds. An over-sized dark wood desk dominated the book-lined chamber. Far too large and ornate, it belonged in the office of a bank president. Such a relic was a curiosity piece, an example of the past. The room resembled a stage play version of a wealthy man's office. The rest of the furniture looked just as ridiculous. The bare desktop gleamed from the spare starlight peeking through the heavy, blood-red curtains.

Even from a short glance, Irma had realized Pierre Gérard never actually did any work from behind this object. Instead, seated in the overstuffed, leather chair, he held court, believing he looked important. The effect was, in her mind, ridiculous rather than impressive or overwhelming.

With a light hope, she had alighted on one of the club chairs. Standing on one foot, Irma had smiled, spotting the pressure pads throughout beneath the large Persian-copied rug. The slight raises in the pattern had given her a perfect clue as to where each alarm point was located in the room. This was an effective system against a casual burglar, allowing Gérard a degree of protection from unwanted visitors. Even slightly more expert housebreakers might fall victim to this protection system. But to Irma Vep, they were merely a source of amusement.

The method of defeating these alarms was to use their strength as an asset. Once engaged, the system possessed a degree of sensitivity so delicate that only a tiny creature, such as a mouse, were immune from the effect. Unless the owner of such devices kept their room bare of furnishings, the pressure pads could not be positioned beneath the various chairs, tables, and desks.

Under such circumstances, Victor's method of motion became precise, exact, and usually involved wire work. Irma, quite in opposition, preferred to see these alarm structures as a chance to engage in a bit of silent fun.

Choosing Mozart's *Magic Flute*, Irma had begun to sing in her mind one of the famous arias from the legendary opera. Dancing from chair to chair and landing on her toes on the desk, the music had caused her to move with even greater grace.

> *"Der Hölle Rache kocht in meinem Herzen,*
> *Tod und Verzweiflung flammet um mich her!*
> *Fühlt nicht durch dich Sarastro*
> *Todesschmerzen,*
> *So bist du meine Tochter nimmermehr.*
> *Verstossen sei auf ewig,*
> *Verlassen sei auf ewig,*
> *Zertrümmert sei'n auf ewig*
> *Alle Bande der Natur*
> *Wenn nicht durch dich!*
> *Sarastro wird erblassen!*
> *Hört, Rachegötter,*
> *Hört der Mutter Schwur!"*

Then she had spotted the purpose of her search: Pierre Gérard's supposedly hidden safe. She wondered why every wealthy man she had ever encountered possessed the same lack of information regarding the location of their secret miniature vault. As always, the safe lay behind a painting behind the desk chair. A pair of pressure pads lay before the painting and a magnet, probably connected to another set of bells and the like, held the ornate wooden frame against the wall.

This had greatly amused Irma. It was a ridiculously simple protection that she could have defeated at age thirteen. Checking the time, she had nodded. Then, she had opened the desk drawers one at a time. Pulling out a battered notebook, she had quickly paged through the journal until she had stopped on a set of numbers.

Moron! she had thought, suppressing a giggle of delight. *Never write the combination down and keep in the same room as your safe.*

Dancing over to the window on another chair and a sofa, Irma had opened the frame and, with a loud cry, released a screeching caw.

The hunting call of the Bonelli Eagle had echoed across the silent lawns.

Irma had closed the window softly and turned back to the desk, enjoying the simplicity of her part of this caper.

Pirouetting back onto the onto the desk chair, Irma had leaned forward and chosen another song for her entertainment. Going in a different direction entirely, she had decided on the lyrics from the silly English operetta, *The Mikado*. The song, "Some Day it May Happen," always made her smile. Victor kept a recording on the music player in their trailer, sensing it was a proper method of disarming her black moods.

Pulling out a magnet, she had maintained the connection between the circuit and swung the painting wide. A simple black metal combination safe lay beneath it, and she b to turn the dial.

The song then rose in her mind…

"As some day it may happen that a victim must be found
I've got a little list, I've got a little list
Of society offenders who might well be underground
And who never would be missed, who never would be
missed!..."*

Just as she had thought-sing the final words (*"I'm sure*
she'd not he missed!"), the safe door had opened.

Irma had examined the contents of the tiny vault, reaching in and running a gentle finger around the edges. Happily,
there were no holes or trip wires protecting the items within.

Without bothering to sort them out, Irma Vep had emptied every item into her satchel.

She had then closed the safe, the painting, slipping out
her magnet, before retracing her path out of the room.

Locking the door again, in less than a minute, Irma had
found herself outside again. There, pulling out a large fire-
cracker, she had lit it and tossed it across the lawn, repeating
the procedure with another wick, tied to a series of smaller, yet
quite loud, bangers.

She had run to the wall and had waited until the first explosion had rent the air. Then, climbing up the wall, she had
paused at the top, only watching the windows with the corner
of her eye.

Much to her relief, she has seen Victor's black-clad figure vaulting out the window and swinging onto the roof.

Irma, her back to the house, yet standing in a beam of
moonlight, had paused for a ten-count before dropping onto
the other side and out of sight.

Do not linger, Victor! she thought, running into the
night.

The waiting was the hardest part for her.

CHAPTER XVIII

Across the Atlantic Ocean, Doctor Cornelius Kramm waved his brother into a seat. The harsh lines of the physician's face appeared deeper, causing him to resemble a disapproving Puritan. In a black suit and a cockle hat, he would have been the very image of a Massachusetts preacher from the first settlement of the American colonies.

Quite in contrast, Fritz Kramm gave the impression of a man about to attend a party at a nightclub. A friendly smile lay across his jolly face and his well-cut suit was well-cut was bright enough to fit in anywhere from a society gathering to a low jazz club.

"Our Parisian employees are experiencing some resistance," Fritz stated.

He knew his brother had already read the report and fully grasped the implications. Still, this was the best method of starting their conference.

"I perused the report. Our collections decreased ten percent and one courier received a severe beating," Cornelius said, tenting his fingers and watching Fritz.

"The courier had in his possession two hundred thousand francs from our illegal armament sales," Fritz explained. "The loss of the funds was terrible, but we can recover. The greater danger is the larger implications. Our position is now quite tenuous among the Parisian underworld. Should news of that spread, we shall find our organization hampered in future operations."

He recited the details from memory, knowing such information should not be committed to paper.

"Who performed the robbery?" Cornelius asked.

He stared slightly above his brother's head, the picture of a man in deep contemplation.

"Unknown. One of the Apache gangs appeared involved. The courier lost an eye and was unable to provide a detailed description other than the costume of the men who committed the attack."

"Your opinion?" Cornelius pressed, his eyes still viewing a location only he could see in the room.

Fritz shrugged broadly and shook his head.

"I would rule out the small gangs of lesser crooks. They comprehend that assailing our position would undoubtedly result in harsh reprisal. Therefore, the architect of this assault must be one who is conscious of their position and our relative strength."

Cornelius nodded approximately two centimeters, a rare physical demonstration of agreement.

"Continue."

"Fantômas?" Fritz whispered.

He appeared to hunch lower in his chair, as if even uttering the name was a means of risking his very life.

"He is dead. He died at sea years ago," Cornelius replied.

"Until I see that fiend's corpse, I will not believe the truth of that statement. Even then, I happen to know he was believed to have been publicly guillotined once, and returned afterward. According to legend, he had placed another man in his cell and that one died in his stead."

Fritz shivered with naked fear and mopped his now damp forehead with a silk handkerchief.

"Nonetheless, we possess no evidence that the creature is still alive. Move along and provide other possibilities," Cornelius said, focusing his penetrating gaze on Fritz.

He did not blink, or at least that was the appearance one gained from this intense focus.

"There is a Prussian organization whose leader we have yet to discover. They call themselves the Gamblers and their strength is on the rise. They are deeply connected to the darker side of the Berlin Metropolis spread."

Cornelius considered for a moment and then stated:

"No, I do not believe their strength is great enough for such an expansion. Your last report suggested their focus is upon the lesser industrial zones in Saxony and Baden. Their operation suffered heavy losses when they clashed with the British in Hanover. Any others?"

"Either the last remnants of the Moriarty organization or possibly Zenith the Albino—though the latter would never stoop so low as to engineer a common street robbery, unless there is a larger purpose."

Fritz opened his cigar case and pulled out a thin cheroot. He placed the tobacco between his lips but did not seek a light.

"Not the Albino, he is in Athens" said Cornelius. "The Moriarty remnants are possible, though that gang may have emerged from an older unit. Go to London and begin inquiries into a long-destroyed group that called themselves the Gentlemen of the Night. We shall speak through the coded system exclusively, unless we are in the same chamber."

Fritz rose and turned to leave. He was not unduly concerned about heading to Europe—the continent was like a second home to him. As an art dealer, he had traveled to many cities throughout a dozen of countries. Just the previous month, he had visited Grand Fenwick, Clerville, and Ruritania and discovered several prized relics which had sold quickly in his gallery in Manhattan. A trip to London would be a nice change, though he doubted there would be many hidden gems there to rival with a dueling sword with the Strelsau arms across the hilt.

At the doorway, he stopped and turned around, reaching for his lighter.

"*She* will be arriving in Marseilles within the hour. You will not be in contact with her except when I report in after my arrival in London."

Cornelius frowned slightly and said:

"Acceptable. She does not require my oversight during her operations. If any difficulties arise, I would prefer my anonymity to remain uncompromised. Maggs and her ilk are incapable of keeping any secrets."

"And if an extreme difficulty arises when I am unavailable?" Fritz asked as he reached for the doorknob.

"Tell Mama Maggs to send a message to Bandello. He is fully aware of cutouts that will provide me with the necessary information. I will send orders back through that same channel until you are near a coded televisor."

Cornelius opened his desk drawer and removed a file. He opened it and immediately began to read it, effectively dismissing Fritz without another word.

CHAPTER XIX

Irma threw her arms around Victor's neck and held him for a full minute. She did not speak, nor did she demonstrate any other reaction to the events of the night. Yet her embrace was tight, her muscular arms holding him with a power that belied her lithe frame.

Then she pulled back and lightly slapped his face.

"I despise that plan. We must find another means of misleading our enemies. There are detectives in Paris and London capable of seeing through the ruse. Oh, and take off that insane mask. I feel as if I was about to kiss a crow."

Victor pulled off the mask and tossed it onto one of the trunks. His pale face dripped with perspiration, like a man that had just ran a great distance in powerful sunlight.

"I believe the intention was to resemble a raven, not a crow, but I understand your meaning. Was the safe difficult to open?"

Irma giggled and released him as she shook her head.

"The imbecile left the combination in a book in his desk drawer. And he used a pressure pad alarm system!"

Victor rolled his eyes as he quickly pulled off his dark clothing.

"What song did you use as inspiration this time?"

She opened her mouth to answer, but was drowned out by a rising tide of noise from outside the trailer. The first sound was that of fanfare trumpets blasting a triumphant song. The sound that followed was also a trumpeting, but not that of a brass instrument. This was the circus's lead elephant, a massive bull named Ptolemy, who led the animal parade into the tent.

"Madame has the animals parading through the tent. We can talk later. Get dressed. I put your costume to your right. But first, towel off! You look like you just ran naked through a rainstorm."

Irma poured him a cold cut of tea as she pulled on her blond wig.

Downing the drink in a gulp, Victor took a moment to wash his naked body quickly before putting on his circus costume. White and black striped shirt, red neckerchief, black tight pants, and a set of soft shoes that resembled boots.

He audibly groaned as he pulled on the tight fitting black pants.

"The Apache? Why? We could just do the blade dance."

"Not memorable enough," said Irma, shaking her head. "You stressed many times that everyone should remember us when we perform, less than two hours from your escape. While the blade dance and the fire escape are impressive, the Apache always stuns the house. Face it, *mon chéri*, when we perform those steps on the high wire, even Sandokan the tiger holds his breath."

"Very well," Victor replied, knowing he'd already lost the argument. "You alerted Madame Defarge? She does not like being upstaged by anyone."

"She knows and shall keep the animals beneath us to add to the danger. We may have to repeat the performance tomorrow at another hour. Valentin and his clowns shall hint to the people that we may appear at any time to do the Apache. Sales shall grow, as they always do when we are at our best."

Irma giggled and placed a red beret on his head at a rakish angle. Victor reached out and tied a cotton scarf loosely around her long neck.

"Throw my hat to the loudest mouth in the crowd," he said. "He will never stop bragging about it and help sales."

Irma rolled her eyes, not moving her hands from his shoulders.

"Thank you, but I was the one who taught you that trick. Just as you shall throw my scarf to the prettiest girl in the crowd. Unfortunately, you usually pick out some cheap painted harlot. You have no taste in women."

Victor squinted her direction and he fought a grin from crossing his face.

"Does that include you?"

Irma nodded quickly.

"Didn't your mother tell you never to associate with dangerous ladies?"

"Probably," Victor replied. "I do not remember if I spoke to the lady. Yet that hypnotist Moréno did say I was fool to stay with you. He said: 'Any woman who names herself Irma Vep can't be tamed even by the strongest man.' Those were his final words."

"What was your response?" asked Irma, cocking her head. "Or do you believe I am just as Moréno said?"

"I told him I agreed with him," replied Victor with a chuckle. "Taming a spirit such as yours would be a mortal sin."

Irma smiled, her face brightening.

"That was the correct answer, *mon chéri*. I would like to kiss you now, but alas, I cannot. That would spoil my makeup and make us late for the performance. I do not like risking Madame's anger, especially when she is standing in a cage full of lions, tigers and elephants."

"I have no luck," Victor replied, pretending to sound morose.

"You shall have some... later," Irma said.

She took his hand and led him from the trailer.

CHAPTER XX

"Get me the Professor," the Great Brain said to one of his followers.

The man, a short Italian named Puzo, bowed and backed out without a word.

Silence reigned over the base of the Children of Giphantie. Unlike humans, the Great Brain found talk without purpose to be an unnecessary waste of time. Humans, like most barely evolved animals, felt the bizarre need to chatter to fill the hours. This was counterproductive—noise for the sake of preventing nervousness. Silence, especially when accompanied by important work, achieved greater results.

This new rule of his had not been easy to enforce, even in a group that prided themselves for being intelligent. The Children of Giphantie, for all their pretentions, still fell victims to their baser urges. They still wished to laugh, sing, procreate, eat full meals as a group, and even drink alcoholic beverages. The Great Brain's demand that they cease such activities had been met with great resistance.

"There are no rules in our society that demands we no longer drink wine, smoke cigarettes, or have sex," Bastien Chasse had said, emphasizing his words by striking his thigh with a clenched fist. "In fact, the Paris temple have a rota in which every member sleeps with another each night. They are the happiest people in the world!"

Chasse was a tall man with a large frame. He possessed the type of personality that rarely allowed others to give him orders. He was not especially clever, nor handsome, nor well trained in leadership. What he did possess, however, was a forceful personality that caused him to be rude to anyone he saw as less important than he. To date, that included everyone on Earth, and possibly Mars too.

"They are also the least productive temple in Europe," the Great Brain had replied, looking at Rotwang's estimates.

"Humans cannot be worked in this manner. We are not ants, sir!" Chase had shouted, this time striking the table with a heavy hand.

"No, you are not. At least, not yet…"

The Great Brain had looked up, his face spreading into what he thought was a smile. The result was more like a rictus grin of the type one would expect from a tortured man seconds away from death. The result was ghastly, a mockery of humanity, that caused Bastien to recoil in fear and disgust.

Since that time, the few remaining members of the Great Brain's staff had complied with his wishes—not that they had any choice in the matter.

Professor Rotwang bustled in, the scent of grease and blood filling the air like a vast noxious cloud.

"Yes, Master?" he asked.

"How many of your experimental units are available for use? I wish to seize all remaining assets of the Blanc organization this evening. I require their instant obedience as well as their funding for our projects."

The Great Brain disliked having to explain his plans to the eccentric scientist, but for now, other difficulties prevented him from merely issuing orders.

Rotwang pondered for a moment and slowly nodded his hirsute head.

"I think five are operational. Two units are still experiencing delirium responses during random moments. I am hopeful ten Brinken shall soon provide a narcotic that shall suppress these lingering personality traits."

"Five," the Great Brain repeated slowly. "I expected more… I require many more to enact my greater plan."

Rotwang raised a hand in the air, as if blaming the very heavens for the past failures of his project.

"We've suffered mass spoilage in the early experimental stages. The humans provided proved unable to complete the transformation process."

"Spoilage?" the Great Brain inquired.

Rotwang flapped his hand, as if shooing a pestering fly.

"My uncle was a butcher. He used the term to mean pigs and cattle which expired during transportation. Steps taken to lessen the spoilage of the meat proved a topic of great conversation to that segment of my family."

The Great Brain nodded slowly.

"Spoilage. I comprehend and accept the term. Yes, quite proper. How may we diminish the spoilage rate in our conversion subjects?"

"That is why you placed the biological laboratory in the hands of that vivisectionist, ten Brinken. Though I find his love of medical sciences to be a waste of time, I do believe his work in that field will be useful. He shall analyze the Oxus compound and synthesize a new solution, one with greater reliability. This should bring the spoilage rate down to nearly nil. Now, may I return to my work? If you require all five units, I must spend time ensuring that their functions will be set at maximum efficiency—even though that will delay my more important work by several hours!"

The Great Brain waved Rotwang away and contemplated the implications of the mad scientist's words. He would soon require bodies for Rotwang and ten Brinken, allowing them to convert his phalanx of troops. Then the real work would begin.

Picking up another jewel, the Great Brain started carving the myriad facets of the stone's face.

CHAPTER XXI

"Sit down," the Woman barked.

Her raucous voice caused Pierre Gérard to flinch and Anton to wince as the sound shredded his nerves. Robert stood nearby, as unperturbed as ever by the recent events.

The Gérard mansion was otherwise empty; the guards and all the other employees had been dismissed with pay for the day. The birds, that often populated the gardens and trees, had failed to appear that morning, and a hush seemed to have descended over the expansive grounds. The dogs and their handler had disappeared into the distant kennel, their barely audible barks being the only sounds breaking the powerful silence.

"This intruder broke into your home and none of you proved capable of discovering any useful details about that man," the Woman continued, "other than the fact that he was fast moving, skilled in both armed and unarmed combat, and wore some kind of bird mask. But the Director already knew these details when you called him after the murder of your employees. Have I misstated your position?"

The Woman walked past Anton and stepped deeper inside Gérard's bedroom.

"It was an effective trap," Pierre started, "one that I used in the past for burglars and enemies. Why, I killed an entire team of..."

His statement was cut off by the Woman who silenced him with a look.

"It was the act of a vain fool," she said. "This man had defeated you before—easily. Did you believe a change in locale would alter this fact? You gained nothing from this encounter. Nothing!"

The tone of her voice caused Pierre and Anton to burst out with cold perspiration.

"But we did learn something, lady!" Anton snapped back.

He placed his hands on his hips and tried to appear threatening, but the effect was quite the opposite. Instead of looking like a dangerous gangster, he resembled a child trying to imitate the posture of an adult.

"Pray tell me what information you received from this reckless, fruitless waste of time and resources?" the Woman asked.

Anton jabbed a finger at the open window, his face pugnacious despite his terror.

"That creature wasn't an ordinary human being. No man or woman could have done what he did when he escaped!"

The Woman turned to Robert.

"You," she said, "explain what he means by that ridiculous comment."

With sepulchral emphasis, Robert recounted the exact sequence of events of the previous night. He concluded with a simple nod, never having added any emotional content to his speech.

"Well spoken," the Woman said.

She walked to the window and studied the scene, leaning outside and staring up and down and to each side.

"Anton is right," Pierre added. "No normal being could have covered such a distance in so short a time. Perhaps the tales of vamp…"

"Shut up, you idiot," the Woman interrupted.

She stepped away from the window and continued:

"Every time you speak, you demonstrate a greater degree of foolishness."

"What?" Pierre asked.

He stood up, his gun now in his hand.

"I am not a man to be insulted in such a…"

At blinding speed, the Woman snatched the gun from his grasp and tossed it onto the bed.

"One more word from you and I shall toss you from that window. Do you, three simpletons, not see how easily you were fooled?"

"But we did see…" Anton muttered.

His voice was cut off as he received another cold look from the Director's envoy.

"What you saw," the Woman explained, "was precisely what they wanted you to see. The art of fooling those without observation skills is an ancient art form. Mountebanks and false prophets have used such trickery since the dawn of time. You three proved as easy to deceive as a desperate gambler in a casino."

"What? How?" Pierre spluttered.

"There were two of them!" the Woman spat out.

"That is not possible!" Pierre said, his voice rising. "Nothing in this house was disturbed. There was one man, only one, who sought my life!"

The woman grabbed Pierre Gérard by the collar of his suit and dragged him to the window. She turned his body with one flick of her wrist, forcing his head to look upward towards the roof.

"See! The rain gutter to the right is slightly bent and the tiles near the edge of the roof are clean. A man jumped out, grabbed the drain, and pulled himself up onto the roof. The sounds of the fireworks muffled his landing and gave his partner time to climb over the wall. It was a case of simple misdirection—and old trick that still works on the gullible. What did you talk about when you thought your visitor had leaped across that chasm?"

"We, er…" Anton began, but was silenced as the Woman cut him off with a gesture.

"You," she said, pointing at Robert. "Tell me the exact words spoken."

Robert cleared his throat and said:

"There were expressions of surprise and concern about the Director's reaction. I could recount the precise statements, if you wish?"

"Not necessary; that is sufficient," the woman said.

She began scanning the walls and floor of the room.

"Where is your safe?" she asked.

"What… er…"

Pierre Gérard first thought of denying possession of such an item, but remembered his precarious position. This terrifying female, who cowed all three of them by her very presence, was the personal envoy dispatched the Supreme Lord of the Red Hand. Lying to her was like prevaricating in front of her master, and such behavior always resulted in swift, vicious, reprisal.

"Well, I have a hidden one down in my study," he finally admitted. "That is the best-protected room in the house. Sophisticated burglar alarm systems protect it day and night."

"Show me," the Woman replied. "Immediately."

With Robert in the lead, they trooped to the other wing of the mansion. Fishing a key from his voluminous pocket, the butler unlocked the door and stepped aside for their visitor.

"Are there any alarms on this door?" she asked, studying the frame slowly.

Pierre shook his head.

"I did not find a system that proved properly effective. Most could be defeated with a simple wire cutter. Instead, I chose an old-fashioned lock with a very complicated key. A burglar would struggle in vain to use a lock pick on such a lock."

"Unless they know how to open old locks," the Woman said, shaking her head. "Very foolish. Let's continue."

All three men expected their terrifying visitor to step inside the room and set off the alarm system, but she did not. Instead, she studied the room from the threshold, tilting her head left and right as she examined the floor, ceiling and walls.

"A pressure pad system? Nothing else? This is your so-called sophisticated method to protect your valuables—and the Red Hand's secret documents?"

She did not bother to hide her disgust.

"But there are over one hundred pressure pads!" Pierre Gérard replied with some heat. "If anything larger than a mouse stepped on one, the alarm would sound and we could catch them within seconds."

"I was wrong, you are not an ignoramus," the Woman said, her voice a low hiss, "you are a complete simpleton without enough basic intelligence to fill a soup spoon. The furniture does not rest on pressure pads! Your burglar hopped between the chairs and coffee table until they reached the desk. That places them within mere feet of that safe that you stupidly attempted to hide behind a painting!"

"But the painting is held in place..." Pierre Gérard sputtered.

"By a magnet, yes," she cut him off. "So long as something maintains the circuit, with a bit of metal and another magnet, the painting shall freely open. I will also hazard to guess that we will find the combination to the safe within one of the drawers of your desk, correct?"

She held up a hand.

"If you lie to me and I prove you wrong, the torment I shall visit upon you before your death shall be make that of the circles of Dante's Inferno pale by comparison. So think before you speak, for your life is in my grasp."

Pierre Gérard frowned, looked down and nodded.

"Er, yes, it's in my appointment book."

Suddenly, he pulled another smaller revolver from his jacket and raised it towards the Woman's face. A few steps behind him, Anton also drew a derringer from his sleeve, the tiny weapon appearing in his grasp in an instant.

The Woman grabbed Pierre's arm, causing the bone to audibly crunch under her fist. She then propelled him into Anton, who fired his gun just as Pierre Gérard appeared in front of him. The tiny, but powerful, firearm released a popping sound and a small crimson hole appeared in Pierre Gérard's forehead.

Anton, surprised, nevertheless reached into his jacket to get his other holdout gun. He had just placed his fingers on its grip when a hard impact struck him in the back. There was also a strange cold sensation, followed by a squishing sound in his chest. He looked down and saw with puzzled eyes a blade protruding from his chest.

"How did that get there?" he asked, his voice a strangled whisper.

Anton tried to turn his head to look at the person behind him, but found that his neck was no longer working.

He frowned as his mouth filled with blood and his vision suddenly became blurry, then dark.

His body crumpled to the floor, a wet rattle emerging from his throat as he convulsed one last time. The scents of urine and excrement filled the air, mixed with the rusty iron odor of spilled blood.

The Woman looked over at Robert Ménard, who fussily cleaned the blood from his blade with a red silk handkerchief. Examining the weapon minutely, he cleaned it for another minute before looking up. The knife disappeared from sight and he carefully folded the cloth before placing the item in a small oilskin pouch.

"Why did you kill your friend?" the Woman asked, his voice not hiding her suspicion.

"These men were not my friends, Madame," Robert replied. "They were mere co-workers who failed to perform their duties as ordered. My employer is the Red Hand, not a mere regional manager who mistakenly believed that his money and worldly possessions raised him to the level of an Emperor."

Robert stood stiffly before her, the pose of a classic butler before his charge.

The Woman studied him for a full minute before turning her back on him.

"Very good," she said. "Disengage the alarm system so that I may determine the extent of this idiot's failure. After that, dispose of these corpses. I imagine you possess a means?"

"Indeed, I do, Madame." Robert said, as coolly composed as ever. "Will you require anything else?"

"Move my bags to the main bedroom. I will require food in precisely fifty-two minutes. You will find my exact dietary requirements in the smaller case's inside pocket. Then await my further instructions."

"Very well, Madame." Robert replied.

He picked up the dead body of Pierre Gérard and headed towards his sausage press.

CHAPTER XXII

"My darlings, you were inspirational this morning," Madame Defarge said as Irma and Victor exited the tent.

She reached a hairy knuckled hand up and gently stroked the head of one of her pet wolves. They were not part of her act, but followed her like silent sentinels wherever she walked.

"This idiot nearly missed me when I flipped forward," Irma said, shooting Victor an annoyed look. Irma said, shooting Victor an annoyed look. "Another centimeter and I would end up failing into your tiger cage."

"You were two degrees offline during your jump," Victor replied, his voice sounding distant, as if he were speaking from a distant location. "I adjusted the best I could in the split second left to me."

Irma rolled her eyes and shook his head.

"Men! I would call him a liar and a fool, but I doubt he would hear a word I am saying."

Madame Defarge frowned and asked:

"What is the matter? Is he sick?"

"No," Irma replied, "Merely concentrating on something else. Time matters not when he is in this state."

"That would be useful if you chose to take another man as a lover," Madame Defarge said, guffawing in a deep, resonant tone.

"Lucky for this idiot, I have no interest in such activities," giggled Irma. "He is all I wish in a mate and I hope he feels the same. Victor is not one to discuss such topics."

Madame Defarge fondly patted Irma on the cheek.

"Little one, you need never fear. Do you remember Patricia, the American horse-woman? She was lovely, with deep dark eyes and hair like a raven's wing."

"Yes," Irma said, practically spitting the word. "She had thick ankles, and a voice that caused the animals to yowl in agony."

"Bernard the Fire-Eater and Inigo the Snake-Charmer had a knife fight over her charms. She threw herself at your young man and he never so much as looked her direction. You two are like my darling Mars and Venus here."

The animal-tamer gently stroked her wolves' thick fur.

"Together to the end" she continued. "Though with your lifestyle, that could be a short life."

Irma impulsively hugged the older woman and kissed her on both leathery cheeks.

"Thank you. It is difficult some days. Men possess all the emotions of a boulder."

Madame Defarge snorted and turned to leave.

"I think you overestimate them, my darling. Go, take your young man somewhere safe. Otherwise, he will be run over or stabbed by some jealous factory worker."

Irma smiled and took Victor by the arm, leading him gently back to their trailer. She folded out a chair and pushed him into the seat before stripping out of her costume. She then, still naked, performed a series of post-exercise stretching activities for another hour. By the end, she was soaked with sweat, her taut muscles rippling in the spare light of their small living space.

Pushing aside a trunk, Irma folded out a small tub, which she filled after working a small hand pump. Dropping into the cold water with a loud sigh, she lay in it for a time before cleaning and draining the tub. She then dressed in a light green dressing grown with a gold floral pattern and read a book as she brushed her thick, auburn, locks.

"How did I get in here?" Victor eventually asked, looking around in confusion. "We were just outside the tent a minute ago."

"Three hours ago, *mon chéri*," Irma said, blowing him a kiss. "I have already stretched my muscles, bathed, ate and drank two cups of tea. You were under your spell for some time."

"Huh," Victor grunted.

He stood up and threw off his clothes. He pulled out the bathing tub, filling it again and climbing inside. Unlike Irma, he did not luxuriate, but merely cleaned his body and emptied the device moments later.

"What are you reading?" he asked as he pulled on a kimono that she had given him a year ago.

She had bought the article while they were on tour in Moscow, having befriended a servant of the Shogun's representative, one Lady Yuki. The young lady, a pretty, kind, highly intelligent woman, had been married to a coarse merchant who had achieved some position of power in the new government. Her husband, who possessed complex tattoos all over his bloated, scarred body, had owned many such kimonos made for far slimmer men, a fact that had angered him every time he had looked at them. Having his wife sell them to a European had made him happy, especially since she had earned a decent profit on the transaction.

"Rudyard Kipling," Irma replied, placing a silk strip in between her pages. "About an Irish boy following a Tibetan lama. Interesting, but just an amusement. I think I shall sell it when I am done. Now, what caused you to fall into a waking sleep?"

"I was processing what you told me about the figures and all the details you saw in the books we stole. I recognized that most of it was in code, but I believe I've succeeded in deciphering some of the contents."

Victor prepared himself a quick meal of apples and cheese and sat back in his chair.

"What did you find?" Irma asked.

Victor began chewing an apple slice slowly.

"We went up a false trail," he said. "These are not the ones that were responsible for the deaths of your gang."

"*Our* gang," Irma said, with an edge in her voice.

Her eyes narrowed slightly and she suddenly appeared very tense. Victor shook his head.

"Only in the sense that you convinced me to stay there and learn their ways. Let us not go over this discussion again… The Vampires kidnapped me. Yes, it turned out to be a good thing, but I did not love them for it. They treated me with fear and loathing. I was their weapon, not a member."

Irma crossed her arms across her chest as her bare foot tapped the trailer in open annoyance. She possessed dainty feet, but they were hard, calloused, and even slightly deformed. These were not the toes of a lady whose main concern was blisters after an evening of dancing. These were the feet of a trained athlete, a gymnast and, most importantly, a cat burglar. The many bumps, blemishes and near deformities were a tribute to the trials and tribulations of her dangerous life.

"Is that how you see me?" she spat back "As one who kept you chained to a pack of criminals? Escaping only because they were wiped out?"

Victor shook his head and extended his hand, but it hung between them like a ghostly tree limb.

"No, I could leave any time. You were the only reason I stayed. The only way I would have left was if you'd come with me."

Irma studied the hand for a moment, her eyes narrowing.

"You never told me that before," she said.

"You never asked. Leaving the Vampires was easy enough. How do you think I could find you so many books and records?"

"You told me you bought them from stores on your free time outside."

Victor smiled and shook his head.

"No. What I told you was I got it from a store. You supplied the rest. I used to come and go as I chose."

Irma's stony expression transformed in an instant into surprise, shock, then open amusement. She entwined her fingers in his.

"You never told me that," she repeated.

"You were a devoted member of the gang," Victor replied. "To tell you would have tested your loyalty. I had no loyalty to them, only to you."

Irma smiled and looked over her shoulder.

"It would take too long to unfold the bed. I hope you re-inforced the table... I will have you here and now..."

Victor smiled back as they reached for each other, grateful their heavily sound-proofed trailer possessed reinforced furniture.

CHAPTER XXIII

Days passed before the Great Brain found himself interrupted again. With Professor Rotwang and Doctor ten Brinken eagerly working on the test subjects, silence reigned over a large portion of the headquarters. The final gem carvings proceeded at a good pace and the Great Brain only interrupted his work for food intakes and the minimum amount of sleep required for him to operate at proper capacity.

"Mardon! I would have words with you!" the Lamane thundered, storming into the Great Brain's main chamber.

The elderly cultist appeared clearly agitated, tapping his heavy staff upon the stone floor with a heavy hand.

"What do you want?" the Great Brain asked, sighing and replacing his tools on his workbench.

The aged advisor to the Nimrod had kept to the shadows, sneaking about and making notes on a wax tablet he kept at his side at all times.

"You... you... are an abomination! You are a vile, immoral, transgressor... a lover of... the horrors of modernities! Then, I discovered your true intent! What you plan to do with those poor men and women is abhorrent to all that we hold dear. You... you are like the serpent in the Garden!"

The Great Brain stopped listening, but did not hide his mocking delight at the white-bearded official of the Children of Giphantie.

This shard of the great Martian mastermind had joined this cult more out of amusement and their employment of skilled scientists than for any philosophical reasons.

Upon landing inside a body on this misbegotten, backward planet, the Great Brain had found himself weakened beyond all imagination. Before, his mighty mind controlled the very elements of Mars. The lightning struck his enemies and the land quaked as his mountain-sized brain controlled ever form of life on his homeworld.

But here, on Earth, other than an uncanny talent for hypnosis, and memories of an alien science beyond the dreams of these lesser creatures, he was as helpless as one of the tiny aborigines of the Red Planet.

The cult of the Children of Giphantie possessed many great minds, but all were hampered by a silly philosophy that anyone with a teaspoon of intelligence could mimic.

They based their beliefs in an odd mythology. According to the Children of Giphantie, humanity had started with a single male and a female in a paradise garden. In that vegetal utopia was a tree that was supposed to contain the entire knowledge of mankind. And, the fruits of this tree affected humans in both positive and negative manner. Some inspired, others weakened the minds of those consuming them.

The Children of Giphantie believe that this so-called "Garden of Eden" had once existed in a hidden location somewhere in Africa. The women and men who had acted as the guardians of this Tree eventually metamorphosed into higher beings, who chose to walk among the hidden places of the cosmos. Those who wished to remain among humanity and not rise to a higher plane of existence, had founded the Children of Giphantie. They a taken human slaves with the understanding that they would someday replace all of mankind's industrious societies with a benevolent, pastoral existence of simplicity, vegetarianism—and, of course, obedience to the leaders of Giphantie.

But within a few decades of the creation of the Children of Giphantie, the human slaves, led by the chief servant known as the Nimrod, had overthrown their masters. Some said that the Nimrod and his followers had entombed the Giphantians alive underground or beneath the ocean. Others whispered these higher creatures had received swift executions. All agreed that they had underestimated humanity's desire for power over their own fellows. The Nimrod and his followers have kept many of Giphantie's original beliefs, but with the intent of ruling all life on Earth.

Which had been a perfect motivation for the Great Brain to join that secret society!

Memorizing their beliefs, he had swiftly risen in the ranks until he had had enough influence to attempt to enact his plans. No longer would he remain a mere crippled human. The Great Brain was a higher being, who fed upon the life of insects such as the humans of Earth.

"Are you done with your complaints, old man?" he asked as the Lamane paused to inhale.

"I... I..." the Lamane spluttered.

The Great Brain chopped the air with one hand while his other hand pressed a button built into his chair.

"Silence!" he spat back. "I do not need to listen to your complaining anymore. You and the rest of your cult of fools shall inconvenience me no longer. It is time you served your true master."

"You?" the Lamane scoffed, rolling his eyes. "But you are merely Mordon, a satrap under the Nimrod. You are not even the senior of the Nimrod's followers! Soon you shall no longer be called by that wondrous title!"

The Great Brain surprisingly nodded.

"That much we agree upon. That silly name and title are those of a lesser being. I am higher than any creature living on this ridiculous, unimportant speck of a rock. The usefulness of your pathetic, misbegotten cult of cretins is nearing an end. Allow me to tell you a secret about the individuals you believe rose to a higher plane of existence. They miscalculated the time and space equations and ended up rematerializing in the center of a dwarf star. The hyper-gravity crushed them and cosmic winds consumed the remains."

"You... you... madman...you..." the Lamane stammered, his eyes grown wide.

He stepped back, holding his staff in front of his body in a defensive posture.

"Hold that statement," the Great Brain said, nodding to the doorway.

Doctor ten Brinken strode in, his face flushed.

"Good evening, Master!" he crooned "The tests results are exceeding all expectations! Soon I shall require subjects to begin the trials."

"Excellent, my servant," the Great Brain replied. "Oh, and point of fact—it is morning, not evening."

Ten Brinken shrugged.

"Night, day, who cares!? The work on unveiling the secrets of life are all that matters, Master."

"Well said, my servant."

The Great Brain chuckled softly.

The Lamane tapped the stone floor with his staff and cried:

"You traitor! You swore to serve the Children of Giphantie! Not this madman who seeks to destroy all we hold true!"

Ten Brinken snickered, causing his eyes to vanish in his face and sending his jowls aquiver. He resembled an English bulldog about to bark or bite as he looked at his former leader.

"I agreed to no such thing, sir," he said. "I agreed to work in your labs with the understanding that I could pursue my own projects. Yet, your organization hampered my every attempt to break through the walls established by the feeble-minded under the guise of ethical standards."

"Your ideas were heresy!" the Lamane screamed, spittle forming at the corners of his mouth.

"You destroyed my mandrake root!" ten Brinken roared.

His face turned purple and his stance changed from relaxed and amused to hunched, tense, and enraged.

"I had such plans for that special subspecies created by the semen of hanged men in their last seconds of life!" he added. "Yet, you and the rest of your fatuous fools threw that rare plant into a furnace!"

"Happily," the Great Brain intervened, "I found another source for you, my good servant. A certain Doctor Caligari from one of the Grand Duchies, Oldenburg I believe, gratefully provided me with a recent sample obtained during a hanging of some political gangsters."

"Oh, thank you, Master! Did it cost you dear? I met that Caligari some years ago. He is not one that easily releases that which he views as his property."

Ten Brinken rubbed his hands together with obvious anticipation.

The Great Brain shook his head and replied:

"I only used some of my recent infusions of funds to pay a few clerks and officials to look away from some of his less licit activities."

"What infusions of money?" the Lamane asked. "You are thieving from our grand body? Is that how low you've sunk, you worm?"

The Great Brain swiveled his head a few inches and mockingly twisted his countenance into one of surprise.

"Oh, Lamane! I forgot you were present," he mocked. "You are a quite forgettable fellow. However, I shall answer your question, although I would remind you that it is quite rude to eavesdrop on other people's conversations. My scientists required subjects for their experiments. Rather than simply taking some innocent souls off the streets, I had my followers attack and abduct criminals. The assets of these evil men then became mine. We are also becoming a major supplier of red lotus to the populace. The narcotic weakens the human will and grants us an additional source of income."

"I cannot believe my ears!" the Lamane said. "I shall contact the Nimrod immediately and he shall expel you and your followers from our organization!"

He shook his head, causing spittle to spatter across the floor and began walking towards the exit.

"Doctor ten Brinken," the Great Brain drawled, "I believe here is your first new subject for procedure one. I do not think, however, that he will survive three, four, or six."

"I agree, Master. The flesh, especially old flesh that subsists on a diet of vegetables and water, is weak."

With that, ten Brinken stepped aside, allowing the Lamane to sweep past.

"I shall put an end to this…"

The Lamane's speech was cut off and he gasped in surprise and pain.

Ten Brinken withdrew the hypodermic needle from the elderly man's neck and placed the instrument back in his coat pocket.

"He shall not collapse, Master," the scientist said. "The psychoactive narcotic I injected him with shall render him drowsy and easily suggestible."

He pulled the staff of the Lamane's office from the man's fingers and tossed it aside.

"When may I use him next?" the Great Brain asked, wincing at the clattering sound of the wooden staff on the stone floor.

"I shall weigh him and prepare the precise amount of the reagent for his body," ten Brinken said. "Too much or too little would result in disaster. Then I shall operate and, with a small period of recovery, the subject's operational capacity shall be acceptable within twelve hours, I surmise. Perhaps two to four hours longer if his organs do not adapt to the compound with alacrity."

He took the Lamane's arm and led the man towards the door.

"Apprise me upon completion," the Great Brain replied as he returned to his work.

CHAPTER XXIV

"This is a very poor idea," Irma said for perhaps the thirtieth time since they had left their trailer.

"It is the only means of discovering the truth." Victor replied as he dropped to the ground by her side.

"They will shoot us on sight," she added as she crouched low in the shadows.

Victor shook his head, the plague doctor's mask casting odd shadows across her heavily made-up face.

"I doubt it. They will find our actions confusing. Anyone capable of building an international criminal organization cannot murder people thoughtlessly. They must first find out what we know, and if we spread the details of their organization to others."

"Which translates into torture and murder," Irma whispered back. "How very delightful. If you consider this an inspirational chat, *chéri*, you are failing miserably. I hope you have a greater plan than to simply hope that a pack of ambitious criminals shall forgive our transgressions."

"I have," Victor replied, "though it hinges on both of us staying alive until we speak to the Lord of the Main Rouge."

"Somehow, I am not heartened by your words."

Irma shook her head, then vanished into the darkness. Beneath his heavy mask, Victor chuckled and soundlessly ran towards the house.

Using the same route, he climbed up, entered through an unlit water closet and walked down the hall. This was the point of greatest danger, where he could be killed in mere seconds. Yet, there was no other path that could lead to the answers they sought.

Unlocking the door to Gérard's bedroom, he stepped inside. The room appeared empty, the furnishings exactly as he had left them days earlier. Even the disarray caused by the fight appeared to be exactly as before—which was odd. Even a poor household owner would have picked up an overturned chair.

Victor was about to leave, when the silvery moonlight coming through the window illuminated a feminine figure. She had landed lightly, alighting onto the wooden floor with a slight thud.

Straightening up, she stood as tall as Victor, with broad shoulders and a narrow waist.

"I was waiting for you," the Woman said, her voice a harsh, abrasive, croak. "I knew you would come."

Victor stood still, watching as the shadowy figure stepped closer. This Woman's step was heavy, yet she moved with impressive speed. It was an odd combination that caused his hackles to raise and his body to tense with concern.

"You must be a madman, you and your partner," she snarled, raising a pair of gloved fists. "You murder our people and rob our funds. I assume Mabuse or Fantômas are paying you well for your actions. It matters not at all. I shall break your body and rip all your secrets from your shrieking form."

Victor grabbed a glass tube from a pocket and poured its contents, a thin powder, before him. Then, taking a step backwards towards the door, he gave her a quick salute and entered the hallway.

The Woman strode forward. Victor waited in the corridor, smiling beneath his mask. As she arrived near the doorway, the powder crackled, and a heavy, yellow gas appeared around her body. She stumbled, unable to see, and fell into a nearby wall.

Victor was about to guffaw when the door splintered. A pair of black-gloved fists emerged from the wooden frame Seconds later, they withdrew, but appeared again.

Victor backed away, no longer smiling. The shattered remains of the door fell away and the Woman stepped into the hallway, revealing herself for the first time.

Despite having lived for years in a circus, Victor Sicarius gasped at the sight before his incredulous eyes.

The being that had stepped out from the shadows was only nominally human. Her blackened dead face was a skeletal, nearly fleshless horror, held together by thin plates of silver-gray metal. Patches of colorless, lifeless hair lay like withered weeds across her scalp. More metal plates held up the head, creaking and clicking with each movement.

Equally terrifying were her arms, or the lack of them. In the place of human appendages were a pair of metal limbs, made from steel, with gears and machine parts that softly whirled and clicked. A pair of black leather gloves pulled over their oversized hands did not hide their inhumanity.

"Clever boy," the Woman snarled, "Are you a chemist? No matter, I've killed scientists in the past."

That said, she exploded into action, moving with uncanny speed. Within a heartbeat her monstrous hands slashed the air inches from where Victor's head had stood. Her frightening firsts shattered the wall behind him, sending a plume of stone and plaster dust into the air.

Seeing that this woman was no mere gangster, Victor mentally prepared himself. Backflipping down the hallway, he landed several feet from the railing next to the marble staircase.

"Yes," she said, her voice a hoarse whisper, "run, little bird. Make this exciting before I rip your arms and legs from their sockets and crush each bone in your body."

Victor did not respond, sensing that his silence would anger his opponent even further. This was exactly what he required for the moment. A furious enemy was one who might make foolish decisions. He needed this woman-thing off-balance until the right time.

As his frightening enemy barreled forward, Victor was not surprised when he saw her skid to a halt a few feet from his position. Though enraged, she was professional enough to know that running his direction while he was near a staircase was dangerous.

Most would would have fled screaming at the sight of this monster bearing down on them with murderous intentions, but not Victor Sicarius. Standing straight and steady, his plague doctor mask hiding his features, he appeared as odd and terrible as the half-human creature raising her hands above her head.

Victor waited for her foot to rise as she stepped forward, then he kicked her with his left leg, his boot striking her in the solar plexus. The Woman fell back, sailing down the hall like a rag doll, landing with a massive crash.

But she bounced back to her feet, her frightening face twisted with fury. Victor knew that a kick to a nerve cluster, such as the one had had just delivered, would finished nearly anyone else. That blow should have caused any opponent to fall to their knees, unable to breathe. Yet the Woman was not injured—if anything, she seemed empowered by the strike.

Waiting until she was in range again, Victor lifted his leg, as if he were about to deliver the same kick. But at the last minute, he shifted backwards, spun low in a tight circle, and his right leg slashed out, sweeping the charging woman off her feet—or at least partially so.

One of her oversized hands slammed on the floor, preventing her from fully falling to the ground. With a creak of metal, she straightened up. Her movements resembled that of a marionette whose master pulled the strings to get her to stand her upright. The movement was inhuman, a motion one would have expected from a clockwork figure.

"Is that it?" she asked, not advancing another step. "A few fighting tricks? I am disappointed, but the sound of your bones shattering will soon bring me solace."

Victor was about to attempt yet another daring maneuver, when a crashing sound originating from down below drifted in his direction.

He tensed, wondering about Irma's safety.

This gave his enemy a chance to close the distance between them and launch a hard punch to his head.

The extended beak of the plague doctor mask shattered under the impact. Victor fell back against the railing.

The Woman stepped closer and grabbed his jacket with a grip of iron. Her mechanical arm whirred and creaked as she lifted Victor from his feet and held him up above her head.

With a lurching step, she then dangled him in empty space, thirty feet above the marble hallway below.

"Will the drop kill you?" she rasped. "If you land on your feet, possibly not. I think I shall test the theory."

Her nearly fleshless face split into a skeletal rictus as her grip slackened.

CHAPTER XXV

Chevalier Bernard Benoît was a harried man. The second son of Baron Clément Benoît, he desperately wished to please his father and increase the family's growing power at the Emperor's court. Neither were easy goals to achieve, for the competition was terrible and fierce. A dozen clans fought daily for the Emperor and Empress's approval, with even more seeking to reach the royal circle of power.

The Benoît clan possessed a few advantages that placed them above most of the new noble clans. Bernard's father and grandfather, along with the military advisor, Duplessis, had been amongst the earliest who had supported the Emperor when he had declared his intent to rebuild the Empire. As a reward for their loyalty, the Benoîts' private bank and new industrial corporation, Machines Lourdes Benoît & Cie., now held the exclusive rights to many new, scientifically advanced, patents.

This had led to their bids to take over several large cities with the understanding that massive manufacturing complexes would be set up there. The Emperor had granted them huge land leases in Marseilles, Le Havre, Lyon, and the Saint-Denis district of Paris. Borrowing from the royal treasury to cover the startup costs, Machines Lourdes Benoît had created giant factories that powered whole cities as well as built everything from small home devices to huge airships. There was a product from their company in every home in the Empire and they competed with the British, Hessians, Ottomans, Americans, and Zulus for the world market.

However, the Benoît manufacturing complexes were always secondary in their output compared with the Americans and the British. They still held a slight lead over the others, but the Japanese and Chinese appeared on the rise.

"You are now in charge of Marseilles," Baron Clément Benoît had informed Bernard. "Improve the productivity or I shall replace you with your brother, Gaétan."

Baron Benoît was tall, with a fleshy, pale face, reddish yellow hair and dark eyes that resembled chips of black marble.

"Do whatever you deem necessary, but do not fail me," he added. "Lack of success on your part means that the facility on Île Royale shall receive a new supervisor."

"Yes, father." Bernard had squeaked.

He knew that his father admired boldness and strength, so he asked a very impertinent question:

"What if I succeed?"

Baron Benoît stared at Bernard, his expression never varying for an instant. This was one of his terrifying gifts, an ability to study anyone without appearing to blink or breathe. The effect was astonishingly off-putting, a method of weakening his enemies prior to negotiations.

"You shall not follow my position as chair of the family corporation. You are not suited for such duty. There is a weakness within you, boy. Fear of failure. However, you possess a unique mind well suited for economic theory and practice. My plan for you is a lifetime in politics. Not running for elective positions—we are Benoîts, after all, not dirty vote grubbers. But Deputy Minister of Industry or Finance, what do you think?"

Baron Clément Benoît didn't bother to hide his Machiavellian schemes for every member of his family.

"Yes, Father, that would suit me fine," Bernard had replied.

He had found his name listed on those raised to Chevalier a week later.

Now, four years later, he did have some successes in his position. Creating an eight-hour, three working shift plan had cost the company more in wages, but less in accidents and mistakes. The increased yield of five percent had kept Bernard in his father's good graces. Sadly, that was the sum total of his success, and the Baron was now growing more impatient with each passing month.

"Five percent more by next month," he had said through the televisor only the week before, "or you shall take the Struan ship, *Dancing Cloud*, and hope you do not contract malaria as you go and stay on Île Royale."

Sitting back in his heavy, leather club chair, Bernard had felt the sweat pooling at the base of his spine. All his other ideas so far had not increased production, though none had caused a drop, so far. This meant he needed to do the one thing he found terrifying: take a risk.

Standing, he crossed to his desk and pressed the fourth button on the keypad near the televisor. A buzzing sound emerged from the device and the face of a pretty woman with long dark hair and wide green eyes filled the screen.

She smiled his direction with plump, bright red lips and tiny, pearly colored teeth.

"Hello, *chéri*. Have you come to your senses and agreed to meet with the incredible gentleman I told you about last month?" she asked.

Her voice was the triumphant purr of a cat who has just consumed a bird and a bowl of forbidden cream.

Bernard exhaled. His dislike of undertaking risky ventures rose again in his mind. Then the thought of living on Île Royale, only a short distance from the infamous Devil's Island, rose again in his imagination. Residing on a scrap of land off the coast of South America, fighting off swarms of mosquitoes, praying he did not contract malaria or yellow fever, was not his idea of fun. Also, all the employees there were convicts, working in the small factory under conditions that were little better than slavery. His decision was not difficult to make with those details etched in in mind.

"Yes, Violette," Bernard Benoît said. "I agree to the meeting. How soon can we speak?"

His shoulders drooped in defeat as he begged for aid from a man who, probably, was quite mad.

"A black Saturne steamer shall pull up to the south gate of your factory. Get on the back seat and we shall transport you to our facility," Violette replied, adding: "You made a wise choice, *chéri*. Afterwards, we shall celebrate your coming success in a very special way."

Bernard straightened and whispered:

"The shepherdess and her favorite ram?'

"Your horns are waiting by my bedside..." she replied, licking her lips seductively before the screen went dark.

Bernard closed his eyes and fought for two minutes to regain some degree of control. Eventually, his erection drooped, and he practically ran towards the door.

First, he would listen to the odd man's offer. Then, a night with Violette. The thought of her in her peasant costume almost caused him to return to his office and he had to think unsexual thoughts, such as the state of his workers as they left the plant, their faces and bodies back with oil, grease, and soot.

The only nagging concern he held as he left the factory and climbed into the car was one he had told himself several times since first learning of this person.

"What type of a name is the Great Brain?"

CHAPTER XXVI

Irma Vep entered the house once again through the servant's quarters, crossing into the kitchen seconds later. The marble floor and darkened halls were much the same as it had been when she had first broken into this mansion. She moved with the same slow, careful motions, never trusting every item to remain in the same location.

Scanning the floor and walls, she smiled broadly as she spotted well-hidden pressure pads across the hallway floor. Someone was attempting to be clever, which was always a mistake. Using that alarm system a second time, especially after she had defeated it with such ease earlier, meant that the owners of this house were either foolishly arrogant or setting her up for a snare.

Believing the latter, she careful stepped around the pressure pads, her every sense alert and ready for the slightest change.

Suddenly, she sensed a movement from an alcove to her right, a miniscule motion that was nearly imperceptible.

A mere heartbeat later, she dove to her left, tucking and rolling another two feet. The pair of throwing blades struck the wall and floor near her previous position. The weapons clattered away, vanishing into the lengthy shadows of the gloomy corridor.

Irma rolled up into a low crouch, resembling a massive, lithe black cat with her long-legged pose.

"Impressive," Robert Ménard stated, stepping into the spare starlight illuminating the passage.

"Thank you," Irma chirped back.

Her accent was now the drawling vowels of a native of Brittany. This was not her natural way of speaking, but one of her favorite ploys for putting people off her proverbial scent.

A pair of knives appeared in Robert's white-gloved fists, long thin blades made for throwing.

An instant later, the silver missiles streaked in Irma's direction, seeking her eyes. Leaping up and flipping to her right, both blades passed harmlessly beneath her spinning body. The weapons struck a wooden table, sinking deep below the surface of the furnishing.

"At least, you chose the fake Louis XIV table to practice your throwing." Irma said, giggling.

Robert paused, his hands raised to throw.

"Pardon me, Mademoiselle, but that is an original from the king's own summer cottage."

Irma smiled, her heavily painted face creating a combination of seduction and oddity.

"Only if the king's summer cottage was a shop in Lille owned by a furniture maker named Vadim."

Robert shook his head.

"No matter. You can't avoid my knives forever, *sale garce*."

Being called a "dirty bitch" was far from new to Irma Vep. In fact she found such insults rather amusing. Part of her training in the Vampires had involved suffering through daily insults, threats and beatings aimed at toughening her against the world. The theory was that, after hearing such degrading words daily for years, the curses and oaths would become meaningless. The idea was sound, but the Vampires had not considered the negative side effects. The experiment had caused the surviving members of the gang to treat outsiders or the weak with derisive, sadistic contempt. Only Irma Vep and Victor Sicarius had escaped that fate, thanks to their connection with each other.

"That depends," Irma said, still smiling. "Are your blades as dull as your wit?"

The killer turned butler inhaled quickly, surprised by the sarcastic quip at his expense. With slow, deliberate movements, he returned the throwing knives to their sleeve sheathes. Using the same painstaking motions, he then drew a pair of matching American Bowie knives.

The weapons glinted and glimmered in the pale, silvery moonlight that peaked out from distant windows. Each blade measured nine inches in length and a pair of simple wooden handles acted as grips. There was a terrible, awful majesty to these killing tools. Just looking at them invoked a disquieting sensation that derived from the ancient atavistic fear of tooth and claw. These Bowie knives possessed none of the majesty of a sword, or even the slim delicacy of the Italian stiletto. These were killing tools, meant for nothing else but the death and dismemberment of another living being.

"Oh, my," Irma said, intentionally giggling again. "Did I make you angry?"

Robert's lips curled back in a silent snarl, then he charged.

He spun his knives in the palm of his hands and sliced through the air. Though massive, he moved with the momentum of a charging rhino. His speed was astonishing, often fooling enemies by closing the distance between them in seconds.

Not so with Irma Vep, however. She had sensed that this man was a trained killer with a love of the blade. Those who specialized in such weapons often possessed exceptional speed. They loved how their fast reflexes enabled them to kill their enemies before they even realized they were under attack.

Quick-draw gunmen think the same way. Idiots, Irma thought as she feinted a high flip and slid down the hallway away from her attacker.

Popping to her feet, she grinned and skipped around the corner, waving as she stepped out of sight.

Robert appeared around the corner, stepping wide in case she stood nearby intent on attacking. But Irma was nowhere in sight, causing him to look left, right, and finally up.

He spotted her standing on the top of a high cupboard, waving once again.

"*Merde!*" he snarled and spat on the floor.

Running forward, he pocketed to blade and reached for the front of the cabinet.

Irma placed her hands on the wall at her rear and positioned her feet on the edge furthest from the maddened butler. Then, pushing back, she sent the cupboard falling forward, forcing Robert to dive to his right.

The butler crashed through a low table, the sound muffled by that of the cabinet hitting the Persian rug.

"That was a priceless armoire once owned by the Marquis de Saint-Evremonde," Robert Ménard whispered as he climbed to his feet.

"Not anymore," Irma replied.

She danced out of the room, humming *In the Hall of the Mountain King* as she vanished from sight. This was intentional as she wished for the oversized man to be angry and follow her.

Snarling, Robert did, but at a sedate pace this time. He muttered oaths under his breath, never having suffered such humiliation in his life before.

The humming grew softer as he walked, forcing him to increase his gait to a near trot.

"I will make her die slowly," he swore, leaving the living room behind and stepping into the main hall.

CHAPTER XXVII

"I still do not understand your idea, Monsieur," Bernard Benoît said, shaking his head. "You tell me that you can get the workers to toil at a faster rate and increase our output immeasurably. Yet, you do not tell me the process you plan to use to achieve that objective."

The Great Brain fought to keep his facial muscles under control. He wished he could sneer at this man's sweaty face. This venal fool held an incredible source of power without fully comprehending his own wealth. Under his management, eight thousand men and women labored in one of the factory's three work shifts. Yet, to Benoît and others of his ilk, they were nothing more than cogs who ensured that the mighty machines continued grinding away day and night. Such a waste of biological wealth!

"How very wise of you to recognize that fact, Chevalier," the Great Brain purred. "I knew you were a brilliant man."

Bernard flushed, unused to such compliments, except from Violette. His father was not a man given to praising anyone, even when a person yielded great success. Only Violette seemed to understand him, although she reserved her uplifting comments for moments after he had paid for her services, or received a handsome gift.

"Thank you," Bernard said, dabbing his forehead with a handkerchief. "I await your answer."

The Great Brain rose and moved to Bernard's side. Placing an arm across his sweaty shoulder, he whispered:

"If I show you, you must swear an oath to tell no one."

Bernard frowned and shook his head.

"I can't. My father will want to know the source of the plant's increased productivity."

The Great Brain stepped back, regretting his decision to leave this man unconverted. But for the moment, he needed

Bernard Benoît's behavior to vary as little as possible. Therefore, he needed to placate the fool for a little while longer.

"You are wiser than I believed possible, Chevalier. Then I shall tell you everything. The concoction I propose that you provide to your workers is a simple drink made from a number of common herbs and minerals. The consumption of this brew shall grant them greater concentration and a desire to work harder and with precision. You shall see an immediate transformation in their behavior."

The Great Brain was telling the truth… at least partially.

"Are any of these herbs illegal?" Bernard whispered, afraid of the answer.

The Great Brain straightened and twisted his face in an expression that approximated outrage.

"*Mais non, Monsieur!* That would be against the law! If that is what you wish, I must ask you to leave immediately!"

The frightened executive's eyes widened and he looked shocked and frightened.

"Please forgive me!" he wailed, raising a hand to stop the Great Brain from saying anymore. "I had to ask in case you were proposing such a practice. I abide by all the laws of God and the Empire!"

"Very well," the Great Brain replied, pretending the words had mollified his fury.

He had learned this tactic from studying humans. If you attempted to give or sell an item to this backward species, they reacted with fear and suspicion. In contrast, if you attempted to prevent them from obtaining anything, they viewed the object as a treasured item. He had used this same tactic when selling the excess red lotus leafs to criminal fraternities. The conversation roughly ran as followed every time:

GREAT BRAIN: "I am only selling to large organizations. Your group is small and unimportant compared to my other buyers."

CRIMINAL LEADER: "That is insulting. We are just as large as those others and we shall pay you in cash immediately."

GREAT BRAIN (speaking slowly and seemingly hesitating): "I am not sure…"

CRIMINAL LEADER (showing anger): "Tell me your price! Now, damn you!"

GREAT BRAIN (naming a price five percent higher than most): "As I said, I can only a spare a few…"

CRIMINAL LEADER: "Done! I expect the full shipment by close of business tomorrow!"

The Great Brain still did not understand why humans behaved in this manner. This was contrary to all life he had encountered during his mental travels throughout the cosmos. This irrationality demonstrated yet another reason why these creatures required the guidance and control the Great Brain offered.

Now, he sat across from Bernard Benoît and said:

"I apologize if I offended you, Chevalier. I am a simple researcher into the human condition and I wish to improve all of humanity. The best route for that is through the common people, the laborers who toil in the massive factories. Do you know that Berlin is now one large complex? Everyone in that city either keeps the machines running or works in some capacity to ensure their daily operation?"

Nodding his head in agreement, Bernard replied in a choked voice:

"Yes. They also possess a wealthy class who live in great palaces of gardens and sunlight above the rest of the city."

The Great Brain, had he been emotive, might have kissed this man for that statement. Clearly, Chevalier Bernard Benoît envied those wealthy lotus-eaters of Berlin, living without the concerns that were heaped on his shoulders every day. This now provided the Great Brain with the lever to move this man according to his every whim.

"I knew you were sagacious, Chevalier," he said. "You now know the reason why I chose you rather than any other industrialist in Europe. You possess the foresight of a Fredersen or a Swift. I am amazed, truly amazed and humbled by your stellar mind."

The Great Brain knew his words were patently absurd, but a nervous, frightened man who desperately wished to please his father required such gentle handling.

Blushing a deep crimson, Bernard nodded and whispered:

"You flatter me, Monsieur."

"I do not," said the Great Brain, shaking his head. "Your mentioning of these wealthy pleasure-seekers with such contempt impresses me so very much. You, who toil away in this small city to ensure that the citizens of the Empire receive full employment; you, a man who works day and night and sneers at such lesser creatures, dancing about like sprites in a fairy tale—I said to myself: this is a great man, a great man. This is a leader who will one day receive accolades from the Emperor himself!"

"Many thanks," Bernard replied. "But you were about to tell me more about your chemical potion. An herbal and vitamin mixture, I believe you said?"

"Of course! The elixir consists of a compound consisting of…" the Great Brain then rattled off a series of Latin terms for garlic root, dandelion, and three types of grass you could find on any lawn.

The list did not matter. Fools such as this one found solace when scientists used Latin to explain common terms. It was another oddity that proved humans required the Great Brain's guidance.

"Will there be any after-effects? We possess a limited medical budget for workers below the sub-executive pay grade. Losing a percentage of the work force would weaken our overall output for the quarter."

The Great Brain shook his head, already tiring of this discussion.

"None at all. Are we in agreement?"

Pausing for a moment, Bernard Benoît frowned. He sensed that this situation was larger and somehow beyond his control. Part of him understood that whatever this odd man called the "Great Brain" offered, it was a false promise, a façade that could destroy everything his family held dear. But he remembered his father's sneering comments regarding the alleged weakness that prevented him from inheriting his family businesses. The old man's statements still stung. No man wishes to learn that his father held him in such contempt, nor that said parent had planned his entire future.

The difficulty lay in Bernard's preferences—he favored the notion of becoming a minister in the Imperial government. There, his duties would involve policies, laws, and currency. People, such as the thousands employed in the Marseilles facility, would no longer haunt his dreams. The life of a minister was not exactly peaceful, but he would reside in Paris and ride in expensive cars to important meetings. It was a much better life than worrying that one of his workers might be attempting to start a union and slow the labor lines.

"Yes," he finally said, sighing audibly.

Part of his mind screamed that this was a major mistake, but he ignored that voice in his head.

"When can you begin?" he asked. "Also, you have not named a price for your services."

The Great Brain straightened, his face seemingly twisting with disgust.

"Money? I do not perform my work for filthy coin, Chevalier! I serve all mankind with my researches!"

Bernard bowed his head briefly.

"My apologies, Monsieur. I have worked so long in business that I always believe others seek profit for their labors. I shall not mention money in your presence again. When can you begin?"

The Great Brain pretended to appear mollified.

"Very well. I believe we shall begin with tomorrow morning's inbound labor pool. You shall see an immediate transformation. I shall send one of my personnel in a steamer filled with jars and cups. One cup per man, woman or child. More would not help."

Bernard rose and bowed, remembering the Great Brain did not like shaking hands.

123

"Out of interest, does it possess a foul flavor?"

The Great Brain chuckled.

"Quite the opposite, Chevalier. You shall find the flavor quite delightful."

With that, Bernard Benoît fled, heading for the home of his mistress.

The Great Brain waited until he had left before clapping his hands together and allowing himself to feel a wave of triumphant delight.

Pushing a button on his chair, he said:

"Professor! Doctor! Come to my chamber immediately. My plans are about to commence."

"Yes, master!" came the joint reply.

Neither man sounded elated, but then, they never did unless the announcement involved their research.

CHAPTER XXVIII

The Woman's hand slackened and she slowly let Victor Sicarius fall a few inches.

He made a sound, which was muffled beneath his shattered plague doctor's mask, but sounded like a cry.

The dreaded Woman let out a gargling sound that might have been a laugh, or a cough, then dropped him.

Victor dropped three stories down to the main hallway. He could have grabbed the Woman and pulled her down with him, but that would have been an unnecessary risk. Her metal arms delivered dangerous strikes, capable of snapping bones. A better idea was to fight her using his mind.

Throwing out a spiked line from beneath his coat, Victor laughed as the metal shaft penetrated deep in the ceiling and stuck fast. This was an old device from the Vampires' gang, a last ditch means of escaping a dangerous fall. The spike was no mere piece of iron, but a complex machine with springs and other items within the small shaft. Upon penetrating a surface, even an inch, the mechanism burrowed deep and secured its position. A clever bit of engineering, one that Victor and Irma still used regularly.

Grasping the line with his gloved hand, Victor stopped his fall and swung in a quick arc. Dropping a few more feet, his legs brought his body completely under control. Now, hanging only fifteen feet above the floor, he dropped lightly and bowed up at the enraged Woman.

"My thanks, mademoiselle!" he said in the same drawling accent as Irma.

"You bastard!" the Woman shrieked.

She leaped over the railing without pausing.

Victor ran back several feet, nearly colliding with the lightly dancing Irma Vep.

The horrible, twisted Woman crashed to the stone floor with an audible crunch just as Robert Ménard appeared around the corner.

"Oh my," Irma said, surveying the metallic woman as she rose from the wreckage that was once a well-made, floor.

Stone chips clattered about her unharmed body and a thin layer of dust flowed about her metallic legs.

"I was about to say the same about your rather large friend," said Victor, as he surveyed the huge Robert and his tightly gripped Bowie knives. "Is he effective with those blades?"

"Adequate," Irma replied, tilting her head left and right. "I do not think much of your playmate. She appears to be of a rather emotional sort."

"Agreed," Victor replied, "Fight or flee?"

"I am in no mood to run" Irma replied. "Let us chastise these two and complete our business."

She turned so that they stood back to back, able to watch the now-wary Robert and his frightening companion.

"Chastise…" Victor mused as he pulled a metal tube from an inside pocket. "I like that term."

"Oh do shut up, *mon chéri*. We are wasting time."

Their palms slapped together and their arms rose up.

"Let's kill them both," the Woman hissed.

She charged forward. Robert's lips rose in a silent snarl and he stepped forward, knives at the ready.

Victor tossed the tube over his shoulder and Irma caught the item in her gloved hand. She pushed an invisible button and the tube extended outward, transforming into a steel staff about five feet in length.

She spun the weapon in her hand, causing Robert to halt his stride forward.

Without warning, using their joined hands, Irma and Victor pirouetted, now facing each other's opponent.

The dreaded, metal-armed Woman swung a metal fist towards Irma, only to find herself batted aside by the spinning staff.

A second later, she was on the defensive, backing up as the cat-suited Irma Vep attacked high, middle, and low. Sparks flew off the metal arms and legs as the Woman struggled to keep up.

Meanwhile, standing just behind Irma, Victor battled the knife-wielding Robert Ménard. The huge man's fast hands slashed and stabbed through the air, seeking to slice open arms, legs or torso. But his attacks missed by mere inches. Victor's sinuous movements always maintained a careful distance from the butler's shining, sharp, steel.

Just as Robert stabbed hard towards Victor's neck, the young man dropped into a full split beneath the blade.

Irma, seemingly without looking, swung her staff in a fast backward arc and caught Robert on the side of the head. The metal slammed into his temple and sent him crashing to the floor, unconscious.

Meanwhile, Victor popped back to his feet, bent at the waist, allowing Irma to roll over his back.

Facing him now, with the staff between them, she winked. The signal! Victor grabbed the staff and threw both of his feet backwards, like a bucking stallion.

Both his booted feet slammed into the approaching metal-armed Woman, sending her sailing into the distant wall.

She rose only a moment later, her steel fists balled. But Victor and Irma had already spun in place, and now stood facing each other, sideways between the fallen butler and the half-human monster covered with plaster dust.

"I will kill you both," the Woman growled.

Her voice now possessed an inhuman metallic quality, as if she had cast off the last vestiges of her humanity in favor of the life of a creature composed entirely of gears.

"Will you?" Victor asked, keeping an eye on her and the fallen Robert. "You do not appear to be succeeding."

"Perhaps she will try harder now?" Irma quipped. "We are ready, *Madame Métal*. Show us your most impressive tricks."

Releasing a shrieking sound that resembled a steel girder twisting and tearing, the Woman grabbed a heavy table with a marble top and flung it at Irma and Victor.

Irma's arms tightened, gripping the staff with the steely fingers of a professional acrobat. Victor stepped on the pole and jumped straight towards the flying table. His black booted foot extended and he shattered it, sending stone and wood splinters flying in every direction.

He landed and immediately ducked as Irma jumped over his shoulders. The staff spun so fast that it was only a blur. Irma caught the half-human Woman in the chest and leg, halting another charge.

The metal arms lashed out, seeking to grab the staff and tear it away from Irma's grasp. But Irma tossed the pole over her shoulder to Victor while diving low to the left, to keep out of their enemy's reach.

Victor caught the weapon in one hand, stopped and assumed a fighting stance. The inhuman entity emitted her screech once again and raced towards him, a deathly smile crossing her face.

Victor moved to stab her with the staff, and the Woman reached out to snatch the tip, only to have the weapon retract with a snap.

Victor, having pushed the button that retracted the staff into a small tube, flipped it back to Irma. She caught it, extended it to its full length again, and smiled. She knew what was coming next and loved this part.

With two swift strides, Irma stood at Victor's rear, weapon at the ready.

Victor, still in the same pose, grabbed the Woman's steel wrists and stopped her progress completely. They heard the sounds of her gears and other unidentifiable parts clicking, clacking, whirring, and grinding as she struggled to push forward.

Victor appeared to be about to fall back, causing the Woman to grunt what was probably a triumphant noise. But instead, using her momentum, he rolled backwards and pulled her towards him.

His feet caught her falling form just as he released her metal wrists. His legs kicked her into the air, causing her to sail over his head and towards Irma. Her staff slashed through the air and slammed into the Woman's face, sending her sprawling next to the still unconscious Robert.

Victor stepped next to Irma. She retracted the staff and their hands came together a second time. He reached into his jacket and tossed a small bundle next to the groaning, nearly unconscious, pair that lay at their feet.

"When you fully waken, contact the one you call the Director," he said. "There is a televisor code inside that bundle and a time to contact us regarding areas of mutual interest. If he does not call us at the exact time, the remaining contents of Monsieur Gérard's files will be handed to the Imperial police as well as the Apache gang in Paris and the Gambler's syndicate in Berlin."

"Had you not attacked us, you would have received the same message, except without the cracked skulls," Irma added.

She opened the front door.

"Au revoir and thank you for the pleasant evening," she said.

Then they left, as silently as they had come in. It was only when they stripped out of their respective outfits that Irma turned to Victor and said:

"Very well, it was not such a bad plan, but I still think we should devise a wiser one next time."

Victor looked in her direction as he filled the tub.

"Are you saying that I was right and you were wrong?"

"There is a first time for everything," Irma replied.

She grinned and dropped her robe. This effectively ended any further debate for the evening.

CHAPTER XXIX

The Great Brain watched as the five men carefully loaded the small tin tank onto the steamer. These men were quite similar despite their different looks and ages. All possessed visible scars on their faces and hands, and stared out at the world with hard, unyielding eyes that did not demonstrate any empathy. Their style of dress also appeared similar: the simple clothing that a working man wore before or after toiling at his given profession. None of whom could be mistaken for employees of the industrial plant, or even shopkeepers.

These men were human wolves, individuals that survived by feeding upon their fellow man. They were criminals, the blood-soaked outsiders of society that fiction writers occasionally and incorrectly idolized. These were men too violent to hold average daily jobs. They preferred a life where they took whatever they wanted, and followed a set of unspoken rules regarding contact with each other. Their lives were short, brutish, and filled with blood and pain.

At least, it had been so until the Great Brain's special operatives, the creations of Professor Rotwang, had taken them to their base. The influence of the once ruler of Mars upon these men was now absolute. With but a thought, these men would fall dead on the ground, all their bodily functions ceasing instantly.

The scent of machine oil informed the Great Brain that Rotwang was coming. The scientist stopped at his master's side, his mane of wild pale hair causing him to resemble a lunatic from the stage or the cinema. Yet, beneath the exterior of madness, his genius raged on, like a vast ocean of malevolent psychic energy. Rotwang was insane by human standards, but possessed a foresight capable of shaking the very heavens.

"I need more bodies, master," he said, sniffing as he watched the gangsters load the truck. "All those that you have provided me are in the conversion process. I need more, many more, if you are to have your army."

"Soon," the Great Brain replied. "First, I must gain control of the factory workers. Once that is done, we shall begin their conversion."

Rotwang's black-gloved hand clicked as he waved towards the criminals nearby. "What of them? Give me half their number. You have twenty, I believe?"

The Great Brain shook his head.

"Twenty-four, and no. I require them all to sell the red lotus and other goods. But in a few weeks, I shall…"

He broke off as a wave of dizziness suddenly filled his mind and body. The Great Brain staggered slightly, grabbing onto Rotwang's stained shoulder to keep from falling to the ground.

"Master? Are you well? Should I summon ten Brinken?"

Rotwang leaned his leader's back against a nearby brick wall and watched him with careful eyes.

"You do not need to summon me," ten Brinken intoned.

He stepped into view, pulled a stethoscope from his coat pocket, and added:

"You do not look well, master."

The Great Brain waved them away with a flick of his hand.

"Doctor, you just added four more to my ranks. How are you here when the operations just occurred?"

Rotwang giggled and ten Brinken guffawed.

"It was a joint piece of genius on our part." Rotwang replied. "I created mechanical arms capable of performing that simple procedure up to four times at once."

"The actual operation is very simplistic. A drill and a bit of a surgical glue I invented some years ago, and we convert another to your service," ten Brinken added. "That is not why I am here, however. I, too, require more bodies for my great work. I shall not be capable of continuing without more living flesh for my experiments."

"You shall not!" spat Rotwang. "I asked first. Also, I approach a critical juncture in my conversion methods."

"I am a medical and biological scientist, not a mechanic. All my trials demand living tissue. You can work with more gears and oils!"

"Enough!"

The Great Brain silenced both men. He slowly straightened up and gazed upon the pair, so alike, yet so very different. Their scientific endeavors were in complete opposition—biology versus mechanical engineering. Yet, deep within the depths of what humans refer to as a soul, these men were as alike as twins. Both rejected any form of ethics beyond their personal requirements. Even the conventions of their chosen professions did not hold them in check. These two were clever, creative, useful tools—who had to die after the Great Brain took over the planet. Otherwise, like the hated humans who had destroyed the Great Brain's power on Mars, they would attempt to dispose of him in the same manner.

Stepping between his two associates, he placed a hand on each of their shoulders. This was as much for supporting his weakened form as it was for reassurance that these two crazed intellects would continue to serve him.

"I changed my mind," he said. "You shall each receive more living bodies for your own uses. Professor, how many fully functioning creatures are ready for full operation?"

"Four," Rotwang replied. "The remaining ones are receiving ten Brinken's formulae and shall soon be capable of any actions you order."

"Four is sufficient," said the Great Brain. "Activate all four and I shall send them into the city. These creations shall harvest those whose presence is unimportant and forgotten by the populace. The first and best two are mine. The rest you may evenly split between the two of you after I choose what I require. Is that understood?"

"Yes, master," both men chorused, exchanging a pointed look.

The Great Brain looked away, seeing the final items being loaded into the back of the steamer truck. A flash of energy caught his eye and he sent his slaves a mental order.

All at once, they ceased moving and turned their backs to their master, their only movement being an involuntary twitch of their basic autonomic functions.

Though unalike in age, height, and other details, they shared one important similarity. Imbedded in their skulls was a small scarlet gem about the size of a thumbnail. The crimson drop of crystal looked like blood at the first glance—as if each of these men had received the same minor wound in the exact same place in their heads—but a second look revealed an occasional golden pulse of power, a flare of energy that vanished as quickly as it appeared.

The Great Brain sent the enslaved gangsters a mental command and waited.

As a group, they each pulled caps out of their pants or jacket pockets. With yanks and slight adjustments, the cloth caps covered the crimson crystals from view.

"Excellent," the Great Brain said aloud.

He slowly walked back towards his rooms. He needed those bodies tonight!

CHAPTER XXX

"…And that is my report," the frightening Woman concluded, speaking to the televisor screen. "I do not understand how that pair defeated Robert and I with such ease. Their skills exceeded ours, and they used only one weapon."

"One weapon was enough to defeat the two of you? I find that very hard to believe," Fritz Kramm replied, glancing at his brother. "Two people, one weapon, fighting you with your mechanical appendages and Robert Ménard, the best assassin in Europe. If I did not know you so well, I would suspect perfidy at the heart of this situation."

"Madame did not exaggerate to any degree, Monsieur," Robert stated, stiffening as he spoke. "The pair appeared almost lighthearted as they fought. Quite unprofessional."

Fritz opened his mouth to reply, but Cornelius raised one long finger. The gesture was a clear indication that the Lord of the Red Hand was about to intervene. Only Fritz knew this as the pair in Marseilles, like all members of the Red Hand, viewed only a black screen with the stylized image of a red hand during these televisor conferences.

"Were both individuals dressed entirely in black?" Doctor Cornelius inquired. "Also, was the woman's face heavily painted while the male's remained entirely hidden?"

Doctor Cornelius tented his fingers and studied the pair on the screen with an unblinking gaze.

"*Oui, Monsieur le Directeur*," Robert replied. "Even after Madame destroyed his ridiculous bird mask, he made no move to cast it off."

"Miss Zanzi, did…" Doctor Cornelius began.

But he was cut off by a screeching snarl from the half-human, half-robot Woman.

"That is not my name!" she screamed. "That person is dead—gone forever!"

She snapped the armrest of her chair with one steel fist.

"Silence,"

The Lord of the Red Hand didn't raise his voice—he never did—but the screaming half-human creature clamped her lipless mouth shut immediately.

"Your name is Nanon Zanzi," Doctor Cornelius continued. "This is a simple fact. Spare me your denials and past traumas. I have no time for such nonsense. They are a waste of my time. Now, we shall continue this inquiry. The male— were his reflexes heightened to an extraordinary degree?"

Glancing at the seething half-human woman, Robert nodded at the televisor screen and answered:

"*Oui, Monsieur.*"

"Final question—did the female hum or sing at any time?"

"*Oui, Monsieur,*" Robert repeated, "She hummed a song called *In the Hall of the Mountain King* from *Peer Gynt*. The late Monsieur Gérard quite fancied that play."

"I have no doubt about it. It is about a feckless fool," Fritz said, snorting with laughter at his own wit. "He probably felt a commonality of mind and purpose. His failures resulted in our loss of seventy-two percent of our income from Marseilles. The supplies of red lotus from the Ottoman Empire and North Africa must now be redirected toward other ports, thereby adding to our cost."

He carefully did not mention which ports they planned to use, knowing that Nanon Zanzi and Robert Ménard had no need to learn such valuable information.

"The red lotus parlors are still quite active, Monsieur," Robert stated. "The prices have dropped by but a small amount since the attacks commenced."

"Because of the wholesale purchases of the stolen tons," Doctor Cornelius stated.

He spoke more to Fritz than the other two. The only reason he did not silence the televisor was that this pair's presence was vital to the reestablishment of the Red Hand in Marseilles.

135

"Within six months," he continued, "the entity behind the destruction of our position in the city, as well as that of other less important organizations, will either have their own sources of the narcotic, or they shall abandon the proprietors and seek their fortune elsewhere. We shall address this then, and the Red Hand shall regain its place of power soon enough. No doubt, our pair in black shares the same concerns…"

"Did I hear you wrong?" Nanon Zanzi asked, her voice a harsh, whispery, rasp. "Did you just say that the pair in black are just as anxious as we are about the destruction of our base in Marseilles? Surely, they're the ones behind the recent thefts and murders!"

Listening to this half-human woman speak was like hearing animals being tortured prior to butchery. The very wrongness and inhuman quality of her intonations caused Fritz to wince. Doctor Cornelius, however. never appeared to notice.

"They are not," he stated unambiguously. "Had they been the culprits, you two would be dead. Furthermore, I know who they are. Frankly, I thought them both long dead, along with the rest of their cult of marauders."

He looked to Fritz without expression.

"I see!" Fritz said. "You mean—those two? But I thought that monster Fantômas had destroyed them all, root and branch, after they defied him in Nice."

"I believe that was a miscalculation on our part," said Doctor Cornelius. "Consider the details provided by Miss Zanzi and Robert. Both dressed in black, the female with heavy face paint and a love of music. The male possessing inhuman reflexes and appearing stronger than expected. His face covered. And they fight as one with incredible skills. Who else amongst our files match these characteristics?"

"Nobody—but. surely, they must be copycats. The originals disappeared when their gang was annihilated. All that our informants in the Sûreté found were a few torn bodies in their secret lair."

"Who are you talking about?" Nanon Zanzi asked, leaning closer to the televisor. "And why does this pair cause you such fear?"

"They are the Vampire and the Eidolon," Doctor Cornelius replied. "They once belonged to a gang that called itself the Vampires, some years past. Their expertise at theft was only surpassed by their uncanny shared fighting skills. They did not possess the cruelty of the dreaded Fantômas, yet many considered that pair his future successors. This, we thought, was the reason why the Lord of Evil destroyed that gang. He would not allow anyone to receive the same fearful accolades as him. Such comparisons could weaken the terror his name brings to any who hear it whispered in the dark."

"Perhaps we should send word to the Apache gangs in Paris?" Fritz suggested. "Then Fantômas may intervene himself and solve our problems for us."

"Not yet," Doctor Cornelius replied. "I believe that the Vampire and the Eidolon battle the same menace that struck at our interests in Marseilles. We shall speak to them at the appointed time and hour. Have you learned the location of the televisor code our pair provided?"

"*Oui, Monsieur,*" Robert replied. "It is the office of the director of the local branch of the Imperial Sûreté. He is away from the office, investigating a theft in Nice."

"Very well. You both shall proceed to that office and await our possible allies," Doctor Cornelius instructed. "If they present themselves, do not attempt to engage them in battle again. Allow them access to the televisor and I shall issue further orders then."

He reached for a drawer at his side, revealing two ink bottles, two silver pens, a notepad, and several blank envelopes.

The scientist's long fingers reached into the drawer and pressed down on a small button on the side. A hidden cavity in the desk opened near Friz's feet, revealing a set of thin, red colored paper files.

Doctor Cornelius reached within and removed the second dossier and placed it unopened on the desk surface.

"Leave them alone! Never! I will tear them..." Nanon Zanzi snarled.

"Silence," Doctor Cornelius snapped back. "Never forget that you serve the Red Hand. For the now, the Vampire and the Eidolon shall assist us in our struggle. Once their usefulness is over, you may destroy them in any manner you choose. But until such time, they are as sacrosanct as the French Emperor. Is this understood?"

"Yes," Nanon Zanzi replied, her eyes blazing with fury.

"Very well. Proceed," Doctor Cornelius said, ending the connection.

"She will not listen to your orders," Fritz said while glancing at the dossier. "That one possesses no self-control."

He was not surprised to read *Vampire and Eidolon* on the file tab.

"It does not matter," Doctor Cornelius said. "Robert Ménard will not support her attempt to kill either of the two former members of the Vampires gang. And he, at least, is obedient."

Doctor Cornelius opened the folder and scanned its scant contents.

"As long as he receives his regular stipend," observed Fritz. "You do not believe either will present themselves at that office, correct?"

"Correct. They have been clever enough so far. Why should they not possess a means of redirecting calls to another machine of their choosing—as we do? If they are foolish enough to show themselves at that office, they are of no use to us. Now, let's find another location to redirect our own call. Perhaps the home of a wealthy idiot away from the city. Do you have anyone we could use as a tethered goat?"

"Yes," Fritz replied, smiling. "An English lord, a real boob who lives part of the year in Brookport, Long Island. He and his bee-loving wife are somewhere in Jamaica. Their house is open and only guarded by a bee pasture in the rear. I saved their televisor unit in case we had an emergency. I had the device installed three months ago when I sold them a Millet painting."

"Very well. I shall study this dossier in the meantime and I also have a minor surgery to perform prior to that conference."

"One question before I go," Fitz asked as he rose. "What is, pray tell, an eidolon?"

Doctor Cornelius looked up, his cold eyes locking with his brother's.

"The word *eidolon* has several definitions, though only have meaning in our circumstances. The first is that of a phantom, a spectral image in human form. The second is the idealized image of a perfect person."

"They do not appear to be the same. In fact, they rather seem to be opposite concepts. Still, you know best."

Fritz strode towards the locked study door and reached for the doorknob.

"No, I think both apply when we consider this man. He may be either the perfect specimen of humanity, or he is a shadow, a being that lives a false life and is disconnected from the rest of humanity."

"Given that his partner is called the Vampire, does the later not appear more probable?"

"Only if you believe that they chose these names for each other. Additionally, the word vampire is not so simplistic a term. There are fascinating undercurrents in this entire farce, Fritz. We must only be aware that this pair resides in shadows and that may possess depths even we cannot imagine."

Fritz Kramm harrumphed and exited without looking back. He needed to get back to the Dawlish cottage and switch on the device in time to inspect a Constable painting that he hoped to sell to that English lord.

CHAPTER XXXI

Etienne Faure counted the coins that rattled at the bottom of his tin cup. He was still four francs short from having enough for the night. Four little francs was the difference between a night of peace and wonderful dreams and one spent shivering on a park bench or on the soft grass of a graveyard.

Etienne had more than enough if he wanted a bed for the night and a small meal of vegetables and a small piece of meat. In fact, he could probably afford a few nights based on what was in his tin cup if he chose one of the wharf side beds. A former sailor, he could easily pay for a hammock and sleep inside for a few nights.

The difficulty was, Etienne Faure preferred scrounging for scraps, eating rats, and stealing nearly rotting vegetables from the market rather than paying for food. This method of living also continued with his non-existent place of residence. Better sleeping in a park, a doorway, or a graveyard rather than paying a solitary *sou* for a hammock or bed.

This indifference towards basic living was not a philo-sophical choice—Etienne despised the food he ate and the hard Earth that made up his usual bed. The difficulty lay in his choices years ago, that had repercussions to this day. Despite all the warnings from his friends, family, the government, and even his source, Etienne Faure was on a path to a sad end.

Etienne Faure was a red lotus addict, who gave himself over to the drug to exclusion of all life. Formerly a sailor in the French navy, he had first tasted the new narcotic while on shore leave in Algiers. He had gambled that night, and won, purchasing for himself a young whore who called herself Samia. She was tiny, very young, and spoke with a light, mu-sical voice and unaccented French.

"Would you like to taste some red lotus?" she had asked after their second sexual romp.

Etienne, who had been reaching for an empty wine bottle, had paused mid-grab and looked at the girl with open confusion.

"Is that a new wine?" he had asked.

Samia had shaken her head, her long, curled ebony locks bouncing with the short movement.

"It is a new leaf that causes happiness. You roll it in a little ball with some lime and place it in your cheek. The red lotus will send wonderful dreams to you as you lay awake."

That time, Etienne had rejected the drug in favor of some more wine and another attempted coupling with little Samia. However, he had heard rumors of the new drug back on the ship, with sailors, and even a few officers, speaking of delightful delusions followed by energetic sex with the girls and boys in port.

"If someone offers you a taste of this lotus garbage," Léon Ranchon, the quartermaster of the ship has said in a heavy voice, "run away. Or better yet, punch them in the face and run away."

"Why?" Etienne had asked, pulling on a line as the officer watched.

"It is a drug, boy," Ranchon had explained, his voice a low growl. "Do you think they offer you the first for free out of the goodness of their hearts? Drug sellers entice you in with a taste of pleasure. Then you crave it until the drug is more important than God, family, or food. When I was in Siam, a friend of mine started smoking opium. He craved it, stole from all of us to get a smoke. He vanished and we found him a month later, dead. The drug had stopped his heart and his body lay in a pool of filth. The poor lad weighed only fifty-five kilos when we found his shriveled corpse."

"I thought that the Benet serum made all opium useless," a young sailor named Rémy had interjected. "My granddad had that shot in him after he lost his leg so that he did not get addicted to morphine."

"Not then," Ranchon had said, nodding and pointing towards the buckets and mops.

His heavy, stern face suddenly took on a mournful, pained expression. For just an instant, the powerful, demanding officer resembled an old man remembering a painful loss in his life.

"Back then, if most people took morphine or opium, they died before they found a way to quit," he added. "The ones who walked away still feel an awful craving every day. That is why I tell you all—avoid this new lotus drug. Do it and you may end up like my poor friend, Marc. Now, get swabbing, lads. Otherwise, the next shore leave you receive will be your retirement day!"

Etienne Faure had remembered that story, right up until Samia, who was still pretty, if a little worn, a year later, had offered him a free taste again. He had paid her the last of his wages and, after an unsatisfying roll, had proved unable to perform a second time.

"Try some red lotus," she had crooned. "You will become a stallion and see dreams as I ride you."

Samia had climbed off the small bed and crossed to a small pot, opening it and removing a single crimson leaf.

That had been the decisive moment, the metaphorical fork in the road determining the rest of Etienne Faure's life. The words of Léon Ranchon still rang in his head, the sadness and regret easy to recall. But interrupting that memory had been the bare breasted reality of the whore, Samia, and her whispered promises of sexual delight.

Reaching for the red lotus leaf, Etienne had quickly forgotten the officer's words, and obediently rolled the small plant, squeezing a bit of lime across the surface. After placing the sopping, rubbery plant in one cheek, his face had begun tingling. Then the colors had grown bright and he could hear a soft humming from the brighter shades. The oddity of this situation, actually hearing colors and seeing them as vibrant, living organisms had never occurred to Etienne before.

His focus had been upon Samia, who had transformed before his eyes. Once a hardened, if still pretty, young prostitute, the red lotus now had revealed her to be the very perfection in female form. Her thin frame and apple-sized breasts had grown larger, the bruises across her visible rib cage and back replaced by silky dark skin and plump, bountiful breasts. Samia had turned into a goddess, the embodiment of ancient fertility and sexual delight.

With a cry, Etienne Faure had leaped upon the young woman, taking her right there on the dusty bedroom floor. The night of delights had continued until he had passed out on her bed. That had been the last night of his shore leave, but he had never forgotten the power the red lotus after he had returned to sea.

Next time he had been ashore, this time on the Ivory Coast, Etienne had ignored the markets and food, and gone in search of another brothel. He had found one quickly—that was never difficult in a port town. After a brief exchange of coins, he had received another red lotus leaf and a Mandika girl whose name he had never learned. The experienced had proved as explosively wonderful as his first occasion.

This had now become Etienne's habit on shore leave, find a woman and some red lotus and use up all his funds in an orgiastic bacchanalia, the period of which had decreased with each trip. The cost of his addiction had steadily risen, since his need for more leaves had increased as their effect weakened.

By the time his ship moored back in Marseilles, Etienne Faure was a fully committed addict, a lotus-eater who required four leaves just to achieve a tiny drop of happiness. He did not even require a girl anymore, having no longer any interest in sex, food, or drink beyond the basics required to get his next fix.

Rejecting reenlistment, Etienne had taken what little funds he had saved and become a full-time addict. By day, he begged, performed little jobs, like sweeping bar floors, and stole small items. Little things like clean clothes and a bed no longer mattered to him; the drug was all he craved, day and night. Etienne had even stopped bathing, having learned that the sweat and oils produced by the skin held the drug inside his body for a fraction of a second longer.

Gazing up at the clock on the top of the distant industrial complex, Etienne smiled. Within an hour, the night workers' shift ended and the morning crew would take their places. The tired men, women, and children usually ignored him, their eyes drifting over him as if he did not exist. A few, a small group who felt pity after their own harsh time keeping the machines operating, often dropped a few *sous* in his cup. The total might be enough to buy eleven leaves and a night of dream-filled, glorious, sleep. Without the red lotus, the night terrors forced him to wake screaming every hour, and Etienne found himself barely able to walk the next day.

A metallic ring broke through his reverie, an almost musical tone like that of a large bell struck in an old-fashion clock. Shaking his head and attempting to clear the fog that threatened to fill his brain, Etienne smiled without showing his broken, red-stained teeth. He knew his look was ghastly, but the only other expression he possessed was to stare dumbly up while gently shaking his tin.

A figure appeared around the corner, its long, broad, form blocking the streetlight. Etienne blinked at the sudden darkness, attempting to discern the identity of the newcomer. He used different approaches in his begging, based on the individual. A military man received a tale of heroism and injury while rescuing a fellow sailor. A wealthy executive or nobleman received compliments in a soft, almost Parisian-accented tones. For each type of person, there was a different sales method for a skilled beggar like Etienne Faure.

Unable to see, Etienne opened his mouth, intending to use his military tone. After all, this was probably a soldier, but taller than any he had viewed in a long time—though that could merely be a delusion caused by red lotus dreams—he could not be sure.

"Monsieur…" he started to say.

Suddenly, a shaft of light from a nearby window fell across the face and shoulders of the approaching person.

Etienne's mouth dropped open and his eyes widened in terror at the sight before his unbelieving eyes. None of his mind horrors approached the sheer terrifying aspect of the newcomer.

Just as he filled his lungs to shriek and call for help, a soft sound sliced through the silence. It was closer to the breath of a child, attempting, yet failing, to whistle.

A sharp pain in the right side of his chest caused Etienne to squeak in pain. The sound, barely audible even to his ears, soon caused his body to feel warm, as if he had fallen into the sea. That was always a problem when he did not have any red lotus for a long time. One time Etienne had woken up in the fountain outside the treasury building. The only reason he had not drowned was because he had apparently slipped in feet first and his head had remained safely outside the fountain.

Trying to look around, Etienne found his head lolling and unable to look upwards. A pair of powerful hands lifted him to his feet and his body was thrown over a wide shoulder.

Etienne tried to open his mouth and protest, tell this giant that he did not wish to go anywhere and that his tin cup lay on the street. Yet no words or sounds emerged from his unmoving mouth.

After that, Etienne fell asleep.

Etienne woke up, feeling cold metal beneath his naked body. A bare stone ceiling hung above his head. His body felt moist, as if he was just waking after taking a bath. A scent of soap and medical alcohol filled the air. He realized that some-one had cleansed him while he was unconscious.

Etienne opened his mouth, trying to speak, only to find that no sound emerged from his dry, cracked lips. He strug-gled in vain to shout for help, though he only managed to re-lease a soft wheezing sound. Realizing he needed to escape from this hospital or lunatic asylum, he sat up.

Or at least, he tried to, but his body remained motionless. His arms, legs, head, and hips refused to cooperate. They re-mained dead weight, simply meat.

Etienne felt the coolness against his back and slowly dry-ing moisture across his torso, which proved that his body was not crippled from an accident. His predicament filled him with fear.

Then he saw a wide flat face with narrow, probing eyes. A slight smile crossed the heavy features of the man, who said in French:

"Ah, we are awake? Good! Do not agitate yourself. You are experiencing paralysis due to a nerve block I introduced into your nervous system. You will breathe and may look about with your eyes and feel any external stimuli. It is essential that I record your responses."

Etienne struggled to comprehend the man's thick German accent, the heavy, growling, intonations overwhelming the smooth French vowels. It sounded as if a bulldog or a bear were trying to speak in a university version of French.

The flat-faced man smiled again, his tiny eyes nearly vanishing in his wide, block of a face. He reached to his left and produced a massive metal syringe, its needle as long as a man's middle finger. A gelatinous amber fluid lay within the metal-encased glass barrel, slowly undulating and quivering in a slow manner that somehow disturbed Etienne more than the holder of the medical tool.

"Now," the German intoned, "let us begin the trials. I must warn you… this shall hurt a great deal. But it is necessary, *verstanden?*"

After that inquiry, the German doctor reached for Etienne Faure and slowly injected the thick sharp tip into the frozen man's arm.

A moment later, the helpless red lotus addict prayed for the ability to scream… or die…

CHAPTER XXXII

The whistle blared, a piercing exhalation of sound, which echoed for miles about the industrial plant. The heavy iron gate on the north side of the complex creaked and groaned, clanked and whirred, as the portal opened. Slowly the grinding noise continued until a gap opened, wide enough for five people standing shoulder to shoulder to pass.

A deep echoing sound filled the air as five filthy men marched outside. Their bowed heads and slumping shoulders told the story of their hard labors, maintaining the machines and insuring nothing slowed production. The men, followed by dozens of ranks of similarly postured people, marched out in an unconscious lockstep, resembling exhausted soldiers in a bizarre parade.

On the south side of the complex, a similar garbed mass of humanity, cleaner than their north gate fellows, marched in the same sad step into the factory. An observer capable of viewing both lines at the same time would have wondered if a ten-mile long line flowed from one end of the complex to the other. The beaten down march of those entering and exiting appeared precisely the same at both sides of the plant.

As the south side-entering employees walked in, their silent reverie was shattered by the loud din emerging from the sides of the tunnel. As always, the foremen stood on steel boxes and watched the incoming employees. These men and women were the company informants, spies that spent the majority of their time looking for dissention in the ranks and exiling anyone with union sentiments to a sub-basement section codenamed "red three."

Usually, these silent spies stood boldly, studying the workers, seeking means of gaining advantages over the weakest. This time, they called out a clearly pre-written statement in strident voices.

"All employees, all employees! A new health program for all personnel is now in place. Upon entering each shift, you shall drink a new health elixir that shall benefit you before and after work. Failure to consume your entire cup shall result in immediate dismissal."

Each supervisor called out the message, using the exact same words.

The line slowed as five men, none of whom were particularly savory-looking individuals, handed out paper cups half-filled with a warm, red liquid. The first rank of workers took their cups, downed the drink in one swallow, and continued onto their workstations.

They later related to their fellows the same question and response:

"What did that taste like?" someone asked.

"Like tea mixed with cheap wine," most replied.

A spare few, five in all, refused to imbibe the elixir when they reached the men handing out the drink. None of the cup holders responded; they merely waved over the guards, who led the offenders towards the exit.

All five, three men, a woman, and a teen boy, realizing their mistake, spoke up quickly.

"I'll drink it, I'm sorry!" the teenager said, clearly frightened.

"I will too," said an older man, a cousin of one of the other men. "Please! I'm married and have two children!"

"Take them back to the line, let them drink," the guard commander ordered, adding: "Refuse again and there will no second chance."

"I'll drink too!" another man claimed, realizing his wife might kick him out if he suddenly became unemployed.

"I agree also," the woman added, speaking for herself and her holdout husband. "Shut up, Sorel! I did not agree to marry you just to starve because you want to play the fool!"

Sorel, a handsome red-haired man with the stained scarlet teeth of a red lotus addict, frowned, but then nodded.

"Very well, but I do so under protest."

"Oh just shut up!" the woman, a pretty girl with sharp features and eyes that appeared too big for her face, replied. "Make your speeches later when you and your friends are at the café."

Complete compliance having been enforced, the servants of the Great Brain left the complex in their steamer.

They returned an hour later, preparing for the next shift of factory workers.

CHAPTER XXXIII

Nanon Zanzi hated waiting. Time was a burden on her, a slow-moving monolith that robbed her of life with each passing second. Each tick of the clock brought her slightly closer to death, the ultimate enemy to all living things.

This philosophical thought process was inherent within her, not a carefully thought out belief system created while surveying her life. Nanon Zanzi rarely allowed herself a period of deep thought. She had not been that type of woman, even before her transformation from a lovely creature with a wounded psyche into the hideous man-metal monster that existed only to serve as the Red Hand's most frightening assassin. This belief had come to her as she, in her twisted, half-human form, attempted to survive each day without turning fully mad.

Born the daughter of a circus owner and a dancer, Nanon Zanzi had possessed a fear of being embraced by men or women. A lovely dark-haired girl, resembling her late mother, few males at the circus had appeared willing to embrace her. The only man she had loved had been the knife-thrower, Alonzo the Armless. She had decided to take him as her first and only lover, but he had died thanks to an accidental blow from the brutish strong man, Malabar the Mighty.

Enraged by the loss of Alonzo, Nanon Zanzi had lit the tent on fire as Malabar had performed an act involving teams of horses pulling him in two directions. Malabar the Mighty, and most of the performers as well as fifty-four people, had died, either from the fire or from being trampled by the horses, elephants and panicked crowd.

Nanon Zanzi had almost died as well—her fancy dress had caught on fire and, as she had rolled on the ground trying to put it out, the frightened crowd had trampled her burned body. She had passed out, the darkness a welcomed relief from the molten agony which had racked her each terrible second.

"Ah, you're awake, I see," a calm, cold voice had stated as she had attempted to open her eyes days later. "Miss Zanzi, are you capable of understanding my words? Merely raise one finger for yes, two for no. Speech, at this moment, will be quite beyond your present capacity. Do you understand my words, young lady?"

That was how Nanon Zanzi had met the brilliant and terrible Doctor Cornelius Kramm. The formerly lovely dancer, now covered in thick, soft bandages, had raised one finger in response.

Nanon had soon realized that only one of her eyes appeared capable of focusing on the acerbic man in the clean white laboratory coat.

"Excellent!" Doctor Cornelius had answered. "The fire, which you caused, has killed many people. As a favor to you, I shifted all blame to the strongman, Arjun Malabar, whom, I believe, operated under the pseudonym of Malabar the Mighty. Is this an acceptable course to you?"

Doctor Cornelius had picked up a pale folder and quickly scribbled a note without bothering to look down at the page.

Yes, Nanon had indicated, lifting one blackened digit up.

The act itself had proved a mighty struggle, her finger barely shifting more than a few inches.

"Very well then," Cornelius had said, closing the folder and stepping a little closer. "You must now make a choice. If you wish to die, I shall inject you with an air bubble. This will result in your death from an arterial air embolism. If you do not, then you must understand the following facts. Your burns cover one hundred percent of your body. The fact that you are still alive is a medical anomaly, entirely unprecedented. I amputated both your legs and your left arm. I believe your right arm shall turn septic within the week. Amputation shall follow before the infection can spread to the remaining organs."

Here, Doctor Cornelius had paused, to adjust his spectacles for a moment, before continuing:

"A grim picture. However, you do appear to possess a spirit with an unusually powerful desire to live. If this is so, I can offer you an alternative. But first, I must ask you a few questions. Is your desire to continue living prompted by the fact that you love someone and wish to be by their side?"

No, Nanon struggled to respond.

Nodding one time, Cornelius had then asked:

"Is your need to survive based on hatred?"

Yes, Nanon had replied.

"Do you hate everyone? Every being upon this planet?" Cornelius asked, leaning closer and staring into her one visible eye.

Nanon opened her lips and managed to wheeze out a croaking, nearly inaudible single word:"

"Yes."

"If given the chance, would you kill these people?"

He had lifted a finger.

"But do not try to speak again. I do not wish any further damage to your larynx."

Yes, Nanon had indicated.

She had known that her single eye had burned with hatred, a fire only the blood of all humanity could quench.

Doctor Cornelius had slowly straightened and nodded again.

"Very well. Then I shall provide you with a means of obtaining your desires. However, it shall be under my direction. If this is acceptable, indicate your agreement."

Yes, Nanon had indicated.

"Excellent. We shall first determine if the arm is salvageable. Then I shall introduce you to a series of advancements made by two young men named Brainerd and Swift. Their facile minds have created devices that, with the proper direction, could replace lost limbs and even damaged organs. Prepare yourself, Nanon Zanzi. The pain shall grow greater, but eventually, your revenge upon the world shall follow."

The mordant Lord of the Red Hand had not exaggerate-the pain—what followed had been terrible, even worse than waking up as a nearly burned out corpse. The graft of mechanical arms, legs and inner organs had soon followed, and Nanon had struggled for a year to master these.

A greater pain, one Doctor Cornelius had not indicated, almost killed her again during the course of her convalescence. It had to do with her new face, or more truthfully, her total lack of a human countenance.

Though known as the world's leading "sculptor of human flesh," Doctor Cornelius had proved unable to restore Nanon Zanzi's previous bewitching beauty. Her face was now that of a goblin, or a troll, or a mythical monster that caused fearful shrieks from adults and children alike.

Nanon had had to shut herself away from the world, satisfying the burning fury in her heart through her missions for the Red Hand. Yet, it had not been enough.

Nanon Zanzi—a name she now refused to accept any longer—had found herself driven mad by an inner bloodlust for her fellow humans, or any other living creature. She only held back from indulging herself in an orgy of blood and agony because of one man—Doctor Cornelius Kramm. There was some power he held over her that kept her in check. She did not understand how, but the minute he spoke, she complied without question.

"Our black-clad attackers appear to be tardy, Madame." Robert Ménard intoned, breaking her reverie.

Nanon did not hate this man, finding his calm, cold manner oddly comforting. His loyalty to the Red Hand aside, Robert did not speak unless he responded to one of her inquiries, and affected no emotions. He reminded her of a clockwork butler lacking any interest beyond its gear-driven duties.

"We are not late," a voice said, suddenly emerging from the televisor screen.

The glass screen shimmered and a yellow glare flared for a moment, quickly replaced by the image of a smiling, heavily painted woman and a man dressed in the now-familiar plague doctor's outfit.

The screen appeared to narrow, with the pair now reduced to a half-size image. The other half remained black, but the voice of Fritz Kramm emerged from the speaker:

"My, my, how interesting. The Vampire and the Eidolon. Still alive despite the destruction of the Vampires. We must update our records. There are no reports saying the Eidolon dresses as a Venetian carnival guest."

Fritz chuckled.

In the office, Nanon Zanzi flexed her terrible, steel fingers. Despite Doctor Cornelius' orders, she planned to rip the flesh off this pair's bones.

The woman first, she thought. *Her pretty face offends me.*

CHAPTER XXXIV

"Master," the Lemane said, bowing deeply before the Great Brain. "You summoned me?"

The Great Brain stood up, feeling life flowing through his mind and body.

He closed his eyes and felt the minds slowly opening to his embrace, increasing his awareness and powers. The intoxicating sensation caused his shuddering form to experience a moment of ecstasy, a human atavistic response to pleasurable stimuli. The difficulty lay in the energy required to maintain such power. He needed more human bodies—preferably living ones filled with vital life energy.

Realizing another slave was awaiting his orders, the Great Brain pointed towards the dust piles near his feet.

"Clean that up. Use the broom in the corner. Did you tell the Nimrod that the inner court of Giphantie must come to this place?"

"Yes, Master," the Lemane replied. "They shall arrive in several days' time. I told them you made a remarkable breakthrough towards the botanical recreation of the trees of life. That is the secret goal of our society."

His elderly body creaked as he knelt on the floor and slowly swept up the dust and grit.

"Yes, yes. Complete nonsense of course," the Great Brain mused aloud. "The plants they think once emerged from your mythical Garden of Eden. Sadly, for you, those plants were in fact a xeno species that attempt to repopulate worlds with their own hybrids after several millennia's experimentation. I think this world may witness their marvels in the next several decades. I doubt their work shall be vegetative. Possibly an implantation of spores as a simulacrum of human gestation? I may allow this to occur, wishing to view the results of these xeno-cuckoos among the sheep of humanity."

The Great Brain rarely indulged in such talk, but the infusion did cause him to rhapsodize regarding the future.

"When you complete cleansing the floors, Lamane, you may consume food," he added. "You shall start with the roast chicken stuffed with ham. Is that understood?"

The Lamane, like all Children of Giphantie, led a strictly vegetarian diet as part of their vows. For a bit of sadistic pleasure, the Great Brain had forced them to eat strictly meat-based meals. No doubt, the small part of the Lamane and his retinue that remained in the mentally enslaved state felt utter disgust at consuming flesh three to five times a day.

"Yes, master." the Lamane replied, never looking up from his work.

"You do enjoy torturing that pathetic little man," Rotwang said.

He smiled and ran his black-gloved hand through his wild locks, causing them to fall back to his head in even greater disarray.

"A minor indulgence," the Great Brain explained. "He and his kind have offended me many times. But I remained silent, knowing in a few short years, my plans would come to fruition. Now, I am like that muscle-bound hero from the Greeks, Heracles."

The Professor followed in his wake, rubbing his hands together with open glee.

"Heracles? I do not believe that mythological character possessed an ounce of brains in his rock-shaped head. Why him?"

"He undertook the labor of cleansing the Augean stables in a single day. According to your human legend, the stables contained one thousand cattle and possessed the muck and filth of thirty years. Can you imagine such a stench?"

"Imagine it?" Rotwang replied, cackling. "Master, have you ever visited the Babel complex in Berlin? The industrial smoke stacks belch out smells that make the dung of a thousand cattle smell like roses on a spring day."

"Yes... Did you not design much of that industrial city?"

"Of course, I did, master. However, Fredersen disagreed with my vision and demonized my genius. He then stole the only woman for whom I ever felt any affection. Leaving that stinking city of fools proved a pleasure. They are all damned with a belief that humanity is of any importance."

Rotwang shaked his gloved fist.

"You damn our species, my friend? That is short-sighted and unworthy," ten Brinken intoned as he strode into the room.

"Humanity is limited, a failed experiment by the universe. They, we, are an evolutionary dead-end, ten Brinken," Rotwang spat back, turning around to meet his colleague.

"In that, we agree," the biologist replied. "Humanity rapidly approaches a point where they shall devolve back to savagery. They demonstrate those instincts in the manner they treat one another. One day, they shall use excuses like natural resources or religion as a means of committing genocide. Did you know that one small political group in Munich blamed the industrial society upon races and religions they despised?"

"No," Rotwang said. "Did they attempt to gain political power?"

The square-faced mad medical man snorted and smiled.

"Apparently, they planned on overthrowing the German government, but the week before their putsch, their leader vanished. They found him hanging by his heels, quite dead. The rest died in a beer hall fire, concluding the power of criminal political gangs."

"Interesting, but you ignore my point. Do you claim that *homo sapiens* is no longer a viable organism? That is quite astonishing coming from one devoted to biology and medicine."

"Not at all, old friend. Our species only rose to something approaching greatness through mutations and evolution. Unless the race receives further prodding, it shall stall. It is my duty as a true scientist, unencumbered by the foolish ethics of the medical community, to help it advance further. Thanks to our good master here, and Oxus' unique biological concepts, I shall achieve a new direction for all life."

"Nonsense!" Rotwang replied. "My engineering advancements shall reduce the need for all but the most basic biological functions in the human organism! Any other path is doomed to fail, since biology is a most imperfect art."

"Enough," the Great Brain said, not hiding his amusement. "You both may pursue your claims under my guidance. However, I don't believe you left your experiments for the pleasure of my company. Why are you here?"

"You first, my friend," ten Brinken said. "I arrived after you and would not attempt to violate the basic rules of courtesy, even for a scientist involved with machines."

Ten Brinken resembled a boulder with a vaguely human carved face and a slight cut that could pass for a smirking mouth.

Rotwang giggled and smiled his familiar rictus.

"How very surprising for a proponent of biology! Do you not always insist that all ethical considerations must stem from an innate, organic drive?"

"Engage in your debate and amusements later, my servants," the Great Brain said, chopping the air with one hand. "I have much to oversee."

"I require more metal, Master," Rotwang said. "The conversions begin at a pace I find almost acceptable. But my stores and the limited foundry I access shall be fully depleted within the week."

"And you?" the Great Brain asked ten Brinken.

"My own facilities are also too small for my needs, Master," ten Brinken said. "I shall soon possess no space in which to operate upon my patients. Unless this situation is rectified, I shall not be able of completing the testing the serum. Additionally, I require more subjects. Preferably a young fertile female with wide hips."

"You shall have your facilities within the next two weeks," the Great Brain replied. "Until that time, I shall provide you with more subjects. Professor, how many units are operational now?"

"Seven, Master," Rotwang answered. "Two others are nearly complete, but to finish them would increase my need for additional metal within three days."

"A delivery of replacement metal shall arrive in the next two hours. Our resources in that area are now nearly unlimited. Within the next two weeks, your foundry requirements and need for additional test subjects shall also be met, but until then, I can provide each of you but with limited assistance. Two weeks. No more. You both must wait with some patience. Human test subjects shall continue to arrive. I will require two or more for myself; the others, you may divide between you. Is this fully understood? Professor? Doctor?"

"Yes, Master." the pair of mad scientists chorused.

They both gave slight bows before leaving the Great Brain's presence.

He closed his eyes and entered a meditative state. He felt his senses expanding; the first hint of smells and sights through multiple eyes shook his human body for a moment. Then, he accepted the greater place, reveling in the first touch of true power. Subtly, he manipulated their minds, creating a hive consciousness with greater efficiency. The sensation was truly glorious.

CHAPTER XXXV

"What is going on here?" Sébastien Masson asked as he exited his office.

A minor supervisor in the assembly department, he was one of the least liked managers in the entire Benoît industrial complex.

The general dislike for Sébastien Masson was far from surprising; he was an unpleasant young man and he knew this for a fact. His father was a minor diplomat; his mother a pretty secretary that he had seduced and impregnated. Sébastien's parents had resented him from birth for their forced marriage. Their treatment of him had never gone as far as actual physical or mental abuse; they had merely treated him as one would treat someone with a disturbingly bad smell. They had sent him to be taken care of by distant relatives and Swiss boarding and had generally ignored his existence. Sébastien had grown up hating them both, and had later discovered that the best means of torturing his neglectful parents was to expose their misdeeds towards each other, allegedly by accident.

Such "accidents" were, in fact, carefully planned by Sébastien, and were guaranteed to embarrass one or both of his parents. For example, his father had conducted an affair with a widow that resided a short distance from their townhouse. His mother had known this, but had ignored the situation because she had herself been enamored of a female poet, who dressed all in black and consumed a cocktail made from absinthe and red lotus.

How best to bring both affairs to light? It had been easy enough if one possessed few scruples regarding the results. To embarrass his father, Sébastien had waited at the widow's home, having learned they were planning to drive to a villa near Cassis for a weekend of lovemaking. Climbing under the car, he had cut deep into the brake line and then had fled.

The car, as expected, had driven off the road before the pair had even left Marseilles. Both had received only minor injuries, but the accident had caused the truth to become widely known.

Angry, bitter, harsh words had followed with long, tension-filled silences, but Sébastien had found this delightful. He had waited two weeks before exposing his mother's own perfidy, increasing the furious fights in their house. This second "accident" had proved far simpler and a great deal more fun to organize.

Simply put, Sébastien had secretly contacted the gendarmes regarding his mother's so-called "friend." Red lotus was a new narcotic and the Imperial police was eager to fight its spread. This poetess, a Russian woman who spoke with accented words and sniffed constantly, held parties nightly in her loft. One telephone call and the gendarmes had arrested everyone.

From that day on, Sébastien Masson's only true source of pleasure had been the misery of others. Using rumors, blackmail, and, if necessary, violence, he had caused harm everywhere he had dwelled or worked. A veritable cloud of despair had followed him from place to place, and he had rarely hidden his joy at the terrible darkness that fell over the souls of his victims. The only thing that had protected him from harm was his fast fists, his willingness to use them, or even a revolver if threatened.

"What do you mean, Monsieur?" his secretary, Honorine Hubert, asked, looking up from her typewriter.

A pale-face, frightened, mouse of a woman with tiny breasts and thin brown hair, she was Sébastien's slave, for lack of a better term. He had broken her through a combination of violence, sexual and physical, threats, and small gifts, Honorine was barely human anymore.

Sébastien stared about, ignoring her and gazing over the workers on the assembly line. They stood in their expected places, their movements quick and following a regular rhythm that did not cease as he watched them work. These men, women and children, resembled the very image of the perfect employees—an impossibility for humans, no matter how motivated or well-paid.

Sébastien's people never worked that silently, not even on holidays when the owners allowed them an early, fully paid dismissal. The workers routinely hurled insults, and sometimes bits of metal, at each other throughout the day. They threatened the weak and stupid, and bullied the children assigned to their lines. Assembly area two-one-four-G barely made its daily minimum numbers because Sébastien Masson kept them battling and mistreating each other under the guise of preventing the formation of a union.

That was how he had received his current position—as a strike-breaker, originally assigned to a coal plant in Lorraine. The Benoît family kept a coterie of men and women whose sole job was to sow enough dissention to keep the ranks from organizing and forming unions. Strike-breakers were the last resort, usually after a failure of other preventive measures.

"A strike-breaker," the elder Benoît often stated, "is a necessary evil. The truth is, they are like doctors attempting to revive a patient dying from poison. The organism is already gangrenous, and it is doubtful that it shall ever be healthy again. It is best to prevent toxins than attempting to cure them after they've infected the body."

As such, Sébastien Masson found the silent, hardworking people quite disturbing. He struggled to find words to explain this situation, when another odd occurrence arose in his mind. Honorine, his weak little slave and informant, stared at him without flinching. Her watery brown eyes did not blink or well-up with tears at the sight of his anger. This was an unheard-of transformation, one as astonishing as the silent employees toiling away on his assembly line.

"Do not speak to me in that familiar tone, woman," Sébastien snarled. "Remember your place. Or must I remind you of who is in charge here."

Honorine Hubert did not react to the threats; she merely cocked her head to the left and stared his direction.

"Monsieur," she said, "did you drink your morning tonic?"

"What business is it of yours?" Sébastien asked, clenching his fists and looming over her desk.

Once again, Honorine's response was not her usual downcast eyes and shivering shoulders. Instead she picked up her telephone and said:

"Please send a team to area two-one-four-G. Yes, Monsieur Masson's. Thank you."

"You little bitch! I will whip the hide off your body once this shift is over! I will…"

Sébastien's rant was cut off by the appearance of Jacques Prévôt, the sector security chief.

Prévôt was a man of medium height with salt and pepper hair, a thick graying, well-groomed beard, and the calm manner of a former combat soldier He stared at Sébastien without any visible expression. Two of his larger men stood a step behind him, young, heavy brutes, with the look of brawlers across their scarred faces. Sébastien knew these men and kept away from them, knowing their reprisal could be greater than his ability to fight back.

"Supervisor 2nd class Masson," Jacques Prévôt said, his accent the rough tones of a Gascon. "You have failed to drink your morning elixir. Failure to do so is grounds for immediate removal from the company."

"I did drink the potion." Sébastien lied. "Honorine Hubert has spread lies about me since I was considering firing her for inefficiency."

Prévôt tilted his head in the same manner as Honorine and then shook his head.

"You have not. You will now either drink it before us or we will escort you out and prevent you from ever working again in this, or any other city."

One of the guards stepped forward and extended a paper cup filled with the same noxious liquid. Sébastien's stomach tightened and flipped at the thought of consuming such garbage. Yet, he did understand that they were clearly willing to expel him and destroy his way of life.

Sighing and shooting Honorine a furious look, he took the paper cup and swallowed the contents in one gulp.

Prévôt and his men stared at him, waiting and watching him for a full minute. They then nodded once and walked away, never looking back.

Sébastien retreated to his office, plotting how he would make Honorine pay for this indignity. Picking up his papers, he read the daily reports with angry eyes and a softly muttering voice.

Within the hour he was still reading them and even writing out the updates he usually left for Honorine's completion.

Three hours later, Sébastien Masson exited his office and handed the work to Honorine.

"Please type a copy for the files and send a second set to the central office. I shall be working on projections for the next quarter until later this evening."

"Yes, Monsieur," Honorine replied, never looking up from her typing.

Neither of them spoke again except on business matters for the remainder of the day. Silence reigned over much of the plant. Only the clink of metal and whir of machines filled the air.

CHAPTER XXXVI

"A black screen?" Irma Vep asked, covering her smile with a black gloved hand. "One would think you did not trust us."

"Clearly, they do not." Victor added. "They hoped we would be foolish enough to present ourselves in that office. After all, they did send Madame Steelfingers and the knife swinging butler to meet us."

"We have no reason to trust you," Doctor Cornelius said at last, his voice cold and precise. "You stole from us and are former members of the Vampires."

"Quite true, Irma stated. "But happily, we are now speaking, and I can state that we have no interest in your operations here."

"So you say," Fritz interjected. "You still hold our dead agent's files."

"If your metallic lady or sharp manservant open the desk's bottom drawer," Irma said, leaning back in her seat and sighing audibly, "you shall discover it contains all the information in question. We do not care whom you rob or what you sell to support your organization.".

Robert Ménard stepped forward and opened the indicated drawer. He pulled the ledger and other items out and performed a cursory examination.

"I believe this represents the entirety of Monsieur Gérard's files, Monsieur le Directeur."

"Then, why did you steal them in the first place?" Fritz asked. "And why was the Eidolon found on the sight of our murdered employees?"

"I should think that would be obvious," Victor replied. "I was looking for clues to discover if the same killer that destroyed the Vampires and many other gangs in France, was the one behind the deaths of your people."

"I assume you are referencing the deaths or disappearances of the Vampires, the Priory of Scion, the Brotherhood of Silence and the Brotherhood of the Ram?" said Cornelius.

"You assume correctly," replied Victor. "All the groups in question, plus three others, existed in an unofficial non-aggression pact. None attacked any of the others. Each pursued its own interests independently. Yet, in a mere two weeks, all have vanished from the Earth."

"How would you know those particulars?" Fritz asked.

Back in his brother's study, he leaned closer to the screen, attempting to discover further details about the pair.

"How else?" Irma asked, her tone dripping with acid. "We checked. This what professionals do, rather than hide behind darkened screens in the United States."

Fritz looked at his brother, concern creasing his face. Cornelius shook his head and asked:

"And what are your conclusions?"

"Simple," Irma replied, "We believe that the same entity that destroyed the secret societies of France are now attempting to destroy other groups, and more specifically, the criminal organizations of Marseilles."

"Ridiculous," Nanon Zanzi said with a choking warble. "A pack of no-good, ridiculous conspirators kill each other and you two hide like rats. Now a gang war commences, and your conclusion is that the same imaginary mastermind committed both crimes? That's idiotic!"

"Our mechanically limbed employee expresses skepticism about your argument," Cornelius said. "Our own theory is that Fantômas simply murdered all his competition in France."

Victor guffawed and slapped his knee as the mirth overcame his whole body. At his side, Irma smiled, shaking her head and ignoring the televisor and those viewing them through the picture tube.

"Care to share the reason for your mirth?" Fritz asked through gritted teeth.

"You believe that Fantômas decided to destroy every conspiracy in France because they were competition? Victor said, still chuckling. "Oh sir, I hope, for your sake, that he never learns you suggested that as a possibility. Otherwise, he might be inclined to demonstrate what made him spoken of in the same hushed whispers as the Devil himself!"

"Fantômas is dead," Fritz spat back. "This a fact known by the entire world."

"We have an old saying about this in France," Irma said. "A wise man never believes in the death of Fantômas, even when looking at his corpse."

"That is not a reasonable assertion," Cornelius stated, "merely a supposition based on a legend."

"No," Irma said, suddenly stone-faced and serious. "That is based on fact. Rumor has it that Fantômas finds the situation just as confusing as we have."

"Besides, you must recognize the similarities," Victor added, his hilarity vanished as quickly as it had appeared. "Secret societies whose members vanish completely, while the rest perish through savage deaths."

"I conceded that makes a very slight, degree of sense," Cornelius replied. "But I fail to comprehend what you wish from us. Are you requesting protection or allegiance?"

The surgeon waved Fritz to silence, shaking his head once.

"Neither," Irma Vep replied. "We do not require the Red Hand's protection. We are fully capable of surviving without your hordes of killers."

"Then what do you want?" Fritz demanded, wiping his brow with a silk handkerchief.

He did not hide from his brother his relief that they would not be inducting the Vampire and the Eidolon into their ranks.

"We have a shared concern for the moment," Irma replied. "You wish to reestablish your position in this very important port city. We wish to discover who murdered the Vampires—and why. We suggest a temporary alliance. Neither of us possess the slightest interest in your organization, but we may be able to help each other. Briefly."

"Ridiculous," Nanon said again. "We do not require your aid. Robert and I shall uncover the truth with ease."

"Oh? You already have a plan of action?" Irma asked, smiling again.

Nanon's skull-like visage twisted into a terrible mask of fury. "You little bitch…"

"We shall conclude that means you do not." Victor replied. "What say you, Monsieur le Directeur? Or does Madame Iron Feet speak for you?"

"She does not," Doctor Cornelius said, stroking his whiskerless chin thoughtfully. "Present your suggestion, if you please."

"You would not trust us to provide you with any information we discover," Victor offered. "We do not trust you either. Therefore, one of us shall work with one of your operatives. This will allow both sides with full access to any discoveries."

"No!" Nanon Zanzi shrieked. "I shall not help these two except into their graves!"

She slammed a fist on the desk top, shattering the wood and sending splinters flying across the office. Robert stepped back, avoiding the sailing shards by mere inches.

"Our operative has strong feelings on this subject. Are you concerned?" Doctor Cornelius asked.

Irma rolled her eyes and shook her shrouded head.

"Of course not. We defeated them with little difficulty in our last meeting. I doubt they will have improved in so short a time."

"I will kill you slowly, slut," Nanon swore. "First, I shall tear your pretty face off, an inch at a time. Then I shall…"

Her fists opened and closed as she spoke. A soft metallic ringing sound accompanied her words, almost musical in tone.

"Oh my," Irma said in mock horror. "She thinks I am pretty. How sweet!"

"If the threats and amusements are at an end, I wish to conclude this conversation," Doctor Cornelius said. "Your arrangement is acceptable. Vampire, you shall partner with Robert Ménard. Eidolon, you shall accompany Miss Zanzi. If we discover you are planning treachery, the entire Red Hand shall hunt you until you are both captured. Then Miss Zanzi's fantasies of torture and abuse shall be granted reality. Agreed?"

"Agreed," Irma said.

"Please meet our operatives at the former home of Pierre Gérard," Fritz added.

"No need," Victor stated.

He and Irma stepped away from the televisor. A moment later, the office window opened inward and they dropped inside the room.

"You!" Nanon Zanzi snarled.

"Yes," Irma said, narrowing her eyes. "You were expecting someone else?"

"I will..." Nanon started to say but she was silenced at the sound of Doctor Cornelius' icy voice.

"You shall do nothing, Miss Zanzi. You are an employee of the Red Hand. You shall obey our orders. Is that fully understood?"

"Yes," Nanon muttered.

"Very well. Where shall you start your inquiries? And must you wear that preposterous bird mask, Eidolon? Unless you plan on causing our enemies to laugh until they reveal their intentions?"

"I did tell you that multiple times," Irma added.

Sighing, Victor Sicarius reached behind his head and manipulated an unseen clasp. Pulling off the plague doctor's mask, he tossed the offending item in the trash basket. But his face did not appear into view—his features were fully covered by a thin black mask which lacked visible eye holes.

"Acceptable, I suppose," Cornelius said. Now, I repeat: where shall you start your inquiries?"

"Where else?" Irma answered. "Among the criminals remaining in this city. The lowest of the low always know more than most realize…"

CHAPTER XXXVII

The second shift of the Benoît complex trudged inside, also stopped by a horde of men who appeared at first sight to be criminals.

As before, the supervisors called out their orders and security were on hand for the rare protestors. Once again, a few attempted to refuse the elixir, and were escorted towards the exit. All save one broke and agreed to imbibe the serum and returned to their duty stations.

The single refusal came from Achille Joly, an angry agitator who had only joined the workforce to start a union. A tall, thin-bodied man with an oval face and a short beard and mustache, Achille did not actually care about the workers he wished to unionize. In truth, he despised every one of them, but concluded they were useful. A man who controlled the proletariat could hold much power.

Having been expelled from three universities for subversive activities, Achille Joly understood that the thesis of Marx and Engel were utopian dreams that could never be realized. For example, take Marx's famous quote, "Workers of the world unite; you have nothing to lose but your chains." The idea that the unwashed masses of society could simply cast aside their proper place in society and serve as equals to men greater than they were, was, in fact, ludicrous. Achille thought as much when that Russian idiot, Lenin, had tried to lead a revolution against the Czar and his forces. His skull, and that of each member of his Bolshevik party, still sat atop the gates of Moscow as an example for those wishing to revolt against the monarchy.

Recognizing that revolution was a waste of time and effort, Achille Joly nevertheless felt that worker's unions still possessed a degree of power, should they arise in the correct places. The industrial cities, like Berlin, Munich, Paris, and Marseilles, possessed thousands of men, women, and children who kept the machines running. Should they serve one man and work only at his command, that individual would enjoy power nearly as great as the French Emperor or the Holy Roman Emperor.

Vowing to be that man, Achille Joly had taken employment at the Benoît plant. He served on the smelting crew, pouring the melted Cavorite into the vast vats and isolating the impurities. There he slowly sought out the disgruntled, the potential troublemakers, and the deeply stupid. The latter he needed most, viewing them as potential martyrs in his future struggle. Achille had eventually gathered ten people, four women, three men, a moronic teenage boy only known as Potato, and two children. Next week, he planned on having them speak to others in different parts of the complex, beginning to spread the word of a change for all that followed his leadership.

Now, all this was in jeopardy, as the leadership of the plant engaged in a very unsavory, secretive action. Achille knew all too well that this elixir was nothing more than a drug meant to dull the spirit. This he could not allow!

"No! I spit at your attempts to drug me and my fellow worker!" he shouted as he tossed his cup to the ground. "This is poison! Workers! Cast down your chains and do not accept this obvious attempt to destroy us for their profit!"

"Follow me, if you please," the security officer standing near the wall said in a dull voice.

He was a small man with wide shoulders, a poorly shaved face with several healing cuts and the dark, lifeless eyes of a cow.

"No! I shall stand here and demand to speak to the master of the plant in person! We shall not allow oppression of our people for their profit. Brothers and sisters, I enjoin you to cast down your chains and I shall lead you to freedom!"

But only a few men glanced in his direction.

"Refusal to drink is a firing offense. It is not poison," the security guard replied.

He took a cup and drunk the contents in one swallow. The few that watched shrugged and took their elixir without question.

"Potato, throw down that poison!" Achille screamed, spotting the boy's odd shaped head two rows away.

"Drink for job. Mama says keep job or I get a whipping," Potato replied.

He swallowed the fluid before trudging inside to start sweeping the floors.

"Follow me, Mister. You are no longer an employee," the security guard said in the same lifeless tone of voice.

"No," Achille Joly finally said, sighing. "I shall drink your foul liquid."

The guard stared at him, his head cocked to the left for a moment.

"Not allowed," he finally replied. "You are not welcome in the collective. You shall leave."

"Collective? This is not a collective!" Achille shouted. "You are the strong arms of the bourgeoisie attempting to prevent the proletariat from rising up and casting off their oppressive shackles! Workers, hear me! These men lie to you and will keep you toiling until your heart breaks! Listen to me!"

But two security guards carried him away. They ignored his words and few workers even bothered to look up as he passed.

Exiting through a loading dock, the security guards placed Achille Joly back on his feet. Both men stood before the door, unblinking human sentries that resembled statues rather than humans.

Achille dusted off his clothing, pretending their very touch was diseased and filthy.

"I shall return and shake this plant to its very foundations!"

"Not allowed," the first security guard said.

He forcibly turned Achille around. A large electric truck lay open near the loading dock and the hapless union organizer found himself propelled inside the gaping back after one hard shove. The door slammed shut on his cry of shock and alarm and, a moment later, the vehicle shook as the nearly silent engine engaged.

"Help! Help! I'm a prisoner!" Achille screamed.

He continued to shriek for what felt like an eternity. His voice went hoarse and his hands were bloody ruins as he beat on the steel walls, begging for rescue.

Finally, the lurching truck ceased moving and the doors slid open with a light bang. A harsh light blinded Achille Joly, causing him to shield his eyes with his bruised arm.

"Please," he whispered, "let me go… please…"

"Let you go?" a German-accented voice said. "Oh no, no, no! I have such marvelous plans for you and so many others. Soon, you shall know the true meaning of greatness. Come with me, my dear man, and you will live forever!"

Hard, unyielding hands lifted him out from the truck's rear.

"Who are you?" Achille Joly asked, trying to smile at the indistinct form dressed in black.

"My name," the man said, smiling, "is Professor Rotwang, and you shall be number eleven…"

CHAPTER XXXVIII

"I will work with you, Miss Zanzi," Victor Sicarius said to the half-human woman.

"Do not use that name!" Nanon Zanzi snarled, raising her steel fists up and shaking them his direction. "That person is dead, ashes on a fairground years before! I have no name and will not accept one from you!"

"Nanon Zanzi, stop this foolishness immediately," Doctor Cornelius said, his voice filled with an icy calm.

"And if you raise that fist to me again, Nameless One, I shall toss you out the window," Victor whispered.

He did not move nor flinch at the fists that were inches away from his face.

Nanon choked again, her version of a derisive laugh.

"You are just a man, flesh and blood," she spat back. "You cannot stand against my steel embrace."

"You will find that I am quite resilient. Additionally, the Vampire and I faced opponents that were far more lethal than you when we were still mere children. Now, either lower those hands or hope you land on a patch of soft ground."

Nanon Zanzi stared at Victor's mask, her horrific face twisting further in her fury. But a moment later, she dropped her arms and said:

"Very well, but I shall kill you both in due time."

"It is good to have ambitions," Irma stated.

She looked at Robert Ménard and asked:

"And you—will you force me to fight you again?"

"No, Madame," Robert said.

"Excellent! I can tell we shall share many laughs in the coming days," Irma replied, stepping towards the window. "Meet me at the Bar des Rougets near the Vieux Port. Do you know it?"

"Yes, Madame," Robert replied.

"I will not take orders from you, Eidolon!" Nanon snapped. "I shall do as I am ordered by the Lord of the Red Hand, but no more."

"Very well," Victor said, shrugging. "Then tell me where we shall begin our search. You do have a plan of action, right?"

Nanon tightened her fists and muttered:

"No."

"In that case," Victor replied, "may I propose that we meet at the red house near Monsieur Gérard's mansion. You can't miss it, its owner loves the color red and it is visible everywhere. He is holding a party and you and I shall be in attendance."

Ridiculous," Nanon said. "You dress as a shadow and I am a monstrosity with a metal body. They shall scream and ruin from us at first sight."

"They shall not, Madame Steelfingers. The ball is a costumed affair and the guests are, in the majority, a club of brainless, wealthy Englishmen. It is there we shall begin our inquiries."

"Excuse me," Fritz Kramm interjected from the televisor, "but that appears an odd choice of assignments. I should think that Miss Vampire and Robert would chose to go to the ball, while the Eidolon and Miss Zanzi would be better suited to visiting a dockside tavern. How did this come about, if I may ask?"

"I am known to those men," Irma replied, stepping up on the window's ledge. "A year ago, I attended one of their parties and left with all their money, jewels, and much of their clothing. I should think that at least one of them might still remember me."

"You are just a common thief," Nanon Zanzi sneered.

Irma slowly shook her head.

"There, you are mistaken, my dear. I am a quite uncommon thief. In fact, I am possibly the greatest cat burglar in the world."

"Better than you?" Nanon asked, glancing at Victor.

176

"Yes," Victor replied, leaping up to her side. "Her skills in this area outstrip mine. Besides, I am not really a burglar. My own talents are quite different."

"If that was meant as a means of sowing dissention, Madame Steelfingers, do not bother," Irma added. "Even Satanas and his entire court could not do so, despite all their wiles, and you do not have their insidious nature... For now, I bid you *Au Revoir!*"

With that, she and Victor leaped out the open window and vanished from sight.

Nanon Zanzi ran to the window and looked out, quickly followed by Robert Ménard. Despite the gathering gloom, their vision was not appear hampered in any way. The fact that neither the Vampire nor the Eidolon were anywhere in sight was more galling to Nanon.

"I hate them, Robert," she snarled. "And I will kill them both, if it is the last thing I do."

"Yes, Madame." Robert replied, following in her wake.

CHAPTER XXXIX

The Great Brain strode through the lowest level of his headquarters, watching as his slaves toiled away at their labors. All the former members of the Children of Giphantie still alive were among this horde, as were other cultists, criminals, and, most amusingly, believers in the practice of magic and demonology. Slowly they worked, their heads bowed, their spirits and minds all but erased.

This was one factor the Great Brain had immediately identified upon throwing the shard of his dying mind into the body of one of these shaven apes—none on this world were his equal. Oh, some may possess cleverness and skills which could be of use in the future. Take Professor Rotwang and his friend, Doctor ten Brinken. Both possessed human level geniuses, causing them to be of use to his plans. By feeding their egos, he could make them create soldiers and other useful tools in his quest for control of the Earth. In doing so, they sped up his design by at least four decades.

Yet, despite their cleverness, they were nothing more than slightly more evolved animals. He cared for them no more than he did the creatures of his native Mars. However, they were quite useful now that he, too, was technically human. Yes, the Great Brain would soon return to full power—if all went as planned. The massive mind he had abandoned on Mars would be as tiny as the human one he currently inhabited.

"Moréno, come here," he said to the dark-haired man who walked with a bent back and possessed the sad eyes of a broken man.

"Yes, Master? How may I serve you?" Moréno asked, staring at the Great Brain's feet.

The Great Brain marveled, as he often did, when speaking to this man. Moréno had once been a feared gang leader whose main talent was an uncanny skill with hypnosis. Now, he was just another slave.

They had met when the Great Brain was still a lowly member of the cult of Giphantie, learning the ways of humanity while planning a new future for this world.

The meeting had come when Moréno, having discovered the existence of the Children of Giphantie, had attempted to bring them into his organization—The Vampires. This was the day everything had changed forever the Great Brain—the day when he had realized his path to power.

"Look into my eyes, fool!" Moréno had said, his voice ringing as he raised a hand dramatically above his head. "Feel my will! Obey my commands!"

The Great Brain had felt Moréno's will crashing against his, a wave of mental energy meant to drown his very thoughts. An ordinary human feeling this power would have fallen to his knees and obeyed this man's every command. While some humans probably possessed the strength of will to resist Moréno's hypnotic powers, most did not.

However, to the Great Brain, the attempted cerebral assault was no more than a slight, soft sensation, like that of a tiny insect crawling across his skin; a slight irritant, but in no way a threat to his mind or body.

Chuckling, the Great Brain had tilted his head to the left and studied Moréno. He was the first to use the power of the mind against him, and the results were very informative. For even in this weak, tiny brain, the Great Brain still possessed powers beyond the dreams of mere humans.

"Do as I order, damn you!" Moréno had said, pointing at the ground with his other hand. "Kneel and beg for me to keep you as a slave."

"Oh, shut up!" the Great Brain had replied.

He had smiled as Moréno's jaws had clicked closed. The Vampires' leader's eyes had grown wild as he had struggled to speak, but his body had refused to obey.

"Answer my questions, idiot," said the Great Brain. "Are you considered a powerful hypnotist amongst humans? Yes or no, do not elaborate."

The Great Brain had often thought that having a conversation with a human was about as useful as speaking to a plant. While the creature was living and breathing, their frames of reference in the universe were too different.

"Yes," Moréno had answered, his eyes going wild as the word had slowly emerged from his mouth.

"I see that you control a secret organization? Are your members known to the world?"

The Great Brain smiled as he learned of the existence of many bizarre cults and brotherhoods that existed On Earth. That day, everything had changed for the former master of Mars.

Now, the Great Brain reveled in the power that he held over this man, and all the cultists and conspirators and criminals he had subsequently enslaved. This was no less than what they deserved, since their aim in life had been to serve a greater cause. Now they only existed because the Great Brain required hands to perform his deeds.

"Have you completed the preparation of tomorrow's elixir?" the Great Brain asked.

He listened to the broken man's answer, given in a voice devoid of emotion or humanity. Moréno and his ilk were little more than automatons, and that was a glorious start towards the transformation of the Earth.

CHAPTER XL

The Bar des Rougets was a surprisingly well-cared establishment for a portside tavern. Built from a thick yellow stone, the location was a bright spot in a zone otherwise renowned for rundown establishments patronized by sailors and many unsavory characters.

According to local legends, the bar dated back to the infamous exiled Roman politician and gangster, Titus Annius Milo. Milo, who had risen from poverty to high office in Rome, had murdered his main rival, Julius Caesar's favored gangster, the well-bred Publius Clodius Pulcher. The result had been exile to Massilia, the present-day Marseilles, where he had developed a taste for red mullet. The Bar des Rougets, named after the fish, was said to have been his last venture before a stone had crushed his skull during a rebellion.

The present-day tavern, of course, was not the original building, nor was it even located exactly at the original site. The first Bar des Rougets had been a wooden structure, which the Visigoths had burned down in the sixth century. The present edifice, however, had existed since the time of King Louis IX, though its ownership had changed hands an untold number of times since.

The current host, for that was the historic title of the owner, was a former soldier named Gaspard Gervais. A man of medium height with graying hair and dark, angry eyes, he was a person of few words and quick action. He held to the tradition of the Rougets, established by Milo back in Roman times—neutrality in all areas.

Roughly, this meant that the Bar des Rougets was a safe haven for those who could afford the price. You could transact the highest and lowest business, hide from the government or your fellow criminals, or store stolen goods in the basement, just so long as you paid Gaspard's exorbitant prices. No negotiations, no credit, just pay the set prices and get out when your time expired. Gaspard, and his band of killers, enforced the rules with violent efficiency.

Robert Ménard knew the Bar des Rougets from the past, having used this place both before and after his employment with Pierre Gérard. The last time he had visited it had been to act as the intermediary in a deal for the sale of a stolen painting. The painting in question, by the legendary master artist, van Klomp, had "vanished" from a small museum in the town of Nouvion.

"The Fallen Madonna with the Big Boobies by van Klomp is a true work of art, one of the great masterpieces! It is worth at least…" Léon had whispered.

The thief was a tall, portly man with a thick mustache and sad eyes. Though probably just out of his teen years, he resembled a tired, hard-working man in his late forties. Despite that, he appeared to have an eye for the ladies and some skill in the art of seduction. The gorgeous brunette sixteen-year-old waitress, Yvette, was planning on following him back north once business concluded.

"Show me the painting, if you please," Robert had said, pulling a loupe from his waistcoat pocket.

Léon had unrolled the painting across the table, adding:

"Also in a private collector's home in the next village over is the lost Cracked Vase with the big daisies by Van Gogh. Give me a good price and I will…"

"Forgery," Robert said, replacing the loupe in his pocket. "A rather poor one, in fact. The painter used camel hair brushes. Such brushes did not arrive in Batavia until sixty-five years after van Klomp's death. Bring me the real painting and I shall offer you a reasonable sum. You may dispose of this piece of trash as you see fit."

Robert Ménard had left that meeting, hearing the curses of the thief behind him, already soothed by the dulcet tones of the long-legged Yvette. They had never returned to Marseilles, or if they had, they had dealt with someone else. Meanwhile, Robert Ménard's role in the Red Hand had evolved, for the better.

Robert knew that his two best qualities were his undeniable skill with blades and his ability to act as a manservant. The former talent, he held as important—a proficiency placing him far above most of the best killers in Europe. As to his ability to keep a good house, and serve food properly, that was simple observation. Chaos and disorder filled the world, some of which Robert himself had caused with his trusty knives. During the times he was not murdering for the State or the Red Hand, he fought against chaos. A perfectly clean home was one that rejected disorder, a state closer to perfection than most humans ever achieved in this life.

Therefore, working with the woman known as the Vampire did not bother him as much as it had Nanon Zanzi. The Red Hand paid his wages and he obeyed their orders without question. Killing Pierre Gérard, like working with this appalling female burglar, were the reasons his bank account never dropped lower than six figures.

"Right on time," Irma said, dropping from above to his side. "I like that in a man."

"If I may ask, Mademoiselle..." Robert started to say.

"Madame," Irma said, "You may report to your masters that the Vampire and the Eidolon were married years ago."

"My apologies, Madame," Robert said, giving a sketch of a bow. "What plans do you have within? The host, Monsieur Gervais, will not allow violence on the premises. Nor will he provide any information. This may be a wasted journey."

"It is all in the way you ask a question. There are always answers to be found, if you know where to look."

"If you say so, Madame," Robert replied, not hiding his lack of faith.

Irma smiled in his direction and threw open the door, stepping in with a flourish.

"Hello, my darlings. Did you miss me?"

"*Merde!* Les Vampires!" A short woman with pale platinum blond hair shrieked.

She threw down a few coins and fled for the rear exit.

"The Vampires? No, it's not possible!" a one-eyed man with a brown beard and the peaked cap usually worn by sailors added.

He stood up and took a step forward, a bottle of cheap wine gripped tightly in his knobby fist. Then, looking at the two newcomers, he stopped in mid-step, his mouth dropping open in shock.

"*Oh, la vache!* She was right ! It's them! Run for your lives!"

"That means the Eidolon may be outside!" an older man with a huge scar across his cheek cried. "That dark phantom's gonna steal our souls!"

The man slowly backed away and lowered himself into a chair, his body quivering with naked terror.

"Oh, you did miss me, darlings!" Irma cooed. "How very sweet."

She waved at a man who stood at least two meters high across the darkened chamber. The giant, who flinched under her gaze, wore a tight fitting red shirt that was the size of a small circus tent. Robert estimated he weighed at least one hundred and seventy-five kilos of pure muscle. Had he lost the vast paunch around his middle, he might still have topped the scales at one hundred thirty kilos. He was a true giant, though one that appeared to wish he were the size of a mouse just right now.

"Dario!" Irma cried.

She stepped up on a table. The men and women eating and drinking, all of whom had fallen silent upon her entry, froze in their seats.

With the slow stride of a ballerina dancing across a stage, Irma Vep approached the giant. She stopped about three feet away, still standing on a wooden table. The people nearby melted away, sliding out of their seats and moving to more distant tables. Nobody objected. All business appeared suspended as the Vampire faced off with the monstrous Dario.

The giant's nickname among the criminal community was *Le Broyeur*, the Crusher, and he had been a professional wrestler who now acted as an enforcer for various gangs.

"You can't touch me here, Vampire. This is Neutral ground," Dario the Crusher mumbled.

His voice was a rumbling growl, though the hint of fear beneath his words was audible to all present.

"Oh, la, la!" Irma said, her chirping voice sounding like the theatrical version of a prim and proper French lass. "Look at you! You are becoming quite the barbell boy, darling. Do you think that will help you from me? Or my dear Eidolon?"

"Neutral ground! Neutral ground!" Dario whined, stepping back against the nearest wall.

"I knew today was an unlucky one, the moment that penny came up tails four times in a row," Gaspard Gervais muttered as he appeared.

His angry eyes surveyed the scene and he shook his head. A heavy hunting rifle lay across his shoulder, but he did not attempt to bring the weapon to bear.

"Bonsoir, Gaspard," Irma said, not looking away from Dario. "You sound as unpleasant as ever. I am here for information and then I shall leave. I may even pay. The longer I am delayed, the more problems I shall cause."

"I'll ban you from my bar," Gaspard spat back. "And your pet monster, the Eidolon, too. Break the rules and all of the Marseilles underworld will turn against you."

"Oh, Gaspard darling, why should that matter?" Irma replied, giving the tavern owner a sideways glance filled with amusement. "We would kill you first and all who protect you. Then, we would start to get angry…"

"Dario," Gaspard asked, sighing. "What have you done?"

"Nothing!" the giant criminal shrieked. "I just did some bodyguard work for a Gambler negotiator. He paid me and now, I'm about to leave for America. I got hired as a professional wrestler!"

Gaspard Gervais looked to Irma and asked:

"Is that what you wanted to know?"

Irma shook her head and giggled.

"I never said I wished information from him, Gaspard darling. I was just saying hello to my old friend Dario. It is with you that I wish to have a long discussion. You have been a quite naughty boy…"

Gasping in shock, Gaspard Gervais brought his rifle up to his shoulder and quickly aimed for the black-clad Irma Vep. The motion was the practiced skill of an expert hunter responding to danger of the worst kind.

"Die!" Gaspard screamed, pulling the trigger.

CHAPTER XLI

"I am here, you bastard. Where are you?" Nanon Zanzi shouted as she stared up the long driveway leading to the red-colored mansion.

The sounds of laughter, singing, and dancing drifted in her direction. The jangle of noise caused her to pick up a rock and grind it into dust as she called out again:

"Where are you, Eidolon?"

"You are a little ray of sunshine, are you not?" Victor Sicarius asked from somewhere above her head.

Still dressed entirely in black, he squatted on the stone gate, resembling a massive gargoyle more than a human being.

"Shut up, you bastard! Stop laughing at me!" Nanon spat back.

Victor shook his head, pitying this twisted woman, but knowing his entreaties would serve no positive end. This Nanon Zanzi existed only as a creature of hatred and anger. Just listening to her and watching her actions, he knew immediately that her soul had long been lost. All that remained was a dark fury, a poisonous desire only fulfilled when she destroyed something beautiful.

"I am not laughing," Victor replied. "I merely observed that you are suffused with anger when we are about to attend a party filled with happy, wealthy people. Walking inside shrieking in rage will not help our purpose."

"What purpose? I do not even know why I am here!" Nanon said.

"Fair enough, you deserve the details. Within that house are a large group of foolish rich men and women. Most merely drink champagne or other wines, but a few shall be addicted to red lotus. I wish to determine their source of this rare narcotic."

187

"Ridiculous!" Nanon replied. "Most will have their own supply, and those that bought some here will not share that information with a French outsider."

"A French outsider, you say? Where?" Victor replied, smiling beneath his mask.

His words and accent had suddenly turned into pure Oxford-accented English.

"How did you do that?" Nanon asked.

"I am a unique individual. Now, shall we go inside?" Victor asked, dropping to the ground near the gate.

"No," Nanon said. "I will not help you in any way. I do not care if the Director takes my arms and legs and throws me back into the night. I will not help you—or that slut."

Victor shook his head, unmoved by the insult. He had learned as a child to examine the source of the nasty words and decide if they were worth his anger. This half-human hateful creature did not deserve his anger, pity, or kindness.

"Very well, that is between you and your leader. *Adieu*," he replied, walking towards the mansion.

Nanon stomped her foot, shattering a small stone and causing a deep rut in the grass.

"That is it? I insult your woman and you just shrug and walk away?"

Victor chuckled and shook his head.

"You are no more capable of insulting her than I am of flapping my arms are flying to the moon. She would not be insulted by your words, and nor will I on her behalf. At best, I may one day find some pity for you, but that is doubtful. Your missing limbs did not cause your hateful ways, Mademoiselle."

"What does that mean?" Nanon whispered, feeling a cold wave fill her body.

"Nobody could possess that much anger from one terrible event. Before your terrible accident, I think you despised people and wished them all dead. The horrors that followed simply enhanced that side of your spirit."

Nanon choked, surprised by the accuracy of this man's statements. How could he know? Not even Doctor Cornelius knew of her disgust of men. She loathed the sensation, which grew to encompass women, children and animals too. The death of the one man she had cared about, Alonzo the Armless, had only heightened that sensation to the point where she reviled all life.

"Die, you…" Nanon screeched, taking a large step his direction.

"Bastard?" Victor replied, neither flinching nor backing away. "Forgive me, but you do possess a limited vocabulary. Point of fact, I am a bastard."

"I am going to rip you into pieces!" she whispered, balling both of her fists up.

"Feel free to make another attempt," Victor replied.

Then he audibly yawned.

"Once again, forgive me but I find your simplistic threats quite boring," he said. "I heard worse in my childhood from men and women whose lethal qualities were legendary then."

Screaming wordlessly from both frustration and rage, Nanon Zanzi rushed at Victor Sicarius, her bloody intent all too visible across her ruined face.

The Eidolon raised his hands but did not move an inch. He knew this was inevitable…

CHAPTER XLII

The massive hunting rifle barked, sending a plume of smoke and flame across the gloomy room. The far wall of the chamber exploded in a shower of stones and plaster dust causing patrons to yelp in pain and dive for cover.

Gaspard Gervais lowered the gun, scanning the room for his quarry. But Irma Vep was nowhere in sight; no traces of her were visible on the floor or near the tables.

Gaspard blinked, trying to penetrate the shadows without success. He was about to step forward and raise his rifle again, when he felt a cold metallic object pressed against his throat. He gulped, recognizing a knife, and froze in his place, knowing there was no escape.

"Lower the gun, please, Monsieur Gervais," Robert Ménard said. "Slowly, by the strap. Let us keep this polite and proper."

He held a long knife in his extended right hand with another blade held tightly in his other palm.

"Ménard? How dare you?" Gaspard snarled, "You are helping the Vampire violate the rules of the Bar des Rougets? Have you lost all your senses?"

But he slowly lowered the rifle to the floor and frowned as Robert placed a heavy foot across the barrel.

"As a point of fact, Monsieur Gervais, she has not broken the rules in any way," Robert said.

"Of course, she has! She threatened the Crusher and then myself!" Gaspard replied, eyes widening.

"Excuse me, Monsieur Gervais," Dario said, looking somewhat shamefaced. "But mere threats are not technically a violation. The Vampire did not violate neutrality. You did when you shot at her."

The older scarred sailor stood up and cried:

"The scoundrel's right. Threats are not a violation!"

There was a loud murmur of agreement, followed by a few shrieks of shock as Irma Vep dropped into view on a table. She was smiling and, with a flourish, bowed deeply.

"Quite true, darlings," she said with a wide smile. "It is you, Gaspard Gervais, who violated the rules of this ancient establishment. And what is the punishment for attacking a fellow patron of the Bar des Rougets? Is it slow death? I am quite adept at providing that…"

Several men and women nearby shuddered and backed away at the sight of her grin.

Raising his hands in surrender, Gervais said:

"This is to be decided between the parties. Perhaps we can come to some private arrangement, Vampire? You said you wished some small service from me?"

"Oh, Gaspard, darling," Irma replied, winking at the bar-keeper, "I knew you would be amenable to my gentle ways. However, you did cause a terrible fuss and may have injured a few of the good ladies and gentlemen. I think a free drink for all would make up for their injured feelings, *non*?"

"Of course!" said Gaspard. "One free drink to all, but only one. Please resume normal opérations."

Then he looked at the heavyset Robert out of the corner of his eye.

"Will you please get that knife away from my neck, Ménard? I find it difficult to concentrate when a sneeze could result in my death."

"Of course, Monsieur Gervais," Robert replied, carefully pulling the blade away from the tavern owner's throat.

The weapon vanished from sight a moment later and he added:

"Perhaps we should conduct this discussion in your private office?"

"A very good idea," Irma said, hopping off her table. "Lead the way, Gaspard."

The bar-keeper narrowed his eyes, sensing mockery in her tone. But he snorted, picked up his rifle and led then towards the rear of the tavern.

Heading down a short flight of stone stairs, he stopped before a small desk and sat on a wooden stool. The basement possessed a sandy floor and every inch appeared filled with boxes, barrels, and crates. A few small electric lights cast huge shadows across the expanse, adding an eerie, dungeon-type feel to this small part of the tavern.

"I do not keep an office," Gaspard said, resting his rifle against the wall near his right leg. "They are a waste of space and become storage for information that is best kept in one's head. All accounts and details of the bar are held by me alone."

"Commendable, if completely unimportant to me," Irma replied, sitting on top of a large crate.

She crossed her legs in a dainty manner, behaving as if she was a high-class lady and this basement storage area was a garden party.

"It is important because I wish you to understand a few facts," continued Gaspard. "First, I will not betray any of my customers. Second, I am now aware that you tricked me into violating the terms of my agreement with my patrons. You shall not succeed in that foolishness a second time. Third, if you or that monster, the Eidolon, ever threaten my patrons again, I shall offer a million francs for your heads. Do you understand these terms?"

Irma Vep nodded and said in an artificially sweet tone

"I do, very much so, Gaspard, but allow me to reply in kind. First, I do not care about any of the baboons you consider your patrons. Keep their secrets, or don't. I doubt any ten of them would be worthy of my interest. Second, I never use the same trick twice. To do so, even to a swaggering fool such as yourself, would be needlessly risky. Third, if you ever refer to my better half in that manner again, I shall hang you by your innards from the tallest spire of Notre-Dame de la Garde. Do you understand *my* terms?"

Gaspard Gervais' face grew pale as Irma spoke, and he eventually nodded. The movement was quick and jerky, but convincing.

"Yes, Vampire, I do. Now, what do you want?"

"Red lotus," Irma said, uncrossing her legs and leaning forward.

"You want some red lotus? But you can buy as much of that as you like upstairs. Why upset me over such a simple request?"

Irma laughed and shook her head.

"No, silly boy. I would not allow that foul plant in my body. My question is about the supply…"

She held up a hand seeing Gaspard opening his mouth.

"Please, stop interrupting me. I do not wish to engage in its traffic either. My question is this: from whom are you receiving your supply? All the major suppliers are dead and buried. However, the flow of that foul plant continues without even a rise in price. Tell me the identity of your seller and I shall leave your tavern without any further questions."

"I do not know," Gaspard said. "And I do not lie," he rushed to add, seeing her disbelief. "A man approached me two days after all my other supplier had vanished. He informed me that his principal was now the new and only supplier, and that he wished to meet with me. They placed me in an enclosed steamer truck and drove me about for an hour. Then I met with a man whom I cannot remember in a large empty room with wooden floors. He gave me a good price and I received a two-month supply. That is the entire story."

"Not quite." Irma said, hopping off her crate. "I know you. You remember everything, from the smallest drink to the largest amount bet upon a single turn of the cards. This, you say you forgot. How is that possible?"

Gaspard nodded quickly, made fists with his hands and punched his thighs.

"You now see my problem. I cannot remember anything about that man. I remember that he spoke with some kind of odd accent, but nothing further. When I think hard on the subject, all I find is an empty gap where the memory of that man should be. It disturbs me greatly."

"If I may, Madame?" Robert asked, looking to Irma. Seeing her nod, he asked: "Monsieur Gervais, do you remember anything about the room in which you spoke to this person?"

"Yes, but it was featureless. No furniture. Just wooden floors and light-colored walls. Nothing else," Gaspard replied.

"Windows," Robert asked. "Were there any windows? If so, how many, and how large?"

Gaspard frowned but then slowly nodded again.

"Yes... Many large windows. They covered the entire wall and looked like doors. They ever went around a curve at the end of the room. I could not see outside. A bright chandelier made a mirror of the long windows."

"Thank you, Monsieur Gervais. Madame, do you wish to question this gentleman any further?"

"No, I think not," Irma replied. "I think we shall leave now."

"Don't go back upstairs!" Gaspard said, waving his hands in front of his body in open desperation. "I have already lost too much business by your appearance tonight. I will show you another way out, through the wall to your right. The tunnel will lead you to a warehouse in the alley behind the bar."

"Lead the way, Gaspard," Irma said, "We shall follow in your steps."

Gaspard frowned and growled:

"You do not trust me?"

"I trust you to behave quite poorly, Monsieur Gervais. It is your nature."

Irma and Robert followed he tavern-keeper into the secret exit.

CHAPTER XLIII

Nanon Zanzi reached for Victor's arms, her metal fists clicked and the gears simulated human muscles. The overwhelming terrible, burning, hatred glinting in her eyes gave her a monstrous quality. With the stars casting odd pale silver shadows across her half-human body, she resembled a clockwork simulacrum of a monster from ancient myths. She was horrific and even Victor felt a cold wave of fear at the malice that seemed to exude from her very being.

Stepping forward, he reached and grabbed her metal arms at the wrists, stopping her progress instantly. Her face quivered in her shock, never having witnessed a human move as fast as her. With a wordless snarl, she pressed forward, knowing her iron arms could shatter flesh and bone with ease.

Her artificial arms and legs creaked, whirred, groaned, and clicked as the powerful servos and other devices came to bear. She had once torn a a huge, monstrously powerful strongman named Hugo in half when he had tried to resist her attacks. Nanon liked the idea of repeating such a feat this evening. Then, she could toss the remains of this man at the feet of his mocking, laughing lover.

Yet, the man she knew only as the Eidolon did not move, did not give ground as her artificial arms pressed forward with overwhelming force. His arm muscles appeared to swell as he held the half-human woman back.

Nanon Zanzi grunted in surprise and summoned all the power in her artificial limbs. But Victor Sicarius neither moved, nor appeared to strain, as his enemy tried to crush him with her mechanical arms and legs. Beneath his mask, sweat poured down his body and he felt his tendons quivering under the terrible pressure.

"Bastard!" Nanon spat out. "How? How are you doing this? No human can resist my strength!"

"Who said I was human?" Victor asked, rolling his eyes beneath his mask.

Such a mystifying statement was one he had used in the past against his enemies. It helped create a supernatural legend surrounding his alias.

Victor knew full well there were no demons, vampires, werewolves wandering about the Earth. The idea of such ghouls was amusing, to say the least, especially with the incredible advancements in the world of science. Said developments explained much of his life, though only a few long-dead men and women knew the truth.

Nanon Zanzi screamed in frustration and fury as she heard the gears in her arm whine as they strained. She only had seconds before the mechanisms failed and required immediate repair. She lifted her leg, knowing a kick from her metal leg could shred flesh and crush bones.

Victor praised whatever spirits might have been listening to his prayers, grateful that the hateful killer's inexperience had led her to this mistake. Standing on one leg made even well-trained fighters vulnerable.

Smiling, he shoved her arms with all his remaining strength. Nanon tumbled backwards, landing on the ground in a heavy jangle of metal and meat. Her servos righted her body, making her resemble a marionette suddenly yanked upright by a mad puppeteer.

Once again, she ran towards Victor and tried to rip the flesh off his bones. But, though powerful and dangerous, she attacked like an angry child. Victor doubted that, before she had received her terrible injuries, she had ever fought another human being. Her attacks were simple, rush, grab, punch or kick. Her metal limbs hid her lack of precision and skill. Fighting her was like battling a toddler with the strength of a mad bull—dangerous, but easily dealt with by a skilled fighter.

Reaching into his pocket, Victor pulled out a steel sphere about the size of a child's marble. With a flick of his wrist, he tossed it under Nanon's foot and watched as she slipped and fell on her back again.

"This is pointless, Madame," he said as she bounced back to her feet in the same inhuman manner. "I do not wish to fight you, but you are testing my patience. Why don't you just leave and discuss your refusal to work with me with your Director?"

Nanon screeched and ran forward again, eliciting a sigh of regret from Victor. Some people never learned, and this frightening female appeared to be one of them. Ducking under one of her wildly swinging arms, he grabbed the limb with one hand, freezing her in place.

Then he struck, his open palm crashing into her metal elbow joint. The metal squealed and the vulnerable parts split and shattered.

Half of the arm dropped to the ground and a spray of lubricating fluid squirted out like a shower of black blood.

Nanon's eyes widened in shock. Victor shoved her back and kicked the twitching, detached, steel hand and forearm aside.

"This is your last warning, Madame Zanzi," he snarled. "If you attack me again, I will destroy you and abandon you to rust in some isolated place to. Your metal appendages will not protect you from the Eidolon. Leave now and remember my warning."

"Bastard!" Nanon hissed.

She picked up her fallen arm and added:

"I will kill you slowly one day."

She then ran into the night, vanishing into the silvery, gloom.

Victor watched her leave and shook his head. He despised it when people used some terrible fate as an excuse to destroy anything or anyone in their path. He knew that folly better than Nanon Zanzi, but he had one advantage over the unfortunate woman.

Thank you, Irma, for rescuing me, he thought.

Then, he turned back to the distant party. Judging by the sounds, the merriment within did not appear to have been changed by the short, violent battle just outside the gate.

"Time to finish the mission," he said, heading towards the house.

CHAPTER XLIV

"Master," the Lamane said, bowing his head as he appeared in the Great Brain's doorway. "The Nimrod and her guests are driving through the gates."

"Yes, slave, I know," the Great Brain replied.

He examined the former advisor to the leader of the Children of Giphantie, surveying the wreckage that remained of this once a proud, thoughtful, philosopher.

The Lamane still wore his robes, the same ones he had worn on the day he in the day he had first met the Great Brain. But these garments no longer resembled the brilliant, immaculate dress of a powerful man; now, they looked like the rags of a suffering slave. Soiled, the ceremonial robes were an odd, unpleasant shade of brown and gray. The stench that emerged from the cloth caused an almost visible odiferous miasma that revolted and disgusted any who were unfortunate enough to encounter the Lamane.

This was the Great Brain's subtle torture of the formerly proud, elderly individual. The tiny piece of the Lamane that still reacted to the world screamed in torment as fleas crawled on his body and his soiled his clothes. Had the Great Brain allowed this man a chance to be himself again, the results would have been a terrorized madman whose lifespan would be measured in minutes.

"Usher them into the back conference chamber," the Great Brain instructed. "Do not answer any questions, but tell them I will be along shortly. There is only one chair in the chamber. Do not allow anyone other than myself to sit in it. Now, go."

The Great Brain touched a button on his chair and chuckled as one of his lesser servants passed on an interesting piece of information. Closing his eyes, he issued a series of mental commands now that everything proceeded at a faster pace.

Five minutes later, Rotwang strode into the chamber looking harried and annoyed.

"I was in the middle of a critical juncture in my work!" he complained.

"Suspend it. I have an assignment for you that you will enjoy. Walk to the car park and get into the electrical sedan driven by the Corsican bookkeeper. He will take you to an interesting conference. Relay to him what you wish to do."

Ignoring the Professor's grumbling, the Great Brain watched his servant's progress and found everything acceptable. Then, standing up, he performed the human act of straightening his clothing before walking through the huge headquarters he called a home.

Throwing open the doors to the conference chamber, he strode past the four ceremonial bodyguards and the Nimrod herself without glancing in their direction. His footsteps echoed across the parquet floor, hushing the whispered conversations instantly.

The one chair in the chamber was a huge wooden throne with a high back and the coat of arms of the Emperor Napoleon III etched onto its surface. A priceless heirloom. The Great Brain had bought it, along with the entire furnishings of the for less money than most residents of Marseilles spent on a daily meal.

Settling into the seat, the Great Brain finally looked towards the mistress of the Children of Giphantie.

"Well?" he asked.

The Nimrod flushed with fury at this supercilious greeting. She was a tall woman with a ramrod back, iron gray hair and an angry expression. The Great Brain knew that her family had once possessed great wealth and position, but lost everything after mass industrialization had started. He had once heard her curse an American company called Scarlotti Industries for having driven her family to near poverty, although that was ultimately less important to her than her hereditary position as mistress of the Children of Giphantie.

One of her relatives, a French explorer whose name the Great Brain had never learned, had discovered the original hidden land of Giphantie and had later founded the group after the mysterious guardians had "evolved." He had called himself "Nimrod," and had passed the title on to his nephew on his deathbed. Since then, only members of that family had held the position, and they ruled the cult with a religious fervor.

"Is that a way to dress in my presence?" the Nimrod spat out.

Her fleshy face took on an expression of disgust mixed with embarrassment and fury.

The Great Brain looked down at his gray suit, white shirt and partially unknotted Cambridge tie. He resembled a conservative English banker attempting to relax in his home after a long day at the office. In fact, he had taken these clothes from an actual English banker named Banks years ago.

The Nimrod dressed as all of her rank did when meeting other high-ranking members of the Children of Giphantie. Her gown, a purple silk affair based on a design from an ancient Roman Empress, possessed carefully gold thread stitched in the images of the mythical plants from the Garden of Eden. A crown of laurel encircled her gray hair and she held with a white knuckled grip a willow wood wand.

"Is there some problem, Nimrod?" the Great Brain asked, smiling.

The bodyguards, four tall men with thick blond hair, pale skin and blue eyes, surged forward. As a body, their faces flushed with fury, enraged by the open insult to their leader. Each wore protective leather jackets and trousers, and they held wooden swords with sharpened obsidian squares imbedded in their sides. The Great Brain had learned years earlier that these weapons, known as *macuahuitl*, were traditional war weapons from the Aztecs. How they had become the traditional bodyguard clubs of the Nimrod's force was a puzzle he did not care to solve.

"Hold," the Nimrod thundered, raising one pudgy hand. "I wish to learn if this man has somehow lost his senses."

The bodyguards bowed slightly, their eyes still on the lounging Great Brain. They took a half-step back but held their *macuahuitl* at the ready. Their eyes glittered with hatred and fury for the Great Brain who openly ignored their long-held traditions.

"Well?" the Nimrod said. "Explain yourself and your disgusting actions. Also, what have you done to the Lamane? He is little more than a walking corpse and smells of... meat and alcohol..."

"He is my slave now," the Great Brain replied, and, glancing at the foul smelling old man standing near the door, he added: "Isn't that right, you old fool?"

"Yes, Master," the Lamane said in a hollow voice.

"Slavery?" the Nimrod said. "But that is immoral and disgusting, as well as against the very laws of the Children of Giphantie!"

She marched up to the Lamane and said:

"You are now free, you poor, poor man."

"Slap her, Lamane," the Great Brain chuckled.

The aged advisor raised one skeletal hand and weakly struck the Nimrod across the cheek.

The leader of the Children of Giphantie cried out and fell back. Her eyes widened, and she held one fleshy fist against her reddening face.

"Oh," the Great Brain added with mirth. "That was impolite. Lamane, strike yourself twice as an apology to our injured Nimrod."

The Lamane lifted his hand and slapped himself hard across the mouth two times. A thin trickle of blood dribbled from his split lip and across his chin. Yet, he stood in place, staring with dead eyes at the Great Brain.

"There now," the Great Brain said, still chuckling. "Let us return to our discussion. You were saying that the keeping of slaves is immoral and against the rules of your organization, correct?"

The Nimrod straightened and shot back:

"You defy rules hundreds of years-old—you, a mediocre third-generation inheritor of our secrets!"

A long, sneering laugh emerged from the Great Brain's lips. He clapped his hands together in merriment and stomped his feet on the decorative wooden floor.

"Oh, my! Oh, mountains of Mars. Third generation, ha, ha, ha!"

The Nimrod struck her willow wand against the flat paddle surface of one of her bodyguards. A loud cracking sound filled the air and her badge of office split, but the noise did quiet the guffawing man across the chamber.

"What, pray tell, is so amusing, little man? I expect better behavior from one of our third-generation leaders."

"Third generation?" the Great Brain roared and stood up. "Nimrod, you half-evolved ape! I'm not even third generation human!"

"You are insane!" the Nimrod whispered, backing away a step.

"Cease your prattle," the Great Brain ordered.

His amusement had vanished as quick as it had appeared, and he now looked at the robed woman and her followers with naked disgust.

"Humans never shut up when they believe they possess a degree of importance, but this will change in the coming days."

"Take this lunatic into custody!" the Nimrod said, glancing over a fleshy shoulder at her troop of bodyguards. "We shall see if we may heal his wounded mind in the coming years."

"I think not," the Great Brain replied.

Suddenly, the doors flew open. The metallic clank and crash of the beings who stepped inside drowned out the screams of shock from the Nimrod and her men.

The five creatures that had just entered the room moved in lock-step, their motions exact and completely inhuman. Each was over two meters high and possessed shining silver bodies that appeared human in design, but looked more like a mockery of mankind than an attempted recreation of the species. Their legs, arms, hand, and fingers resembled that of a human being sculpted in metal. However, there was an odd, inhuman imperfection to these molded men, as if their joints had been redesigned for utility rather than similarity to the human form.

Their faces resembled steel simulacrums of classic angels from religious iconography. They appeared sad and mournful as they stared with unblinking glass eyes at the Nimrod and her guards. Imbedded in each forehead were crimson jewels that pulsed periodically with yellow energy, though never at the same instant.

"What in the name of the Tree of Knowledge are those abominations?" the Nimrod cried, shrinking back at the unwinking gaze of the newcomers.

"Those are my soldiers, my personal army" the Great Brain replied. "They grow in numbers each day, and soon I shall possess thousands. My servant, Professor Rotwang…"

"Rotwang?" the Nimrod shrieked, "That arch-heretic who seeks to destroy all that is natural upon the Earth? The designer of these terrible machines which despoil our planet without regard for the consequences? You allowed him in our sanctum?"

"Allowed him? I sought him out specially. He and his comrade, Doctor ten Brinken, serve me with loyalty I did not believe possible for *homo sapiens*. Soon, my true goal since arriving on this too warm world shall be achieved. Now, stop talking, I wish to answer your earlier question. Rotwang named these creatures the *Maschinenmensch—les Hommes-Machines*—the Mechanical Men, in your languages—a successful merger of humans with mechanical parts. Their minds are under my complete control and they are the perfect fighting force."

"Kill him! Kill this twisted, evil creature! Whoever takes his head shall rise to the inner circle immediately!" the Nimrod screamed.

The bodyguard closest to her, a powerful man with short hair and a thin mustache, raised his club and surged forward. But a steel body blocked his way and a metallic fist grabbed the wood and obsidian sword. With a loud snap, the razor-sharp edges shattered under the inhuman, grasp of the *Maschinenmensch*.

The remaining metal men stepped closer and held the bodyguard's arms. The man screamed as the flesh and bones shattered beneath the *Maschinenmensch*'s hands.

The metal man standing beside the Nimrod did not grab her body. He merely stood by her side, a steel sentinel whose very presence froze her in place. The Nimrod shivered beneath the inhuman orbs, frozen in place with the same terror than a rabbit feels under the gaze of a serpent.

"Take those three," the Great Brain said, pointing towards the bodyguards who had not attacked.

He did not need to speak aloud, having mental control over the drones. He did so because it added to the terror and pain felt by the Nimrod and her followers.

"Take them to Dr. ten Brinken with my compliments. Take the other one to Professor Rotwang and hold him in restraints until ordered otherwise by Rotwang or myself. As for you, Nimrod…"

The Great Brain turned towards the leader of the Children of Giphantie.

"…You shall come with me to learn your very special fate."

•

CHAPTER XLV

Victor Sicarius opened the second-floor window of the Gérard mansion and swung inside.

The formerly wrecked room appeared perfectly in order and he saw no traces of the battle he had fought earlier with Gérard, his driver, and Robert Ménard.

He still found the room quite gaudy, wondering who could rest in such an overdone décor.

Heading down the hallway, Victor walked down the stairs, spotting the hole he had made in the ceiling with his climbing spike. However, the plaster dust below had been cleaned away, another tribute to the butler's impressive skills. Even the wreckage along the walls, still very evident, appeared to have been swept and scrubbed, only waiting for someone to repair the walls and floor.

"We are in the library, *mon cœur*," Irma called out, her voice barely audible from where he stood.

Heading through the hallways and rooms, Victor spotted the open door leading to the impressive library.

Irma sat cross-legged on the desk while Robert dusted a set of leather-bound volumes.

She smiled when he entered and crooked a finger his direction.

Lifting his mask a few inches, Victor approached and they instantly embraced, kissing with unbridled passion. This continued for several minutes, with Irma's legs wrapping around his waist and holding him tight.

"Ahem," Robert said, standing at attention.

"If you do like what you see, Robert, do not look," Irma replied over Victor's shoulder.

"No," Victor said, glancing over at Robert. "We owe him some courtesy. We shall continue later."

"You shall owe me, and I shall collect tonight," Irma replied, releasing her lover. "Do we have a feather duster, a silk cord, and a stethoscope?"

Victor turned around to sit beside her on the desk.

"Yes," he replied, "I restocked last week. But we will need extra ice."

"Only if you injure your neck again," Irma said, laying her chin on his shoulder as they spoke. "You should try to be more careful."

"If I may interrupt," Robert piped in, "partly to return us to business, but also because I wish to avoid hearing more of this, where is Miss Zanzi?"

"I assume," Victor replied, as he pulled down his mask, "that, based on your question, she has not returned? Well, Madame Zanzi grew enraged by my presence and the costumed party in the distance. She attacked me, and I disarmed her... quite literally..."

Victor then explained the details of Nanon Zanzi's insane attack and the results. Her paused once, hearing Irma giggle when she understood the meaning of his "disarmed" comment.

"It is quite distressing, Monsieur," Robert said, his voice growing colder. "And I do find your account rather difficult to believe. Defeating her in the manner you describe would be beyond the powers of even the strongest man."

"Do you have a coin in your pocket, Robert?" Irma asked.

The giant knife-wielding butler's forehead wrinkled as he puzzled over the simple request.

"Yes, Madame, but why?"

"Toss the Eidolon a penny," she stated, her grin growing wider.

Robert stared at her for a few seconds and then reached into his pants pocket. He removed several coins and examined two pennies carefully. After a moment, he tossed a copper piece to Victor, who caught it easily.

Holding the coin up between thumb and forefinger, Victor Sicarius bent the penny in half. He then tossed it back to Robert and waited as the huge butler examined the object.

"That is impressive," Robert finally conceded. "I have heard of similar feats in the past, but until now, I had dismissed them as mere exaggeration and fanciful talk. How are you capable of such exploits? Was this a result of some experiment by the Vampires?"

Victor and Irma turned their heads and stared into each other's eyes for several seconds. Their behavior resembled that of long-time married couples who knew each other well enough to exchange entire discussions with a simple look.

"That would require a longer conversation than we are prepared to have today," Victor said.

"Plus, you work for the Red Hand," Irma added. "We have no desire in either battling or aiding your organization. We have different priorities."

"That comes as something of a surprise," Robert said as he replaced the bent penny back in his pocket. "I thought you were cat burglars."

"The Vampire is a cat burglar, the best in the world after Fantômas," Victor said. "I learned a few useful skills in that area although I, myself, am not a burglar."

"Then what are you, Monsieur?" Robert asked. "The patrons of the Bar des Rougets fled in fear at the sight of Madame la Vampire. Yet, they appeared even more frightened by the very idea of your presence."

"I am…"

Victor paused for a moment as he thought for a moment, then said:

"I did not know the criminal world still feared us."

"Oh yes," Irma replied, giggling. "Dario the Crusher nearly cried as I spoke to him."

"Ah, reputations… They serve us in so many ways… Tell me of your exploits at that tavern of iniquity and I shall regale you with my brief encounter with the English lotus eaters."

He then listened without interruption to their tale of their dealings with Gaspard Gervais. The details of how Robert had extracted additional information from the criminal procurer especially captured his attention.

"I am glad your idea of annoying the patrons until they attacked you worked," he said. "It was a risky idea, but you did discover quite a bit."

"The challenge is still there," Irma said. "We must now find a large, empty home located within one hour by automobile from Marseilles. That could be just outside the city, in Cassis or Aubagne... We are closer than before, but our enemies are still quite a distance from our clutches."

Then she added:

"Unless you have additional information from your encounter with the English?"

"Not as much as one would hope. This is what occurred..."

CHAPTER XLVI

"Oh my, look at you!" a voice cried out as Nanon Zanzi wandered down the avenue.

She had been wandering randomly across the neighborhood, having just reached the edge of the city. She walked like a woman in a fog, unable to see anything, stumbling over the smallest objects. So far, nobody had crossed her path. Had they done so, Nanon's unthinking mind may have snapped and caused her to murder at random.

Now, having a person speak of her in such a manner caused the return of her hate-filled mind and poisonous spirit. She snarled and spun in place to discover a wildly staring man with random tufts of white hair standing out across his wrinkled pate. He grinned her direction, a mad look that paused her instant assault.

"What did you say?" Nanon hissed, her horrid eyes narrowing.

"I said, look at you! You are on the edge of pure perfection, a blend of machine and life. Though you were left incomplete and the workmanship performed was shoddy, at best. You deserve so much more, my dear woman."

Rotwang stepped forward in the light of an electric street lamp.

"You dare insult me? I am a monster!" Nanon screeched, taking a step his direction, her face twisting with fury.

Rotwang dramatically raised his gloved hand and ripped off the leather covering. Beneath lay a hand made from dull gray iron, the fingers clicking as they slowly flexed.

"Am I a monster too, young lady? Do I repulse you? I merely wear the glove so that I do not crush delicate parts in my work."

Stopped by the sight of this man's mechanical hand, Nanon whispered:

"Who are you?"

"I am Professor Rotwang, Doctor of science and mechanical engineering. In the past, I have designed entire mechanical cities, but I have now abandoned such works as a waste of time. My true passion lies in the replacement of a wasteful humanity by higher beings, a merger between homo sapiens and the perfection that is the machine. What you should be, young woman."

Rotwang stepped closer. His artificial hand remained raised at his head level as he approached.

"What I should be?" Nanon repeated, her voice nearly inaudible.

"Yes!" Rotwang cried, shaking his metal fist. "Flesh is weak, useless, and disgusting! Steel and iron are superior, stronger, without the stench and weakness that is meat and bone. Whoever gave you those wondrous limbs and chest cavity possessed the right intentions; however, they lacked the proper skills and provided you with only half-measures. Your arms and legs are at least twenty years behind my own work."

Nanon's skeletal jaw dropped in shock This man... his messianic words... He understood her completely. Before the fire, she had loathed the touch of a man. In truth, that was probably too simplistic a statement. Nanon Zanzi, though possessing a bewitching, dark-eyed beauty that enticed many and caused them to pursue her, despised the touch of *anyone*. Male or female were repulsive in her eyes. They exuded oils from the blubbery, rubbery skin covering their bones that made them smell like animals. They drooled from their gaping mouths and resembled apes in a zoo. Just being around people had proved a trial for Nanon since birth; she perpetually needed to keep from shrieking in horror at the touch of humans.

Now this Rotwang offered her more, a chance to be free of the horrific bonds that still chained her to her humanity. She hoped, even mentally prayed, that he was telling her the truth.

"Tell me more," she said, her voice cracking from her unexpressed emotions.

"Come with me, Mademoiselle..."

He stopped and looked puzzled.

"Forgive me, I do not know your name…"

Nanon shook her head.

"I abandoned that name long ago, no matter what anyone else says. I have no name since the accident that destroyed my body."

"Destroyed? No, it merely robbed you of some unimportant meat and bones. I shall complete the job and you shall be the true future of mankind. Then you may choose your new name. Is that acceptable?"

Rotwang pulled the glove back across his hand.

"Yes," Nanon Zanzi whispered.

She hoped that this man was not just another liar. If so, she would make his death slow and vastly painful.

Rotwang smiled, his full madness visible for an instant.

"Follow me around the corner. My van awaits, and we shall proceed to my laboratory and begin your transformation at once. To use a disgusting analogy, you are about to enter your cocoon and metamorphose into something perfect. Come along, every second we waste is another preventing you from casting off the shackles that held you tied to humanity."

Nanon did not reply, but followed in Rotwang's wake. She clutched her shattered arm against her chest. For the first time since the death of her dear Alonzo, she had some hope for the future.

Soon, Nanon Zanzi would be able to forget her past and start anew as something greater…

CHAPTER XLVII

"Dusting myself off after the fight," Victor began, as he embarked upon his story, "I strolled towards entrance of the red mansion..."

Crouching beneath the open window, Victor listened to the laughter, the sounds of clinking glasses, and the songs played by someone on a well-tuned piano. The accents varied, but most appeared to possess the same drawling vowels of the Oxford colleges.

"...a shark. I screamed and swam away just in time..." came the snatches of words.

The voice was that of a young woman, her accent clearly demonstrating her excellent upbringing.

"Rubbish... flat fish..." came a man's response.

He spoke with an accent that was an equal mixture of lowland Scot and English public-school.

"Tuppy, how could... fat bore..!" the girl replied, close to tears.

Tuppy? Victor thought, creeping away from the brush. *This is a name?*

Staying in the shadows, he walked up to the front door and raised his fist to knock.

Just then, the door flew open and a tall, thin man dressed in a bright white mess jacket with shiny brass buttons appeared. The outfit was rather ridiculous, but no more so than the horse's mask hiding his face.

"May I help you, sir?" another man, one with black hair sprinkled with gray, asked.

He wore the tight, precisely pressed suit that all English butlers appear to wear as their standard costume.

"Hullo, hullo," Victor answered, speaking in the same accented voice as those inside. "My name is Darcy. I'm an old pal of Tuppy who's come to see what's what."

"Yes, sir," the butler replied.

His cold tone possessed a degree of disinterest that impressed Victor as he stepped inside the mansion. The man's eyes stared through him as if he was a wooden statue rather than a human being.

Heading further inside, Victor spotted three distinct areas filled with well-dressed gentlemen and expensively clad ladies. The library contained a small knot of people, the majority of whom appeared to be listening to a lecture from a tall willowy woman with platinum blond hair. Based on her pose and sharp motions as she spoke, Victor sensed this was a highly intelligent, imperious young lady.

Exactly the type which I must avoid, he thought. An intelligent, strong personality might see through his ruse and summon the police.

The second room held a collection of men and women, including a bulldog-faced man and a weeping young lady. They stood near the window and were apparently the young couple he had heard quarreling earlier. Therefore, it would be a poor idea to stay in that room in case someone had heard him claim to be "Tuppy's friend."

The third and final area was a room that overlooked the back of the house. There, men and women stood about in loose groups, drinking, smoking and talking amiably. Drifting in that direction, Victor spotted a pretty girl with bright red hair and a mischievous smile rolling a pair of small, ill-looking red lotus leaves.

"I say," Victor said approaching her, "where did you get such excellent leaves?"

"That's it?" Irma asked, laughing. "You just put on a silly accent and asked the feather-headed idiot where she bought the most illegal narcotic on five continents?"

Victor shrugged.

"Sometimes the simple approach is the best. I asked, and she told me it was from a tobacco parlor owned by an English lady located near the Palais de justice."

"*La Tabatière*? Is the owner English now? Last I'd heard, it owned by a lady from Paris obsessed with mysteries of the Templars and other silliness. She prattled on for hours about secret chambers in famous buildings in Paris."

"Yes," Victor replied, "a Miss Milverton, said to be a very unpleasant sort, though she sells whatever the English require. The building was closed by the time I arrived. We can attempt to determine if she possesses any further knowledge tomorrow. Unless, Monsieur Ménard already knows the lady?"

"Alas no, Monsieur. Monsieur Gérard did not speak directly to customers of, er, lesser prominence. She purchased her narcotics directly from the Blanc brothers."

"Then we shall leave and return tomorrow evening," Irma said. "Robert, will you please inform your masters of the behavior of the frightening Miss Zanzi."

Irma hopped off the desk and led Victor out the door.

"What if I must speak to you earlier? Or if the Director wishes to have another conference?" Robert asked the retreating, black-clad pair.

"Remain patient. It helps the soul," Victor said.

They vanished from view.

Robert frowned and walked to the dead Pierre Gérard's desk. He needed to speak to his employers and discover their views on the present situation. He doubted they would be delighted by the actions of their favorite assassin, Nanon Zanzi.

CHAPTER XLVIII

The Great Brain sighed as the last infusion filled his body with energy and power. He felt the ever-growing army of minds, their numbers climbing and strengthening every eight hours. He already held control over all employees, high and low, from the Benoîts' industrial complex. Now, his men and women enticed newcomers in and added them to his ranks. Twelve gendarmes, six unemployed fools, and a small group of shopkeepers near the factory had just joined the collective gestalt under his influence.

"Influence" was a better description right now, though his power grew daily with each infusion of the elixir. The drink, made from a few psychoactive plants, plus a healthy dose of sugar to mask the flavor, held one important element: the granulated remains of a Martian blood crystal. This item, mistaken by the foolish earthmen for a mere piece of colored quartz, was the secret of the Great Brain's future. Finding it in the hands of a band of silly Satanists had granted the former master of the Red Planet an opportunity to return to his mighty power, or even exceed his previous prominence.

His first task, back then, had been to secure the crystal and destroy any record that it had ever entered the Earth's atmosphere. It had been a simple enough goal, given his mastery of the simplistic mind-control techniques the humans referred to as hypnosis. The deputy leader of the cult, an international group that had called itself the Brotherhood of the Ram, had been a psychically empowered, slightly seductive fat man who went by the name of Mocata. He had believed he possessed magic powers, which had amused the Great Brain to no end.

"There is no such thing as magic, Mocata," the Great Brain had told the man, trying to keep from laughing. "Some humans possess a small degree of psychic talent as part of their genetic makeup, that's all."

216

"Now, that is sadly ignorant rot," Mocata had wheezed back, reaching for an half-empty box of Swiss chocolates. "I could demonstrate the contrary, but you would not survive the experience. A demon from the depths of the Abyss would require a life in recompense for its actions."

"Which gains you strength? You feel invigorated and wiser after one of your so-called familiars destroys your enemy?" the Great Brain had asked as he examined the ram's head ring on Mocata's hand.

Its jeweled eyes were Martian blood crystals, just as he had known they had to be. They acted as psychic amplifiers, either heightening the wielder's powers briefly, or rendering them open to psychic control.

"Yes, I do," Mocata had replied, smacking his lips as he consumed another candy. "I say, for a man who does not believe in magic, you do appear quite learned in some areas of the subject."

"Apparently so," the Great Brain had said, as he sardonically wondered how this species had ever achieved mastery of their planet.

They did not even understand their own capabilities, viewing simple psychic life-leeching as summoning mythical creatures from the dark.

"Yet, all know that even hypnosis is nothing more than charlatan's trickery. Unless you can prove me wrong…"

Mocata had chuckled and flexed his delicate pale hands.

"As my instructor, the late, great Oliver Haddo, believed, one should always demonstrate one's power to the most unbelieving in the world. Very well, look into my eyes…"

The Great Brain had smiled, and done as instructed. He had felt a slight sensation of power emerging from Mocata's mind, a very tiny whiff of energy that might have overwhelmed a weak-willed human. But to the Great Brain of Mars, this foolish magus' power was a mere drop of water compared to the ocean of psychic might that was his. Even in this weakened human body, a tiny shard of the mountain-sized entity that had once controlled the entire Red Planet, he was still a thousand times mightier psychically than Mocata.

The Great Brain had stared into the attractive, light-colored, heavily-lidded eyes of the Satanist. He had not hidden his boredom and amusement, watching as Mocata struggled in vain against a mental barrier exponentially greater than any he had ever encountered before.

"How...?" Mocata had mumbled, falling back into the sofa cushions.

His pale face had glimmered in the gaslight from sweat and he had appeared to be completely drained.

"How did I deflect your weak attempt at mind control?" the Great Brain replied. "The literal answer is, easily. The rest, you do not need to know. I do have some use for you, Mocata. Now, to repeat your clichéd statement, look into my eyes..."

The Great Brain had seized control of the magus's mind in an instant.

From there, it had been simplicity itself to gain control over the minds of the remaining members of the Brotherhood of the Ram. The small supply of blood crystal they held proved an adequate start for his plans, most of which he achieved while convincing the Children of Giphantie that he was serving their own interests.

Heading down three levels, the Great Brain entered the crystal nursery, spotting Mocata slowly and carefully nurturing the new stalks. The blood crystal in the back of the former magus' head pulsed as he transmitted his sensations to his master. Mocata was the oldest and longest serving of the slave class, the last remaining pieces of his will having been crushed a decade earlier. He was little more than a skeletal automaton, an elderly set of hands who served the Great Brain until his body would eventually fail.

The massive chamber containing the blood crystals was a low-lit room laid out in a distinct grid. Each section held growing crystals of various sizes and shapes. When they were a deep crimson, the stalks were ripe for harvest. On Mars, the Great Brain had lived inside a mountain abundantly studded with these minerals, and had used them to increase his power over Mars.

But this had also proved to be his greatest mistake. A human of Earth, one Robert Darvel, had discovered a means of siphoning electrical power away from the crystalline mountain. This had destroyed the Great Brain, forcing it to hurl a shard of his mind out into space and ultimately into the body of an inadequate human male.

Learning from the past, the former master of Mars had designed a plan to take over Earth and become even more powerful than he had been on Mars. The blood crystals were the key, but this time, he would not make the same mistake with them than he had on his home planet.

"Begin harvest of all ready crystals and transport them to the preparation chamber," the Great Brain ordered mentally.

The nursery was twice the size of the house above, covering most of the grounds he owned.

Heading up one level, he found the preparation area thriving with activity. Men and women, all of whom possessed a crimson shard buried in their skulls, silently toiled at their stations. Their actions did not resemble the assembly line of a modern industrial complex; their movements were too precise and synchronized. Their actions possessed an almost insectile quality, resembling a hive of ants instead of humans.

A perfect division of labor was organized across this smaller room. Some slaves ground the crystals into fine powder, sweeping the dust into silk bags. Others carried these bags to the far side of the chamber, leaving them for another group to pour them into large vats, which contained the elixir that had been forcibly administered to all the workers of the Benoît complex. A last small cadre of mind-controlled humans slowly and precisely shaped each larger crystal for use on additional slaves made by Rotwang.

"In less than a week, Marseilles shall be mine," the Great Brain said. "Then I shall move outward and spread to other cities—Toulon, Nice, then north toward Lyon and, finally, Paris, and the Emperor's court in Fontainebleau. In a few short

years, every human on Earth shall be part of my consciousness. I shall be greater than ever before... I shall rename this
world and remake it in my image..."

The Great Brain felt contentment. The hive mind grew
and, once complete, would expand throughout the universe.

"In a decade, the Earth. After that, Mars and, maybe, beyond..."

CHAPTER XLIX

The *Tabatière* was located on the posh section of the Canebière boulevard; it was a combination of a tobacconist and a tea shop in the English style. Inside were seven small round tables, each draped with lace table cloths and Lancaster linen napkins. Two pretty, young waitresses in traditional, if slightly risqué, uniforms appeared from time to time and provided various teas or tobaccos from around the world. The cakes were the only concession to the small detail that they were not on the wind-wiped shores of England. The local bakers created these confections in the Neapolitan style and they had proved very popular with the patrons.

The mistress of this English establishment was Marilyn Milverton, a British expatriate who had purchased the business and moved in the same day. She was a tiny, rotund woman who wore a bright yellow wig that she always kept pinned in a severe bun. Miss Milverton always appeared to smile at everyone and everything, though the merry look never seemed to reach her tiny, agate eyes.

"Nadine, my dear girl," she purred at one of her waitresses. "Once again, you are speaking too fast for the customers. If you do not slow your speaking voice, I shall be forced to keep you after work for additional training."

Nadine, a slip of a girl with short dark hair, lovely light eyes, and lovely, creamy fresh, flinched at the words from her employer. She curtsied deeply and said,

"*Oui*, Miss Milverton. Please forgive me, Madame."

"That remains to be seen. I shall be watching you, my girl."

Miss Milverton spoke an almost perfect French in a girlish, high-pitched voice that resembled that of a merry child rather than an adult woman. As always, she dressed in a high-necked Victorian style gown whose skirt fell to her wide ankles.

The daughter of a professional blackmailer, Miss Milverton was as horrific as her murdered father had been. She had taken up the family business, paying maids, footmen, and other servants for compromising information to use against the great men and women of the British Isles. Though not as effective as her infamous father, she had managed to build a dangerous network of informants, and soon, her wealth had grown to impressive heights.

Then she had made a mistake—a costly one. She had obtained the letters that one Fred Porlock was sending to his sweetheart, letters that detailed the life of the equally infamous Colonel Sebastian Moran. Porlock, a former lesser member of Moran's criminal fraternity, had written pages upon pages on the illegal exploits of the legendary Victorian adventurer, including some of his activities on behalf of Her Majesty's intelligence service.

Knowing that the elderly Moran possessed a vast fortune, Miss Milverton had sent her standard demand of twenty thousand pounds, threatening the make the letters public. She had been prepared for grumbling threats, the police, or even tears, but what she had not expected was a visit from the aged, infirmed Colonel, his mistress, and a brutish cabbie who spoke with a Cambridge accent.

The cabbie, whose name was James, had ripped away the gun she always kept in her handbag. He had tossed her bag into the fireplace and had pinned her into a chair while the aged Moran had wheeled his chair closer. He had examined for a moment with dark eyes that resembled a pair of gun barrels.

"You, dear girl, are weak and foolish," he had said, sneering as he had peered into her face. "Your late daddy knew better than to dance with his betters."

"May I kill her, darling?" the woman had asked.

She was a pretty lady in her late forties or fifties with dark hair and a habit of oscillating her head back and forth in a serpentine fashion.

"Not sure," Moran harrumphed, stoking his thick white whiskers. "What say you, girl? Should I give you over to my dear friend here? Or do you wish to beg for your life?"

"I... I... please... no..." Miss Milverton had whined.

She had even wept.

"Typical," the elderly Moran had harrumphed again. "Blackmailers! They have spines of water and break faster than a lily-livered coward before a Ghazi charge. Killing this one might be a kindness."

His female companion had frowned and shaken her head.

"Well, we would never want that..."

"Agreed," Moran had replied

He had turned back to Miss Milverton,

"You there! Cease that sniveling at once! Where do you keep your files?"

"The safe... in my bedroom... behind the painting of daddy..." she had replied, breathing a little easier.

"And your copies?" Moran had asked, waving a wrinkled, spot-covered hand. "Do not lie or I will have you killed here and now, and we will find them anyway."

"In the mantelpiece. Press the fourth brick to the left at the top and the secret compartment will open."

Miss Milverton had begun weeping again. All her work, gone forever.

James, following her directions, had removed several thick packets of letters, photographs and other files. The pretty woman had exited and returned a moment later with the contents of the safe. Only then did Miss Milverton realize she had never provided the combination to open it.

"Blackmail files, several grotty jewels and one hundred thousand quid in large bills," the woman had reported, displaying the contents. "Looks like being a blackmailing worm has some benefits."

Moran had grunted and looked at Miss Milverton, stroking his whiskers again.

"Very well. You may keep ten percent and anything else you can grab in the next hour. Then James shall drive you to the East Docks and buy you a ticket to anywhere on the continent. You are no longer welcome in these islands, Miss Milverton. Return, and you will not enjoy your remaining days."

"She needs a reminder, darling," the woman had added, gently stroking Moran's surprisingly blemish-free neck. "Father always liked to ensure they never forgot his lessons."

Moran had grunted in what was obviously assent.

"That was the academic in him, my dear. However, the old boy did possess an uncanny mind, by God. What do you suggest?"

James spoke up first.

"The yellow bottle," he had suggested.

The attractive woman had clapped her hands.

"Oh yes, the yellow bottle? May I, darling? May I, please?"

Moran had harrumphed again.

"Yes, yes, but do be fast. I have a dinner at the India Club and it would not do to be late."

The smiling woman had stepped in front of Miss Milverton and removed a tiny bottle painted a repulsive, sickly shade of yellow. She had extended the miniscule container and said with a wide, smile filled with madness:

"Drink every drop. If you do not, James will remove all your teeth with a pair of pliers and pour it down your bleeding gob."

Spotting a happy smirk on the face of a massive cabbie, Miss Milverton had taken the bottle, uncapped it, and drank it down in one swallow.

The flavor was odd, like a combination of peppermint and cod liver oil. The taste had vanished a moment later and, though slightly warm, Miss Milverton had felt no after-effects.

Two days later, however, while bathing in her cabin, en route towards Marseilles, everything had changed.

Her lustrous, blond tresses, probably her finest feature, had fallen away from her head like leaves in autumn. At first, a small patch, then great handfuls. Within two days, she had become totally bald.

Since then, Miss Milverton had worn a variety of blond wigs, painted on her eyebrows each morning, and wished Moran, his insane woman, and the massive James, to the Devil.

She had used her depleted funds to purchase *La Tabatière* and taken up a less respectable duty in life as a narcotics seller. There were always well-off traveling English and Scottish ladies who wished a little red lotus and found purchasing the items from common sources vulgar. Therefore, she subtly sold them their leaves at a rate fifty percent higher than if they had simply gone to a dockside den.

The living was good, more profitable than blackmail with far less risk to life or limb. Yet the indignity of transforming into a common criminal had soured Miss Milverton even worse than her previous life as a blackmailer had. Before, she had been a cold, cruel, grasping creature, very much her father's daughter. Now, she was like a woman possessed by the soul of one of Torquemada's torturers. A remarkable feeling of sadistic delight filled her as she subtly inflicted pain upon all within her world.

One of her favored delights was to sprinkle a tiny dose of red lotus on unsuspecting patrons, first-time visitors to Marseilles. Wealthy elderly ladies were especially her target—the ones who would not so much as touch a small glass of sherry. Just a few flakes of red lotus on their tea and cakes and wave them as they left. Within hours, Miss Milverton learned, strictly through gossip, of these women suddenly behaving odd-singing and dancing for the first time since they were little girls, marrying young fortune hunters, or leaping off buildings because they suddenly believed they could fly.

It was a wonderful amusement, almost as delightful as the small petty cruelties she liked to inflict upon her staff. The local girls who took employment with Miss Milverton were always pretty, innocent, and weak-minded. Each learned fast that the smiling, sweet lady who had hired them never truly existed. Beneath the soft-spoken words and sweet demeanor lay a violent taskmaster who perpetually held the threat of a poor reference if they attempted to leave her service before she agreed. Her girls suffered harsh, painful, pinches, spankings, and being forced to work extra hours without pay for fear of losing their jobs.

Therefore, the *Tabatière* always looked clean, with not a speck of dust or a napkin out of place. The spoons, cups, and saucers gleamed from constant polish and the waitresses appeared neat and properly servile. Exactly what one should expect when entering an English tea shop.

The silver bell on the door chimed with a light tinkle as a pair of young people walked in.

Seated in her place near the door, Miss Milverton quickly assessed them. The female was pretty, with short blond hair and a wide smiling mouth. The man was tall, with dark hair, broad shoulders and the sour disposition of a Puritan. She wore a light summer dress that looked both posh and sexually enticing. His clothing, while expensive and well-tailored, appeared both conservative and a decade out-of-date.

Miss Milverton categorized them immediately, having past experience with such types. The man was a banker or a high-ranking officer in his family's aged, but affluent, business. The woman was his mistress, an actress or an artist's model who wished to rise above her stature, and reside in the comfort of established wealth. She would laugh a great deal and he would barely acknowledge the staff as human.

Miss Milverton despised the type with a deep fervor. Their life of power and ease did not come from hard work or intelligence, but rather an accident of birth. The woman had the fortune of being born with milky white skin, luminous eyes and long, shapely legs. Her male companion possessed acceptable male beauty, though his perfect life derived from being born into a wealthy family. This pair was everything she despised and she would not bear their happiness a moment longer.

Nadine appeared a moment later, curtsied and said in a soft voice:

"Darjeeling tea with Turkish delight, Madame?"

"I shall prepare this order, Nadine," Miss Milverton ordered. "Go in the back and straighten your seams."

She had not even looked at the young waitress's legs; why would she bother. Miss Milverton did know the nebulous rebuke would keep Nadine busy for a while. Exactly the necessary time needed to add a dose of red lotus to her new patrons' mid-afternoon repast.

Nadine swept back in a moment later, curtsied again, and left with the tea trolley.

Miss Milverton watched as the young French waitress gently placed the pot on the table as well as the small plate of overly sweet confection.

Oddly enough, the pair merely stared at the contents of their cups and the Turkish delight. After a moment, they nodded at each other and the man said something to Nadine. She nodded and fled, heading straight for Miss Milverton.

"Madame," the young waitress said, looking confused. "They asked for you by name. Something quite urgent, according to the gentleman."

Miss Milverton frowned, hiding her trepidation. As in her previous business, she kept herself very much in the background. Poor Daddy had died because he had become careless and let too many people know his name. Still, one must not behave rudely, even in the presence of those only worthy of her favorite method of poisoning.

Checking her wig and makeup in the mirror, she swept over to the table and gave both young people a small smile.

"Good afternoon and thank you for patronizing my shop. I am Miss Milverton. How may I assist you on this fine day?"

This was a speech she had once heard in a tea shop in Oxford. The woman speaking the words had believed in her statements with an almost religious zeal, a factor that had surprised Miss Milverton. She remembered the small speech and used it whenever an irritating customer requested her attention.

"Do sit down, Mademoiselle Milverton," the woman said.

Her musical voice fit her image and her French-accented English sounded simply delightful.

"Oh, no, I mustn't," Miss Milverton said, slowly and, falsely, appearing sad. "That simply is not done."

"Sit down," the man said, his voice heavy with a Liverpudlian bur.

"But really, I must not..." Miss Milverton said.

She was silenced as the woman took her small hand.

"Sit down," the woman repeated. "Or my companion will be forced to shoot you in the knee. Then we shall sit and talk."

The man placed one hand on the table, revealing a metal object protruding from his large fist. A tiny black steel barrel extended from beneath his index and pointing fingers.

Miss Milverton brought her hand to her mouth and suppressed a cry.

"An Apache revolver?" she whispered, staring at the man's hand in open terror.

"*Oui*," the woman said, nodding towards a chair. "*Mon chéri* could shoot the wig off your head if he wished. Now, sit and answer our questions."

Miss Milverton sat heavily down and whispered:

"Who are you?"

The man and woman exchanged a fast look and appeared to make a mutual decision. Once again, they nodded as if they had just held an entire conversation.

"That is a fair enough question," the woman said, smiling brilliantly again. "The answer will not cause you happiness. You have probably realized that we are in disguise..."

"One intended to draw you out," the man added as he poured himself a cup of tea.

He then placed the cup and saucer before Miss Milverton and pushed the red lotus-laden, Turkish Delight in her direction.

"We investigated you and found all the answers we needed within an hour," the woman explained, her smile growing even wider. "You are quite sloppy in your evil activities, Mademoiselle Milverton."

"Are you with the police?" Miss Milverton whispered, her eyes widening.

"Do not be ridiculous," the man answered, rolling his eyes. "If we were those gentlemen, we could arrest you based on this table alone. No, we are criminals, too, after a fashion. Allow me to introduce you to the legendary figure known as the Vampire."

Miss Milverton released a quick cry of shock, covering her mouth in hopes of suppressing her terror.

"The Vampire? The infamous woman whose very name caused other bandits to flinch in fear?"

"The same," Irma said, waving a languid hand towards her companion. "And this, of course, is none other than the Eidolon. Do not scream, dear lady. It would not do to make a scene. Then my companion might become... unpleasant..."

"What do you want?" Miss Milverton asked, hearing the crack in her voice.

She knew many tales of the pair known as the Vampire and the Eidolon. According to legend, the Vampire had once broken into the Tower of London and left her calling card on the crown jewels. She had done so purely to demonstrate that nothing was safe from her. As for the Eidolon, Miss Milverton had once seen one of his victims, a notorious pederast and child killer—the man's still-living body had long haunted her nightmares...

"Only information," Victor said. "Provide it and we shall leave. We shall even pay for the tea."

"From whom and where do you receive your red lotus?" Irma asked as she pushed the drugged Turkish delight in Miss Milverton's direction.

"I can't..." the Englishwoman started to say, casting her eyes about the room.

The waitresses were not in sight and the few patrons did not appear to realize the terrifying events occurring mere feet away from them.

"She is stalling," Victor said. "If she lies now, I will remove and eat her left eye."

Irma tutted and shook her head slowly.

"My dear Eidolon does not like liars. He had an unfortunate childhood made worse by those who used falsehoods. I suggest you should think twice before you utter your next words."

Miss Milverton bit her inside cheek and tasted the tang of her own blood as she stared at the pair in horror. The pain and the iron flavor prevented her from causing a scene.

"Very well," she replied. "The new suppliers of the drug made me step inside the rear of a large vehicle that lacked side and back windows. I was kept there, seated upon a wooden box, for one hour. They drove me about, but that was a stupid ruse."

"That was my understanding, too," Irma said. "Do continue."

Emboldened, Miss Milverton leaned down and said *sotto voce*:

"They drove about the streets of this filthy city, often circling the same neighborhoods on several occasions. As if one could not hear the same sounds, the fools! They then ushered me into a newish home…"

"Newish?" Irma asked.

Smiling with superiority, Miss Milverton slowly shook her head.

"Yes, young lady, not one of these small palaces built by vulgar, jumped-up, button sellers who think their money equals class. The walls and floors revealed some age, but were no more than a hundred years-old. The floors I trod upon were wooden and swept, but not polished. A large house with some age that does not entertain with regularity."

Victor nodded to Irma and circled one finger for a few seconds. Irma nodded back and turned her smile back towards Miss Milverton.

"One final piece of information," Irma said. "Please describe the person you met inside this… newish, house."

Miss Milverton frowned, causing a crease to appear between her eyebrows. She sat silently, clearly concentrating and becoming more disconcerted. Eventually she sighed and shook her head.

"I cannot recall. I know that person was a man, but my only impression was that he was a foreigner of some type. Odd, I cannot even picture his face or clothes. Normally, I am quite discerning in such matters."

"She is not lying," Victor said, placing his hand on the table.

Irma beamed and nodded at Miss Milverton.

"Excellent! Now, drink two cups of tea and eat three pieces of Turkish Delight and we shall pay and leave."

"I shall not," Miss Milverton replied.

She screwed her face into her more resolute expression—the one she reserved for salesmen and children.

A small clicking sound emerged from Victor's hand, causing Miss Milverton to glance downward with terror. What terrible weapons did he hold in his hand along with the revolver? Apache weapons, products of the terrifying gangs of Paris, it could be anything. In the past, she had seen one with a spike knuckleduster, a six shot pistol, and a knife. Horrible weapons, usually used by men and women for whom violence was but a daily facet of their lives.

This was the clear difference between Miss Marilyn Milverton, her late father, and most criminals. To most crooks, violence was the first choice of action. To a Milverton, fighting only occurred when all other options had failed. Best to retreat when attacked and use the force of the law against any would-be hero or enemy. As such, true confrontation left Miss Milverton quite faint.

Her worst fears proved correct as she studied the Eidolon's large, scarred hand. A four-inch blade protruded from the bottom of his fist. The razor edge of the knife glinted in the strong sunlight, blinding the former blackmailer.

Miss Milverton gasped and recoiled, almost losing her composure.

"Two cups of tea and three pieces of Turkish Delight," Victor repeated. "Or I will not be happy."

"And you should strive to avoid that, *Madame l'Empoisonneuse*," Irma said. "As I said, you are sloppy. *Mon chéri* detected the narcotic you placed in the tea and on the candies. You do not possess the stained teeth of a lotus-eater, yet there were minute traces of red dust on your fat little fingertips. Therefore, we give you a choice. Drink the two cups and eat the three candies and we leave. Refuse and we shall slice off your nose and feed it to you. Then, we shall leave."

"I'll scream," Miss Milverton whispered, filling her lungs.

Irma giggled, hiding her smile beneath one hand.

"Oh, please do! We shall then harm you quickly and escape. You shall be *sans* nose and eyes, and we shall remember you with fond amusement."

Irma paused and dropped her hand, her face serious, her eyes blazing with open disgust and hatred.

"Choose now, Madame. Scream, or begin drinking and eating. Choose, or we shall make the choice for you at the count of three. One…two…"

Miss Milverton lifted the cup in a shaking hand and took a small sip. The tea was slightly cool, but still excellent. She did not detect any noticeable difference in the flavor or aroma and took a second swallow.

"Finish it all," Victor said, shifting the knife slightly in his hand.

He looked as dour as ever, but his white-knuckle grip on his weapon told a very different tale.

Miss Milverton shuddered and drank down the rest of the tea in one gulp. She then consumed the three little oversweet sugary cakes and swallowed another cup of tea without tasting anything.

"There, I completed your ignoble demands! Now leave my establishment and never return!" she said.

She stood up, causing her wig to fall askew and marched away from the table, her head held high.

Miss Milverton never saw the evil couple as they strolled away. She sat down at her desk and started working on the accounts, updating them to the very last hour. Partway through an entry, she stopped, stared at her hands, and giggled.

"They look like tiny little, fat spiders!" she mumbled

She put down her pen and watched as her silly little hands crawled about the desk, creeping and crawling like bugs in her Papa's basement.

"Oooh," Miss Milverton said, remembering the fun she had as a girl, killing all those creepy-crawly creatures.

Reaching for the hammer in the top drawer with one hand, she giggled as her fingers creeped across the desktop.

"Tally-ho!" she cried as she raised the hammer...

CHAPTER L

"Bernard?" The voice over the televisor said, "Turn on your screen, you young fool! I wish to speak to you!"

Bernard Benoît, who had been asleep after working fourteen straight hours arranging transport of the overwhelming supply of goods the factory complex produced, flipped on the switch. He did not know the time, but that did not matter. Father would brook no delays.

Turning on the light by his bed, he noticed it was three o'clock in the morning. This was both good and bad in the larger scheme of being a member of the Benoît family. Good because father would be unlikely to explode with rage over him sleeping while the sun was up. The old man flew into near murderous rages at the thought of any of his children, i.e. employees, sleeping past sun up.

The bad part of this situation was that he only broke the necessary peace of sleep for critical business. The elder Benoît respected the need for peace and relaxation to ensure proper attention to necessary duties. Lack of sleep could result in a tirade about proper health as well as trips to doctors and prescribed courses of food. The supposedly healthy food often tasted like a horrific combination of dirt, paste, and rancid vegetables and possessed a scent capable of sending swine fleeing for their sty.

"Good evening father. Or should I say, good morning?" Bernard managed to mumble as he turned on the televisor screen.

"Evening for me, morning for you," the elder Benoît said. "I just concluded a trade agreement with the United States. My airship leaves in three hours. Enough nonsense, now to proper business. My office tabulated the output from all divisions. You exceeded all others and achieved a thirty-five percent increase in productivity."

"Point-of-fact, father," Bernard said, "The increase was thirty-four point three percent."

The master of the Benoît empire smiled slightly.

"Precisely true. As such, you have earned your promised reward. Your brother will arrive in the morning to take your position. You will leave by the last airship to Paris. You have until then to turn over all duties and arrange for your mistress and any other items you wish transported to your new residence. Your wedding is next week so you…"

"Wedding? What wedding?" Bernard asked, recoiling.

The elder Benoît glowered into the televisor screen.

"Your wedding to Comte Duplessis' elder daughter, Louise. You cannot possibly believe an unmarried deputy minister exists in this world? Louise is an excellent hostess who will help your career. She will bear your children, help your advancement, and has no interest in your trollop."

"I… um… do not… um…" Bernard stammered.

Baron Clément Benoît stared at his son without blinking.

"Do not lie to me, child. I know of your little strumpet, Violette. Arrangements for a small townhome in the company's name are already in place. She will be available for your visits and shall remain there so long as her expenses do not exceed a fixed amount I shall allow you each year. Do not believe you are clever, boy. I know your every movement and peculiar choice. None of them interests me in the slightest as long as you remain useful. Should that change, I always have openings in locations like Devil's Island or our Siberian mines."

"Understood, father. Thank you, father," Bernard gasped.

He wondered how his father always managed to know everything that each member of the family did or considered doing. Could the old man have spies shadowing them all day and night?

"You are welcome. I will see you in three days," the elder Benoît said, ending the call.

Bernard smiled and punched his pillow in delight. No more heading into the stinking industrial complex and hoping the employees did not revolt or join a union that day. No more living in Marseilles, where the only culture came from house parties thrown by American and English imbeciles, or poor operas staged by a bearded idiot named Svengali. Leaving this city would be a pleasure, one that could keep him smiling for days.

"Leo! Charlotte! Get up! I am moving out and I need my clothes and personal items packed," Bernard yelled.

Happily, the servants stayed with the house as company employees and he did not have to provide their pay or transportation.

Reaching for the televisor, he dialed in Violette's number. Despite the early hour, she would celebrate the news...

CHAPTER LI

"Welcome, Master, welcome to my humble abode," Jakob ten Brinken said, smiling and waving the Great Brain into his laboratory.

The rusty scent of blood mixed in a noxious cloud with the ammonia tang of urine and the earthy, fear-inducing odor of feces filled the room. But the Great Brain knew these smells well, having induced many versions of them since arriving on Earth. These scents represented the Terran equivalent of fear, a scent that all living creatures on this too-warm world exuded in periods of stress. This odiferous odor frightened living creatures and induced atavistic flight or fight responses within seconds. But not in the former master of Mars.

To the Great Brain, these scents had the opposite effect. To his alien mind, this musk only invigorated his spirit. Though sharing the same body as these barely evolved simpletons, the Great Brain was no longer a man in any significant way. He was a vampiric alien entity. whose power derived from the minds and bodies of his many victims.

Doctor ten Brinken's laboratory, once a pristine example of a modern medical facility, now resembled an abattoir from the worst slums of society. Bodies, dead and dying, lay on steel tables, their entrails spilling across the floor, putrefying under the harsh electric lights. There were no distinctions between age, sex, living or dead, in these dozens of torn and tattered corpses. Aged men and women shared tables with children, young men and women, and none of them appeared to be whole. This was not medical science, but an insane vivisectionist's fantasy brought to grisly life.

"You do not appear to have preserved any of the living beings I have sent you every night," the Great Brain observed as he stepped over the headless, limbless torso of a man.

"Them? No, they were not fit for my true works of art! This detritus are the testing creatures I used when preparing to create true beauty. They were refuse, Master, just useless meat. But if this disturbs you, then I shall find a means of disposal. Possibly, we could sell them to sausage-makers and use them as food for the masses?"

The Great Brain chuckled at the notion.

"Nothing disturbs me, doctor. However, I like your suggestion. We shall implement it immediately. Now, why did you request my attention at this critical juncture?"

"Simply put," the Germanic doctor replied, kicking aside a decaying hand that lay in his path, "I require a new location for my work. My current experiments are nearly complete, and they shall serve your needs. However, if I am to pursue my research beyond that great height, I will require a larger laboratory with a private operating theater."

"Show me your progress, doctor. Then I shall decide if your research merits such an enormous expenditure of our resources."

Ten Brinken clapped his hands together and rubbed them furiously while performing a valiant attempt at a beaming smile.

"Follow me, Master, and be prepared to be amazed by my genius!"

Pushing aside a long curtain, ten Brinken waved the Great Brain forward.

"This is the area where I keep my true masterpieces. Obviously, they are just past the embryonic stages, but I think you shall agree that they can serve your cause with even greater precision than what Rotwang has achieved with gears and lubricants!"

The Great Brain strolled along slabs, wordlessly examining the specimens. He stopped before one and looked quizzically at the medical man.

"This one is the product of your work? Yet its outward appearance varies little from regular *homo sapiens*."

Ten Brinken bowed,

"Master, that is my perfect creation. She shall be a shining jewel in the days to come. This one is proof that the mind of man is greater than any mythical deity dreamed up by religious idiots."

The Great Brain listened to ten Brinken's report with only partial attention. His eyes now inhabited much of this city and, as such, processing all that input proved taxing. He... *they*... now were comprised of thousands of minds, each with its own task. Fortunately, the Great Brain remembered when, on Mars, such actions were merely its daily existence. All the former master of Mars now required was more time... and energy...

"Your request is approved, Doctor ten Brinken," he finally said. "Soon, Rotwang shall control a large portion of the factory complex. I... *We* think your work requires a similar expansion. We shall find a suitable location immediately."

The Great Brain sent a series of mental orders to three of his followers. As he left ten Brinken's lab, his men were already driving off, heading east.

"A diversification of resources," he said to himself. "We did not consider that in the past and because of our lack of it, nearly met our end on Mars. But we shall not fall victim to it again."

The Great Brain studied one of his slaves, an elderly woman, as she walked by. He looked at her heavily lined face, bent back, and sparse, filthy, blond hair. She was another of his original slaves, a Satanist who had been Mocata's second in command.

"Stop," he ordered.

He stepped in front of her. At some point, this woman when she had been in her thirties, had been lovely, her thick blond hair shimmering like golden sunlight in Mocata's gloomy, Satanic church. She had possessed a face like that of a classic goddess—Artemis, or possibly Hecate, with lush pink lips and a figure that she knew how to show off to her advantage. She had been a stunning sight—at least, for humans. But to the Great Brain, she had possessed all the allure of a dairy cow or a sow grunting in a sty.

Humans' view of mating, as a pleasure activity as well as one used for procreation, had made little sense to the former master of Mars. He had soon realized that this oddity in these semi-evolved creatures would remain a mystery to him, since he had no desire to comprehend it otherwise.

The beautiful woman had looked at the Great Brain when he had first appeared at the Luciferian Temple and asked:

"Who the fuck are you? You are not one of our circle."

The Great Brain had smiled and, using the blood crystal, had seized control of her mind.

Soon, the entire temple had fallen to his control and his work had begun.

Most of the members had perished as they served as shock troops against other secret organizations that the Great Brain soon overtook. Few humans, like Mocata, had survived to this day, and seeing this woman still in his service proved a small surprise.

"You must possess a strong life force," the Great Brain mused, as he studied the drab creature who stood motionless in the dark, stone corridor. "Ah, I see. We ordered you to clean all the floors since we took you over in Paris. And here you stand, still ready to clean... Shall we send you on your way? There shall be many, many more floors for you to scrub when Rotwang's conversions commence. Also, ten Brinken's endeavors are rather messy. We could send you to scrub his floors. Would that please you? No, probably not. In our early days, we did not yet possess enough precision in our mind-control assaults. We destroyed all that humans refer to poetically as their soul. You are less than Rotwang's drones now. You are nothing but a biological version of a clockwork automaton. Who knows how much time you possess before your organic functions fail? You could last decades, or minutes. The chaos of the universe allowed your survival this long. Or possibly the scrap of your true self that remained and refused death. No matter, we are growing hungry and your life shall sustain us for a time. This is our gift to you, after surviving in

240

our service. Follow us and your end shall be quick and useful."

Without looking back, the Great Brain headed back to
his private chamber where he fed.

The second oldest slave in service proved an excellent
meal.

CHAPTER LII

"No," Robert Ménard said, shaking his huge head. "That is not a private home, but a sanatorium. The people who reside there are wealthy patrons seeking a cure from gout or dipsomania."

"We should go in and verify," Irma said, tapping a finger on her teeth.

Her boredom as they surveyed the many maps of the city grew with each passing day.

A full week after their intelligence gathering expeditions, they now met nightly, with occasional forays checking on the many large houses built over the last decade.

The difficulty lay in Marseilles and its surroundings. Since the creation of the grand industrial complex, and the massive increase of shipping trade, enormous mansions had become the norm in the posh, eastern districts of the city. Some merely looked aged, others were new ones, built by wealthy industrialists from all over France and the North African Imperial provinces. This made the search quite tedious and tempers were growing short.

"Already checked," Robert said. "Monsieur Gérard possessed a distrust for such institutions. He sent the Blanc brothers in to investigate it six months ago. Other than viewing a battle between a tramp and a large man with a huge mustache, they discovered nothing. No, I misspoke. The Red Hand controls the laundry services for that and other similar businesses."

Robert reached for his pen. Dipping the brass end in the inkwell, he then drew a large X across the location.

"Mother of God this is boring," Irma mused. "Is this how the gendarmes behave when they seek out criminals such as us? They must be the most colorless, dullest men upon the planet!"

Robert examined another location and consulted his notes. Victor looked from a book in hand and said:

"Colorless or not, how many times did we nearly find ourselves in their hands? I even had to break you from custody when that reporter blamed you for the death of his lover."

He had taken to reading books from the deceased Pierre Gérard's library as they worked. Today, his choice was an amusing tale by the legendary purveyor of tall tales, Eugène Sue. Irma rolled her eyes and shook her head.

"That was not the police, but one particular dashing reporter and his associate. They possessed panache, unlike the gendarmes. However, you did not assist in my escape, I was already through the bars and on my way to freedom."

"With two men holding onto your ankles and a third on their heels," Victor replied, lifting an eyebrow.

Irma tilted her head and narrowed her eyes.

"Should I remind you of the occasion when I rescued you from the Clerville forces who were only seconds away from piercing you from several dozen directions?"

"Then I would be forced to bring up the escapade in Mad King Ludwig's palace... how far was that drop...?" Victor asked, closing his book and placing it in on a table near his elbow.

"Do that and I shall discuss your difficulties in the depths of the Pankot Palace. Who thought that that operation could be completed in only a few hours?" I

"If I may interrupt your amusing recollections," Robert said, "we still have four more maps to study, and these diversions are only slowing our progress. If you must bicker, please do it on your own time."

"Bicker?" Irma asked, "You consider that an argument?"

"Of course, it was an argument," Robert replied, sighing. "You two bicker constantly over every subject."

Irma threw her head back and laughed as Victor snorted in amusement. Shaking his head, he said:

"Have you ever viewed a steam engine?"

Robert blinked several times and finally nodded,

"Of course. Smelly, loud, filthy devices."

"Yes, very true. Though remember the attempt at petrol vehicles? You would find their scent even more distasteful. However, that was not my point. The pipe at the rear of an automobile slowly releases a stream of water-filled gas into the air. Do you know why?"

"Yes," Robert replied. "It prevents an explosion from the engine."

"Correct," Victor said, nodding his masked head. "That is why the Vampire and I appear to argue. Such discussions prevent a true explosion from our inner engines. It is a method we arrived upon years ago and, because of it, we are in no danger of parting."

"There may be some danger if you are comparing me to the tailpipe of your metaphorical automobile!" Irma said, standing and crossing her arms across her chest.

"I was not calling you a tailpipe," Victor replied. "Our method of discussion was that item. I think I shall refrain from using analogies with you from now on."

"That would be a wise course, if I may say so, Monsieur. Now, will you look at this?" Robert said, tapping the next page with his finger.

Irma blew Victor a kiss and looked down at the map.

"Ah! There, near the sea. That is a massive home!"

Robert shook his head and reached for the pen.

"That is not a home, Madame, it is a palace. The Palais du Pharo to be accurate."

"Tell me more," Irma said, placing a hand over the map. "Staring with why a palace is not a home in your estimation."

Robert frowned for a moment and then picked up his notes.

"It was built in the 1850s by Emperor Napoleon III for his Empress Eugénie. The structure is now owned by a wealthy gentleman. The Blanc brothers investigated it and determined the location was useless to us, and its owner was too close to the Imperial government. They found him quite unmemorable otherwise."

Irma looked over her shoulder at Victor and they both shook their heads.

"Like confronting lambs in a pen, no, *mon chéri*?"

"I wouldn't necessarily call such behavior embarrassing," Victor replied. "We have seen cases of similar blindness from our own gang. The Red Hand is probably no better than Satanas and the others."

"What gang?" Robert asked. "You told us that you two worked alone. Are we now working in concert with another organization? The director will view that omission poorly."

Irma giggled and shook her head.

"Silly man, you misunderstand us. We once were members of the Vampires. But they vanished without a trace while the Eidolon and I were away. Only the body of one of our leaders, a chemist who called himself Venenos, remained. That is to say, we found his head and part of one arm."

"The Vampires?" Robert replied. "Forgive me, I thought they were but a myth."

He tapped the map again.

"But we are moving away from our main topic. Why do you believe the Pharo possesses some connection to the organization that killed our men? As I mentioned, the Blancs already looked into it."

"I think you failed to hear what we three actually discovered," Victor said, standing and crossing the library. "We found that the witnesses could not remember the face and identity of those who supplied them with the narcotics. This occurred three times, and now we learn that the deceased Blanc fools reported exactly the same thing. Therefore, this is a common denominator. What causes such memory gaps? Obviously, an advanced form of hypnosis or mind control."

"Do be serious, Monsieur," Robert sneered. "Such parlor tricks are limited to the stage or penny dreadfuls."

Irma curled her gloved hand in a fist and looked at Robert. Her normally merry expression vanished, replaced by a cold, violent anger that triggered a wave of cold fear down the butler's spine.

"A man, a criminal leader named Moréno, once attempted to take control of my mind," she whispered. "He possessed powers capable of overwhelming almost everyone he met. His plans for me included sharing his bed, among other indignities."

Robert, despite his normally placid exterior, flinched at the glittering fury in the eyes of the Vampire. There was something horrific and terrifying about her and her lover.

"He failed," Irma continued, her voice taut with unconcealed rage, "because the Eidolon had taught me a method of resisting mind control when we were children. I then killed Moréno, quickly despite wishing I could have made his suffering long and lingering."

"My apologies, Madame, Robert said, bowing slightly. "All my previous training has taught me to deny the notions of mesmerism and hypnosis. Do you have any additional suspicions based on what we know?"

"Large, empty rooms with wooden floors" Victor mused. "Many windows and the view carefully hidden from the eyes of those within... All occurring within the city limits... This Pharo may be our best choice."

Victor stepped to the nearby window.

"Feel free to be amazed, Robert," Irma said, regaining some of her light tone. "The Eidolon was trained in observation by an English criminal mastermind. You will find it quite irritating if he decides to tell you what you were doing and where you were based on some fleck of dust on your sleeve."

"Very well," Robert replied. "I shall inform the Director at once."

"Yes, you do that," Victor said, stepping onto the window sill. "And we shall determine if there more to our theory than just a series of wild guesses."

With a quick wave from Irma, they vanished a moment later.

Robert Ménard pulled a handkerchief from his sleeve and mopped his perspiring forehead. He was not one for feeling fear, but the look upon the Vampire's made-up face had caused him to sense his mortality for the first time in many years.

Still, it would not do to remain standing in the library shivering with fear. Exhaling deeply, Robert reached for the televisor unit.

He now had to report their findings to his employers.

CHAPTER LIII

"I am surprised that you agreed to my plan," Irma said as Victor landed by her side. "You generally disagree and demand we perform separate entries."

Victor studied the well-lit palace and shook his head.

"We are confronting a master of mind-control who may have destroyed the Vampires in a single night. I will not feel safe until we are back in our trailer, heading for Italy or Spain."

Irma reached out and squeezed his hand for a few seconds.

"Whatever we confront, we shall do it together, *mon amour*. I promised you that when we were children."

Victor nodded once and squeezed her hand back, slowly releasing his grip and looking back at the house.

"Odd. I smell lubricants, and a great deal of other fluids… and… rotting meat…"

"That is not unexpected. I counted six vehicles when we climbed over the wall. The meat could have many explanations."

"What I do not smell," Victor continued, "is the scents of cooked food. Nothing was cooked in this building in at least a month or more. You cannot believe that that can be easily explained. In addition, I detect no wine or any form of drink other than water. Is that simply explained, too?"

Irma frowned and shook her head.

"No. Quite the opposite. Unless someone is using this great palace as a warehouse for automobiles? But that would be quite unlikely. And it still doesn't explain the meat…"

"A mystery then," Victor said. "Your plan to stay together is becoming a better idea with each passing moment."

Clasping hands for a moment, they ran with stealthy steps through the shadowy lawn.

Irma pulled a hood over her makeup-covered face and appeared to become more insubstantial as she moved through the darkness.

Seconds later, she slithered up the wall of the palace, moving with the sinewy grace of a serpent. Victor followed in her wake, skillful but clearly still a student when compared to her masterful excellence in the art of cat burglary.

Built in the shape of a massive letter H, the Palais du Pharo stood three stories high and possessed dozens of massive bright windows. It appeared as if huge candelabras were lit in each room, creating a massive golden glow across the structure's stone facade. Periodically, the light dimmed in a window as a body stepped across it.

Despite those movements, no sounds escaped from the windows. An unsettling hush covered the palace like a vast invisible blanket. A sense of incongruity caused a shiver up Irma's spine and Victor's motions to slow, becoming warier as he stepped towards the corner of the building.

Irma took Victor's hand, her finger tapping a silent message on his palm. This was a communication system they had invented as children. Members of the Vampires often cooed and clucked over the eleven-year-old boy and the girl who walked everywhere hand-in-hand. None, not even the vastly observant Great Vampire himself, had realized the pair held long conversations using a code they had invented.

"I do not like this place. Did you bring my devices?" Irma said through a series of touches and squeezes.

"Yes, left side jacket pocket. I smell many people inside. None are clean. None are talking, and all are moving." Victor replied in the same manner.

Irma reached in and pulled out several items, placing each one on her belt. Then, with a final reassuring touch, she turned and vaulted onto the wall.

Within seconds, her slight, shadowy form slithered up the heights of the palace, impossibly quick and silent in her motions.

Victor followed a short distance behind, his motions slower and less precise.

Arriving at the top corner, Irma walked along the tiny ledge, her motions as relaxed as one strolling along a park. She stopped next to a window and looked inside, tilting her head left and right as she studied the scent within the chamber.

A moment later, she opened the window and stepped inside, her hand motioning that Victor should follow.

He dropped into a small room, an attic space that appeared to have once served as a servant's bedroom. It possessed a pair of lamps that lit the tiny chamber, revealing two men and a woman crawling along the floor, their tongues extended.

Each licked the floor with dry tongues and cracked, chapped lips. Their elderly emaciated bodies, dressed in rags, slid across the parquet with slow, painful motions. They each appeared unaware of anything beyond their activities. The stench wafting from their filthy forms activated Irma and Victor's gag reflex. They fought down the growing nausea and watched the bizarre actions of the three horrific wretches as they crawled across the floor. Each constantly bumped into the others, or the walls, as they cleansed the floor with their diminishing saliva.

Joining hands again, Irma sent:

"What is wrong with them? They do not see us, or even each other?"

Victor studied the trio and replied:

"They have something red on the back of their heads."

Irma studied the three for a moment and nodded.

She reached into Victor's pocket and removed a battered pen. Reaching down, she gently moved aside the tangled mass of stiff, grease-covered hair from one of the men. She then stepped over to the remaining woman and man and performed the same action.

Finally, she returned to Victor's side and placed the pen on the window sill.

"Gems," she sent, "the color of blood. They are embedded in their skulls and occasionally pulse with yellow light."

"This is bad," Victor sent back. "Worse than we imagined."

Irma was about to send back a question, when all three elderly floor-lickers looked up. Their stark white eyes gazed at Irma and Victor with unblinking intensity. As one, they then spoke, the words emerging simultaneously from their toothless, diseased lips:

"We recognize you. You are the Vampire and the Eidolon. The burglar supreme and the dark killer. You shall serve us well."

"We do not serve anyone," Irma replied.

"All say the same. Humans are such predictable creatures. Soon you shall be part of us and it shall not matter. Individuality is a disease We shall eliminate this plague. Come to us, or we shall bring you to our side. Come to us…"

The voices in the room soon joined a chorus of others from the hallway. Men and women slowly shuffled into the doorway, their filthy frames blocking the light from the hallway.

"I smell at least forty," Victor sent to Irma. "All diseased and wasted, and coming our way."

"We do not have time for such nonsense." Irma replied.

She turned around and dove out the window. Victor followed a step behind, grabbing the ledge and swinging down after her.

A moment later, he landed at her side on the ground, rolling to his feet and staring up at the open window above. A horde of emaciated arms protruded, resembling a bizarre cilium from a monstrous undersea creature. The skeletal limbs waggled and waved, their claw-shaped fingers pawing through the air, enhancing the otherworldly horror.

"That was astonishingly unpleasant, *mon chéri*," Irma said. "You do take me to the most unique places. Are those sad wretches slaves to some alien creature, I wonder?"

"I have no way of knowing," Victor replied. "But these poor souls did not smell right."

"I could tell," Irma replied. "We must learn more."

She jumped and climbed to a first-floor window. Seeing nobody inside, she unlocked it, and stepped back into the palace. Victor followed her. They linked hands again, intending their conversation to continue by touch since they were back inside the building.

"That is not what I meant," Victor sent. "Those creatures upstairs... I am not sure they are truly alive."

"Thank you," Irma tapped. "I was hoping you would terrify me as well as fill me with disgust. Well done, *chéri*."

"You are welcome. I smell machine oil." Victor sent as they slowly stepped through the room and approached a doorway.

The room that followed proved as empty as the last. It was a square chamber with light and dark parquet, swept clean. Embedded in the walls were dusty carvings, detailed etchings of the late nineteenth century French Imperial style. Irma spotted two Napoleonic crests almost invisible due to the layers of neglect.

Victor stopped, releasing Irma's hand, and squatting on the floor. Slowly, he lowered his head to the parquet and examined several discolored patches, barely visible despite the powerful electric lights in the shape of candles hanging along the walls.

Rising a moment later, he said:

"Machine oil of some kind. More than one type. Also saliva, old and new."

"This is one who deserves death. Forcing slaves to lick floors clean is an abomination!" Irma replied.

The search of the enormous ground floor took a half hour, though the results proved confusing. Other than one throne-shaped chair in a south wing chamber, the rooms were completely empty. The floors, as confirmed by Victor, possessed the same equal parts of lubricants and saliva. The

252

scrollwork across the walls and ceilings appeared neglected, as if intentionally ignored by the still missing owner.

"Upstairs? I do not love the idea, but we must explore further," Irma said aloud.

Victor frowned beneath his mask, surprised Irma had not used their usual communication method. However, she was the professional cat burglar and her instincts rarely failed her.

"I think that would waste our time," he said. "There are at least forty wretches above us, slowly moving towards the stairs. Had there been someone with a working intelligence, the poor, mindless creatures might not be bumping and stumbling over one another. We are missing something. Was there another house on the grounds?"

Irma sighed and shook her head.

"You shall never make an effective thief. I try and try to teach you the fundamentals, yet you do not attend."

Victor raised his hand in surrender.

"This much is given. What did I miss this time?"

"*Mon chéri, et très cher imbécile*, an effective night-crawler must be equal parts burglar, alienist, and detective. No wealthy man or woman wishes to place their goods in a position where any hapless thief with a crow bar may lay hands on them. This is why understanding your victim prior to entering his property is as important as mastering burglary techniques."

"I hope this is leading to something profound," Victor replied, glancing up above their heads.

"It is, so attend for once." Irma said. "We are facing a disgusting creature that despises humanity. We are individuals. This means it views us as a disease. One that it must destroy. This creature seeks control, absolute control. Think of the unfortunate slaves licking floors clean. This monster has them perform humiliating menial labor until required for something important. That tells us we are dealing with one that sacrifices human lives, just as we do toe nail clippings. They do not live, they are just appendages to a greater whole."

"Agreed," Victor said, adding: "Please conclude with greater speed. The wretches above are nearing the stairs."

Irma took his arm and led Victor through the myriad of empty corridors, continuing as they strode towards her goal.

"Now consider the palace in which it resides. Massive, capable of holding a number of followers with ease. Yet every room, save the one with the throne, sits unused and empty. The creature does not prize possessions either. This location was chosen for its size and relative solitude. Close to the city, yet far enough for whatever madness is in his plans. This tells us this palace is but a shell, a device used for meetings with humans who are not yet under his control."

"Like those to whom they sell narcotic in Marseilles?" Victor said, nodding.

"Correct. This tells us that this monster requires a great deal of space and privacy. Hence the palace above is empty, but his true home is not."

Irma stopped beside a door and threw it open, revealing a set of clean stone stair leading downward into murky depths.

"*Voilà!* His true lair is underground."

"Brilliant!" Victor whispered. "Perhaps there is more to the art of cat burglary than I realized."

Irma reached out and tweaked his nose.

"I have told you that since we were children, *mon chéri*. Despite your other assets, you are very slow in some areas."

Victor did not reply. Instead, he stepped down the stairs, his movements slow, his senses probing the gloom. Reaching back, he sent:

"There is nobody down there. I smell dead bodies, many of them, and also chemicals."

"You think this is the only level of that monster's lair? This one would kill a whole town if it helped his schemes even a little."

Just as they reached the bottom of the stairs, the lights rose brilliantly and a soft, metallic chuckle filled the air.

"Hello again, Vampire and Eidolon. It shall be my pleasure to tear you to pieces."

CHAPTER LIV

"Robert," Doctor Cornelius asked, having absorbed his underling's detailed report, "do you believe the Vampire and the Eidolon surmised correctly?"

"*Oui, Monsieur*," Robert replied.

He stood stiffly before Gérard's televisor, unwilling to sit in the deceased criminal's desk chair.

"They did not appear interested whether I would follow them or not," he continued. "They are rather... unusual, Monsieur."

"How so?" Fritz Kramm demanded. "They are a professional thief and a murderer. Fantômas is both and we do not revere that creature."

"I believe you are correct, Monsieur," Robert said, running a finger along his mustache, "However, they are unlike many criminals. The Vampire and the Eidolon are closer in behavior to one of those gentlemen cracksman. They behave with seriousness in the moment, but approach all situations with pleasure. Even when they defeated both myself and Madame Zanzi, they acted as if this was a pleasant outing together."

"Bored amateurs? How disappointing!" Fritz said, shaking his head unseen on the other end of the televisor. "We killed one that dressed as a clown and fought crime. He and his crimson costume are now a part of an off-ramp in New Jersey."

"My apologies, Monsieur, but you are incorrect. I can testify neither are what one would deem amateurs. The Vampire is a professional cat burglar, whose ability to scale walls, open locks, and move silently, is without peer, and makes her a true danger. Additionally, she is also an expert in hand-to-hand combat. But it is the Eidolon who quite unnerves me. He was stronger than Madame Zanzi and, frankly, my better with weapons and unarmed combat. In a sense, Monsieur, you were correct earlier. If you were to split the infamous Fantômas into two persons, one would find this pair."

Robert Ménard rarely spoke so long on a subject, preferring a minimalist approach to discussions. However, his employers required full information.

"I think he likes them!" Fritz squawked, "Are you tendering your resignation in favor of service with the Vampire and the Eidolon?"

"Certainly not, Monsieur." Robert said, stiffening. "One may admire the lethal beauty of a poisonous serpent, but one never befriends such a creature."

"Well," Fritz said, "that is good to know at least."

"Yesss," Doctor Cornelius said, drawing out the word into a near hiss. "We have no desire to continue associating with that pair. Whatever they face at the Palais du Pharo is of no interest to the Red Hand. If they die fighting this foe, we win, for that will eliminate a threats which may hamper us in the future. And if they destroy their foe, we win, too. All of Marseilles shall return to our control, possibly to an even greater degree."

"What do you require of me, Monsieur le Directeur?" Robert asked, unsurprised by the callous behavior of the Lords of the Red Hand.

"While you served our interests in Marseilles, we conducted a series of discussions with a few other organizations. We made an alliance with an older group called the Companions of the Silence. A Count Fosco from Naples shall arrive within the week and take full control of the operations. Once you've made him aware of all the activities in the old city, the tenements, and the harbor, you shall then travel to Paris. We are about to undertake a gang war thanks to another alliance with an Apache gang. Your knives will be required and we shall increase your pay. I think a thirty percent raise, as well as some other benefits, will be in order, Monsieur Ménard."

Robert bowed deeply towards the televisor screen.

"Very generous indeed, Monsieur. Thank you for your confidence. I shall prepare the house and all relevant papers for the Count in that time."

The televisor went blank and Robert reached for his dusting cloth.

He felt a moment of trepidation for the Vampire and the Eidolon, but that passed when he spotted a thin layer of dust on the bottom edge of the third table on the left. Taking care of such disorder was far more important than the fate of a pair of amusing criminals.

CHAPTER LV

"Mademoiselle Zanzi," Irma said, smiling beneath her mask. "You have changed. I do like the current fashion, French rococo meets German industrial, I believe."

"Shut up!" Nanon Zanzi screeched as she slapped her hands together.

A metallic clank filled the air, echoing throughout the roughhewn stone chamber.

"That is not my name! Nanon Zanzi died in a fire in the United States. I am Roboterfrau, the first of a new race!"

Roboterfrau stood a meter and a half high and shimmered bright silver in the electric light. She possessed female characteristics such as a lovely, if cold, metal face, a curving body and large flaring steel breasts. The effect was bizarre, a woman of metal, a statue that walked, talked, and even ranted with anger. The sheer artificiality, yet attempted simulacrum of humanity, caused confusion and an unsettled feeling into both Irma Vep and Victor Sicarius.

"You are now entirely made of metal?" Victor asked.

"Yes!" Roboterfrau cried.

Her voice possessed some of the tones similar to Nanon Zanzi. Yet now these sounds held an electronic undertone similar to that of a well-tuned wireless set.

"Then how can you be the first of a new race? Biologically, you appear unable to complete such a task..." Victor replied.

He heard Irma suppress a laugh.

"Bastard! You die first!" Roboterfrau snarled.

She ran forward. Her body moved with uncanny speed and grace, her motions smooth and holding a fluid grace.

As she reached for Victor, he dove forward and slid between her legs, rolled, and halted at the far end of the room. Remaining crouched, he taunted:

"Still very slow, Miss Zanzi. The seasons move faster than you. Also, you still appear quite untrained."

Irma dropped to his side, having vanished as Roboterfrau focused her fury on Victor. How she had moved to the other end of the room with such speed and stealth was a mystery only she held.

"Be fair, *mon chéri*. She does move better than before... though previously Madame Steelfingers strode about with the grace of an ape suffering from polio."

"Very poetic," Victor said.

They joined hands.

"I think we are making her angry," Victor added. "We had best pay attention to Madame Zanzi now."

"My name is Roboterfrau and I shall kill you both right now," she hissed, stalking forward.

"As I said before, it is good for the soul to possess ambitions," Irma remarked. "Though I must say, you shall find that quite difficult, new limbs or not."

She and Victor took fighting stances.

Roboterfrau screeched again, and ran forward. Her speed was uncanny, a blur of silver that appeared inches from where Irma and Victor stood. At least, that is what she had planned. When the former Nanon Zanzi halted inches from the Vampire and the Eidolon, they had already moved aside. Their new position, now three feet from Roboterfrau, placed them near the stairs going up towards the mansion.

"Cowards!" Roboterfrau cried.

She dashed forward, hands extended.

Irma, standing three steps above Victor, leaped forward.

Using the Eidolon's shoulders as a platform, she flipped over Roboterfrau's head and landed near the metal woman's rear. Kicking backwards like an angry horse, she struck the inhuman creature behind her knees and sent her stumbling towards Victor.

Reaching out, he grabbed Roboterfrau's wrist and shifted his hips. She sailed over his body, flying end over end and crashing back first on the stone stairs.

The loud, heavy, metallic jangle sounded like someone dropping a set of heavy pots and pans on a kitchen floor.

"That was simple enough," Irma said as Victor rejoined her.

She was about to say more, when he cut her off with his hand.

"Something is coming. I smell more metal and lubricants."

His head swiveled back and forth.

"She is on the stairs, beginning to stir," Irma said, pointing at the twitching form of Roboterfrau.

Victor shook his head and signaled left and right, down a pair of passages that joined the chamber.

"No, they're approaching from both directions. Get ready."

Indeed, a minute later, two maschinenmensch drones strode into view. Their heavy, iron feet crashed on the stone floor as they marched in lockstep from opposite directions.

Each stopped at the same moment, filling the large gaping corridors with their enormous silver frames. The only signs of life were the gentle energy pulse that illuminated the crimson gems embedded in their massive foreheads.

"Run about and play your games," Roboterfrau sneered from above. "You shall eventually tire, but we do not suffer from such problems of the flesh. Then I shall tear you apart, one piece at a time."

"You really must find a new threat, Madame," Irma quipped. "Hearing this desire of yours over and over is quite tiresome."

She and Victor turned back to back.

"I do believe you will quip at your own funeral," Victor whispered.

"I certainly will at yours, *mon chéri*," she replied as the half-human creatures strode forward.

CHAPTER LVI

Across Marseilles, men, women and children froze in their activities. Thousands came to a literal standstill, with even their eyes no longer blinking. As one they lay down their tools, food, or any other object in their hands. Those in vehicles halted their progress and stepped out onto the street.

Over ten thousand people headed out of their respective businesses, streets, or dwellings, and turned towards the Palais du Pharo.

The Benoît industrial complex ceased operations, much to the confusion of the new manager. Running from his office as the machines ground to a heavy, screeching halt, he waved his arms about and yelled.

"Stop! Stop now or you are all fired! Stop, stop now!"

He yelled over and over to the disinterested masses, but none so much as glanced in his direction.

Their bodies jostled him aside as they strode out of their respective departments and headed for the exits.

Wordlessly, they marched, the biomass of the city, heading for the Pharo. Within moments, their motions became precise, each step exactly in time with others across the city. No matter the age, size, or sex, the mobs of Marseilles moved in perfect step.

The result was, to the few outside observers witnessing the mass exodus, the diminution of these being's humanity. Though outwardly humans, their actions, their unceasing attention towards their goal, and most of all, their silence, stripped them of the individuality that was the main characteristic of mankind.

Instead, these men, women, and children appeared to transform, at least in that indefinable inner essence that most refer to as a soul, into creatures more insect than human. Their apparent shared consciousness transformed them into a terrible weapon, thousands of unthinking hands controlled by a single consciousness.

All headed towards the Pharo, summoned by their terrible master... The being who inhabited them, mind and body, since they had consumed his blood crystal-laced brew... The vampiric, alien intelligence known as the Great Brain of Mars.

CHAPTER LVII

Pulling a pair of telescoping fighting staffs from Victor's jacket, the Vampire and the Eidolon spun their weapons with blinding speed.

None of the three metal beings heading their direction, Roboterfrau having joined the two maschinenmensch, slowed, their inhuman minds apparently unimpressed by the blur of weaponized steel.

Victor struck first, the end of his staff, striking the knee joint of the closest robotic drone. Though a loud clanking sounded, the metallic creature did not slow or appear diminished by the attack. The knee joint was not even dented by a strike that would have rendered a human crippled for months.

A second behind Victor's, Irma's staff lashed out and struck a maschinenmensch's steel skull. A noise like that of a clapper striking a bell sounded and the staff bent slightly from the contact. But the drone's hands grabbed the weapon and, with a quick pull, wrenched it from Irma's nerveless fingers.

Hurling his own weapon into the face of his attacker, Victor and Irma immediately dove to the side. It was a simple trick: engage the enemy's hands and get past them long enough to regroup—or flee. It was a good strategy, at least in theory, that they had often used with success in the past.

Unfortunately, the maschinenmensch did not react in the same manner as humans or animals. The steel staff bounced off the metallic skull, clattering to the ground. The huge iron hands snatched up Victor, forcing Irma to crash into his back. She fell backwards, straight into the hands of the other drone.

Both Vampire and Eidolon found themselves forcibly pulled upright, their feet barely touching the ground. Harsh, unyielding fingers kept them still; the grip on their arms was both painful and confining.

"That was the best you could do?" Roboterfrau asked, swaggering closer

She halted several feet from the black leather-clad duo.

"You two, who have humiliated me before, now know the truth."

"And what truth is that, Madame Steelfingers?" Irma inquired, her voice calm and seemingly unconcerned.

Roboterfrau's hands balled into fists for a moment and her lovely, inhuman silver face stared at Irma.

"I will enjoy hearing you scream, slut. The truth you are learning is that all flesh is weak. Metal feels nothing. We are a higher life form and shall replace all life on this planet."

"*Merde!*" Irma said, shaking her head. "Another one. Oh, la, la, I do believe Europe is overrun with megalomaniacs."

"What is that supposed to mean?" Roboterfrau demanded, raising one hand and reaching for Irma's masked face.

"It means, my dear, that the Eidolon and I have faced many others with similar, ridiculous and quite insane plots. Six in the last…"

She stopped as Victor interrupted her flow of speech.

"Five. The lunatic who created the human-bat hybrids served the Master of Strange Deaths."

"No," Irma said, shaking her head. "I counted them as one. Did you forget the Dwellers in the Dark?"

"I had. My apologies, it was six. Do go on."

Irma turned her head back towards Roboterfrau. If a cyborg could seethe, the former Nanon Zanzi managed the feat. Her silver shell vibrated as sounds of exasperation leaked from her unmoving metal mouth.

"Dear me, I am so sorry," Irma continued, insincerity dripping from her every syllable. "We do tend to forget we have an audience. As I was saying…"

"Shut up, shut up, shut up!" Roboterfrau screeched. "Do you think I care what you say or think?"

"Well!" Irma replied, her voice full of feigned, almost comical annoyance. "That was very rude! Do you behave in this manner with all your guests?"

Roboterfrau released a grinding sound from her mouth

"This nonsense is at an end" she finally said. "Prepare for your slow and painful demise."

"One final request?" Victor asked.

"Speak quickly." the metal woman replied.

"A last kiss before we die?"

Roboterfrau stared at him for a moment and released a crackling sound that was the probable approximation of a laugh.

"Pathetic biological figures! Granted—but you shall not remove your masks, nor be released from your drones' grips."

With crashing, echoing lurches, the maschinenmensch drones stepped closer, placing Irma and Victor inches from each other.

Their hands joined, and their black hooded faces pressed together for several seconds.

"Enough," Roboterfrau said.

The drones pulled the pair apart.

"Time to die," she added. "I hope you are prepared."

"Oh, we are very prepared," Irma said.

And she giggled.

CHAPTER LVIII

"You laugh?" Roboterfrau said. "I think I shall remove your tongue first!"

She turned in Irma's direction.

"You are a tiresome being, Madame Steelfingers," Irma said.

She then clicked her heels together, an action echoed by Victor.

From the toes of their boots emerged steel spikes, four rounded blades that glinted in the harsh electric light. At the same instant, they kicked out their booted feet flying above each other's head. Their targets were the crimson gems in the center of the maschinenmensch's skulls.

The gems shattered under the harsh impact, raining shards onto the stone floor.

The maschinenmensch froze. Then their hands spasmed and opened, releasing the Vampire and the Eidolon.

The metal creatures shrieked, their arms and legs flailing about with hysterical motions. For an instant, they resembled clockwork toys with failing gears as they convulsed and barely managed to stand upright.

"Aaahhh! What is happening to me? It hurts, it hurts!" the maschinenmensch near Victor screamed.

"Why is my face so cold? Why can't I feel my hands? What is happening to me?" the other drone shrieked as it fell over, causing a crack across the rough floor.

The brief touch exchange between Victor and Irma as they had pressed their cowled heads together had caused this incredible occurrence.

Red gem on their heads, Victor had sent to Irma as their hands joined.

Same as upstairs, in the heads, Irma had sent back.

I break yours, Victor had replied.

And I yours. I knew we would need these boots.

Is this the right time for such discussions?
You hate to admit when I am right.

Before Victor could add another reply, Roboterfrau had concluded their conversation.

Now they leaped in different directions as the maschinenmensch's true minds returned to their bodies.

Roboterfrau was standing still, her metal skull scanning the screaming, stumbling drones as they thrashed across the floor.

"Find the demon behind all this evil, *mon chéri*," said Irma, "and leave this one to me."

She blew Victor a kiss.

"Stay safe," Victor replied, returning the gesture. "*Je t'aime,*" he added.

"*Moi non plus,*" Irma said, laughing. "Now go and kill someone evil."

Victor turned and ran down one of the hallways, vanishing from sight seconds later.

Irma then kicked the fallen staff towards Roboterfrau, the steel shaft clattering as it crashed against her leg.

"Now," Irma said, "shall we continue our discussion? Did you say you wished to tear things from my face and body? Forgive me, I grew bored and failed to listen to your threats."

The mocking words and clashing metal woke Roboterfrau from her trance and she spun Irma's direction.

Without a word, she ran towards the Vampire, her hands extended. Irma stood in place, neither retreating nor moving to leap aside. Instead, her long gloved fingers reached into her belt, removing a small glass sphere.

With a flick, she tossed the ball between herself and Roboterfrau before diving and rolling to her right.

The sphere shattered, spilling a clear liquid pool across the floor.

Roboterfrau's metal feet stepped in the puddle and she immediately lost her footing. Both feet flew out from under her and she fell to the floor with a jangling din.

"Frictionless fluid," Irma explained as she straightened. "Very useful when fleeing the gendarmes or other criminals. It should keep you from standing up for a few minutes."

She stepped a little closer and her voice grew colder as she reached into her belt.

"Now, let us see what we can use as a can opener..."

CHAPTER LIX

Victor stepped into the room at the far end of the hall, unsurprised to find one man seated in a large chair. The arms and desk before the man were made of metal and possessed long rows of buttons and switches. A series of tools lay on the desk's surface and Victor recognized them as diamond cutting instruments.

The man seated in the massive chair was of medium height and possessed a skeletal body, a thick, tangled, greasy brown beard and mustache and oily brown hair that probably had not touched soap in months. A feverish stench of rot wafted from his gray robed body and his eyes were a sickly bloodshot red.

"We are the Great Brain," he rasped, "once master of the world you call Mars. We recognize you. You are the one called the Eidolon—wanted for murder throughout this tiny planet. You may serve us and kill for us as we remake this world in our image. Join us and we shall grant you your every wish."

"I am not that foolish" Victor replied. "Creatures such as yourself cannot have servants for long. You said so yourself. To you, individuality is anathema."

"Then you shall join us as another appendage," the Great Brain intoned. "Bow before us. Kneel before your master, Eidolon."

"I think not." Victor replied.

He chuckled at the shocked expression on the rash covered face.

The Great Brain invoked all its massive mental might and sought to envelop the rebel's mind. The former master of Mars reeled back, open-mouthed, unable to touch the bizarre brain of the being that stood calmly before his throne.

"You..." the Martian overlord gasped. "You are not human!"

Victor Sicarius chuckled, though very little mirth filled the sound.

"Better to say, only half-human," he replied, removing his hood.

His amber-colored eyes, now unhidden by contact lenses, did not resemble anything close to human. Then he smiled, flashing sharp, ivory-colored upper and lower canines. He removed his gloves and extended pale curved claws from each of his wide fingertips.

"What are...?" the Great Brain started to ask, when he stopped after a gesture from Victor.

"Two questions," Victor said. "First, I need you to answer two of my questions."

"Very well," the Great Brain said, languidly gesturing as he sent out mental commands to other of his appendages. "We shall answer honestly."

Reaching into his jacket, Victor removed a curved yellowing square of paper. He tossed the item onto the lap of the Great Brain and asked:

"Do you know those men and women?"

The Great Brain lifted the aging photograph and recognized Mocata and the other Satanists instantly. They sat in a very prim and proper line, with the high priest's fat form in the center. It was a dour image, like most daguerreotypes of the Victorian age, with each man and woman staring at the camera with the same blank, unsmiling expression.

"Yes," the Great Brain answered. "They were our first slaves. A circle of fools who believed they possessed magical powers. There is no magic in the universe—that is mere superstition. We took control of their little minds in one evening. Why?"

Victor tapped the image of a lovely blond woman, the same one that the Great Brain had consumed recently to keep up his mental energies.

"That one was my mother. I assume that you killed her?"

"Yes," the Great Brain said, sending more frantic signals. "Do your mammalian atavistic instincts require you to slay us for consuming your parent?"

Victor snorted and took back the picture.

"No. I just wondered. Her life or death means nothing to me. She sold me to a scientist who used me as a subject of his torturous experimentation."

"Then you should…" the Great Brain began.

But he stopped as the Eidolon dropped another, larger photograph dropped into his lap.

He picked it up and studied the image with a frown.

The large group of men and women were unpoised, some sitting, other standing, a pair locked together seemingly dancing. All appeared merry, laughing and drinking and few gazed into the camera.

"The Vampires," the Great Brain said. "They joined us shortly after the Luciferians. Are you about to tell us that one of the males was your father?"

Victor chuckled and took back the picture.

"Most definitely not. However, they did rescue me as a child, and I owed them some debt. Not enough to care who killed them, though. They were not good people. More importantly, the woman I love counted them as her family, and their loss wounded her deeply. For that, and that alone, I will now kill you."

"Then this has nothing to do with criminals and secret societies?" the Great Brain asked, bloodshot eyes widening.

Victor shook his head.

"I feel some sorrow for their deaths, but not enough to kill in their name. No, I will now kill you for the woman you know as the Vampire. You should not have taken away her family."

The Great Brain opened his mouth and a pitiful wail emerged from his cracked lips, ending in a gurgling moan seconds later…

CHAPTER LX

Roboterfrau slid across the floor, slamming into a wall, then rebounding a few feet while still spinning.

A high-pitched squeal emitted from her mouth and she babbled a series of disjointed syllables that resembled speech but were indecipherable.

"Hmm," Irma said, examining her bent staff. "Your shell appears quite impervious to harm. I wish I had thought to bring a chisel."

She tossed the useless weapon aside and searched her pouches. She pulled out a half-broken set of wire cutters, a thin, Italian-made stiletto, and a bent hammer.

"Very impressive, yet frustrating. However, every safe possesses a weak point," she mused.

That was when the odor drifted her direction. Looking up the stairs, she spotted the mob of ragged men and women. They staggered as they stepped down the stairs, their inhuman eyes staring her direction.

"*Merde!*" she spat.

She tossed her last glass globe onto the stairs. The first of the barely living beings tripped and fell, their bones snapping as they struck the stone steps. They lay unmoving and others followed, falling and remaining motionless where they landed.

Soon, a carpet of shattered human forms lay upon the stairs and the staggering, stinking slaves could step on their fellows, untouched by the frictionless fluid.

Snatching up her bent, nearly broken staff, Irma stepped forward and attacked.

Her weapon shattered heads, necks and legs, dropping the weak, barely living beings with each attack. Twenty of these starving, weak, tortured, victims, might have overwhelmed her, but their nearly destroyed bodies caused them to move with slow, tottering steps like those of a newly walking infant.

Still, hands gabbed at her arms, legs and body, bruising her despite the weakness of the attacks. The number of strikes wore her down, weakened her, and left her panting, if elated, as the last pathetic wretch fell to the floor.

"Well done," Roboterfrau said, still struggling to stand. "Such impressive fighting skills. Now, what shall you do with the others?"

That was when the loud tromp, tromp, tromp, of the enslaved populace of Marseilles entered the Palais du Pharo.

The front ranks of the thousands ran towards the sub-basement level, appearing at the top of the stairs only seconds later. Their unblinking gazes were as inhuman as those of the slaves Irma had just defeated; yet, these men, women, and children were fresh and unconsumed by their master's appetites.

"You will die, Vampire!" Roboterfrau crowed, emitting that strange laugh of hers once again. "Not by my hand, but I shall see your end!"

"I shall not give you the satisfaction, Nanon Zanzi," Irma said.

She ran the way Victor had headed. Her slow, painful gait proved far slower than her usual youthful stride and soon the mob was on her heels.

Irma Vep glanced over her shoulder, seeing the blank pale face of a boy, probably no older than ten, with a tall, very pretty, dark-haired woman at his side. They ran with quick, efficient steps, slowly gaining on her with each passing second. Their hands extended like claws, reaching out, just missing her legs and back with a swipe.

Their pace increased and the girl's fingertips just grazed Irma's shoulder. The boy's hand lowered, reached out, and collided with the Vampire's flashing feet.

Irma stumbled and recovered, but the woman grabbed her arm and Irma stopped for fear of falling. The remainder of the mob appeared and slowed, their step returning to a normal walk as they reached for Irma Vep.

A second later, a dozen or more hands held her in place, their grips tightening as others reached towards her.

Then, suddenly, they stopped.

Their arms dropped, their faces appeared puzzled.

The hands fell away from her body and they looked about them with eyes that regained intelligence with each passing second.

Not one to wait, Irma turned and ran, nearly colliding with Victor who was stepping out of a doorway. He was in the act of pulling his mask back in place and he inhaled in shock as she staggered into view.

"Get us out of here, *mon chéri*," she whispered.

He placed a comforting arm around her waist.

"Did you find the monster?" she asked.

"Yes," Victor replied, smelling fresh air down a different corridor. "He was the only living man in the building… and he smelled like something rotting from inside. But he is dead now."

"Good," Irma replied, sighing.

They spotted a flight of stairs leading up.

"Time to vanish for a little while, perhaps," she said. "Paris? Madrid? London? Moscow? Then it can begin again."

Victor did not reply.

He knew she was right. Irma always knew best.

CHAPTER LXI

"…Drones are no more. The loss of control caused them to lose all ability to survive," Rotwang reported. "Roboterfrau, as an independent being, is still fully operational, Master. With ten Brinken's help, I shall find a different means of suppressing the biological functions for an advanced form of maschinenmensch."

The crazed scientist looked even more unhinged as he smiled at the silver form of Roboterfrau. He had repaired her dented panels, grateful she had survived the disaster in Marseilles.

So much had been lost, especially his drone creation devices that were almost fully operational in the Benoît factories. Still, his masterpiece stood as his side.

"My first two successes are present, just outside the chamber. Shall I bring them forward, Master." ten Brinken asked, smiling, his eyes vanishing in the folds of his blocky face.

The pair that entered were as unalike as two beings could be, and still belong to the same species.

The woman stood a head shorter than ten Brinken and possessed long, lustrous golden blond hair, large blue eyes, milky white skin, and a heart-shaped face that resembled an artist's view of the goddess Venus. She wore an unadorned white linen dress and somehow caused that simple outfit to resemble a fashionable evening gown.

The male at her side stood almost three meters high with a blocky body covered with monstrous, oversized muscles. His skin was a light gray and seemed made of leather rather than ordinary flesh. The bones holding up his massive form looked thicker and more substantial, as if he was both human and beast. His face appeared only partially formed, like the first draft of a sculptor's work. The nose was a simple triangular bump with huge circles for nostrils and the mouth was a slash from one end of the square face to the other. The man moved with heavy steps and his black eyes never blinked.

"Meet the finest of my creations, Master" ten Brinken explained. "This is Alraune, my daughter. No man or woman can resist her charms and she will kill anyone we wish. She is, in fact, the perfect killer.

"And this is Skrýmir, the strongest being alive. Bullets will bounce off his hide and he can bend metal. He is a one-man-army and completely obedient."

"Excellent, my servants," the Great Brain said. "Our failure in Marseilles proved disappointing, but we have just begun our work. We shall try again here in Paris, and soon the world shall fall under our sway."

The Great Brain frowned and added:

"Oh, and you had best call us Mistress now."

The Great Brain, now in the body of Bernard Benoît's lover, Violette, smiled at her followers.

"The battle for the world had just begun."

EPILOGUE

Meanwhile, elsewhere in Paris, Irma sighed as she locked the door of their room behind her.

On the floor below, the *Cabaret de l'Épi-Scié* still resembled what it had been in the days of old, a poor drinking establishment for a low clientele, located in the neighborhood of the Temple, near the Grands Boulevards.

Each night Irma sang silly songs and Victor juggled knives as the masses guzzled the cheap wine, danced and laughed.

It had been a simple life, an easy way of relaxing. No doubt, they would leave sooner or later, but for now, the work provided a much needed relaxation from their previous struggle in Marseilles.

"So, this is where the Vampire and the Eidolon hide?" a voice said from a patch of shadows. "A stinking rathole only frequented by the lowest scum of the city? Pathetic."

Irma and Victor stood together and stared into the void.

"Who would think to look for us here?" Irma asked.

"I did," the voice replied. "Consider this the end of your retirement. I have use for both of you and you shall do me this service."

"What do you require of us, Fantômas?" Victor asked, joining hands with Irma.

"You can call me father, boy. We have much to discuss," the voice replied.

The glint of a smile appeared from the shadows. The elusive Lord of Fear stepped into the light.

The world would soon live in terror of his name again!

Afterword

If characters such as Fantômas (created by Pierre Souvestre & Marcel Allain in 1911) and Rotwang, from Fritz Lang & Thea Von Harbou's classic film *Metropolis* (1927) need no introduction, a few of the more prominent characters featured in this dystopic novel do. So, without further ado…

French Filmmaking pioneer Louis Feuillade (1873-1925) launched his popular serial *Les Vampires* [*The Vampires*] at Gaumont in 1915 in order to compete with the American serial *The Perils of Pauline*, starring Pearl White. A novelization of *Les Vampires*, penned George Meirs, was released the following year. Its success was due in great part to the character of Irma Vep played by Musidora, a voluptuous, dark-haired stage and music-hall performer who did all her own stunts. Musidora, who occasionally posed naked, virtually defined the French canons of female beauty for the next decade, and her character, identified by her black tights and mask, slinking down corridors and escaping over rooftops, shaped the archetype of the villainous *femme fatale* for decades to come.

In *Les Vampires*, Philippe Guérande, a reporter working for *Le Mondial*, and his friend, Oscar Mazamette, investigate the eponymous gang of criminals. Its leaders change from episode to episode, going from the nameless "Great Vampire" to Moreno, to Satanas, and finally, to Venenos. Irma Vep is introduced as a cabaret singer who is Moreno's lover and also moonlights as a cat burglar. Although she dies at the end of the serial, the gang reappears in Feuillade's 1918 sequel, *Tih Minh*, in which it conspires to avenge her death and take over the world.

In spite of its huge popularity, *Les Vampires* was too anarchistic for the bourgeois sensibilities of the times, and

Feuillade was compelled to feature a real crime-fighting hero, Judex, in his next project.

The Great Brain of Mars originally appeared in *Le Prisonnier de la Planète Mars*, a.k.a. *The Vampires of Mars* (1908-09)[1] by Gustave Le Rouge (1867-1938), a novel hailed as one of the masterpieces of French scientific romance and a significant precursor of the American subgenre of "planetary romances" pioneered by Edgar Rice Burroughs in *A Princess of Mars* (1912).

Planetary romance was not the only subgenre anticipated by Le Rouge. *The Vampires of Mars* also contains a strong element of the "cosmic horror" that H. P. Lovecraft was to attempt to develop in Earthly settings in "At the Mountains of Madness" (1937) and Clark Ashton Smith exported to Mars in "The Vaults of Yoh-Vombis" (1932) and "The Dweller in Martian Depths" (1933). Indeed, the narrative swings so frequently between cosmic horror fiction and interplanetary heroic fantasy that its characters are continually metamorphosing from helpless bundles of gibbering terror into swashbuckling he-men, or vice versa, between paragraphs.

The Mysterious Doctor Cornelius,[2] also by Gustave Le Rouge, introduced the eponymous villain, his brother Fritz, and their globe-spanning crime cartel, the Red Hand, in eighteen weekly installments published in 1912-13. It was Le Rouge's most successful work.

Gustave Le Rouge was born in Normandy on July 22, 1867. As soon as he arrived in Paris, he supported himself by taking a series of casual jobs, including working in a circus. By 1898, he was determined to make a living with his pen. Teaming up with Gustave Guitton, he wrote *The Dominion of*

---

[1] Black Coat Press, ISBN 978-1-934543-30-6.
[2] Black Coat Press, ISBNs 978-1-61227-243-6, 978-1-61227-244-3 & 978-1-61227-245-0.

the World (1899-1900),[3] a long, thriller in which a cabal of American billionaires plots the conquest of Europe with the aid of robots and hypnotists. They are ultimately thwarted by a young French scientist and his aging mentor.

Le Rouge and Guitton eventually quarreled and split up. By then, the craft of fast composition had been perfected by Marcel Allain and Pierre Souvestre, the creators of Fantômas, who produced a book in ten days flat. *The Mysterious Doctor Cornelius* was ideally suited to that format, being in effect a series of 18 novellas which could be read independently of one another, like the American "dime novels."

The Mysterious Doctor Cornelius tells of the conflict between the eponymous villain, the so-called "sculptor of human flesh," a significant prototype of the megalomaniacal "mad scientist," and his heroic adversaries. Whereas *The Dominion of the World* featured a band of American plutocrats as its villains, in *The Mysterious Doctor Cornelius*, wealthy Americans become the targets of the Red Hand, whose three mysterious "Lords" are Cornelius, Fritz, and the renegade son of one of their victims.

Le Rouge continued to produce *feuilleton* fiction, most of it exotic adventures. In 1907, when his career was in full swing, he met the famous Swiss poet Blaise Cendrars, who was twenty years his junior. (Cendrars later painted an affectionately colorful portrait of Le Rouge in his memoirs.) Although Cendrars does not seem to have collaborated with Le Rouge, one of his books is made up exclusively of lines borrowed from *The Mysterious Doctor Cornelius*, carefully redeployed and remixed—a project which, Cendrars reported, failed to convince the thoroughly disillusioned Le Rouge that he really was a poet, and a surrealist to boot.

Doctor Cornelius Kramm is not unlike Paul Féval's infamous Colonel Bozzo-Corona from *The Black Coats*. But the fact that Cornelius is an experimental scientist rather than a

---

[3] Black Coat Press, ISBNs 978-1-61227-095-1, 978-1-61227-096-8, 978-1-61227-097-5 & 978-1-61227-098-2.

mere gang leader has many interesting ramifications, transforming the nature of his conspiracy and generating precedent-
setting features.

The notion of an evil scientist employing his genius in
the service of a vast criminal enterprise was not entirely new
in 1912, but it must have seemed logical to Le Rouge that anyone trying to run such an enterprise, and make war on a tech-
nologically-progressive society, had to have scientific expertise. That logic was conspicuously lacking in much of the
crime fiction of the times, and as tentative as it appeared in
The Mysterious Doctor Cornelius. Le Rouge was in the fore-
front of the early-20th century evolution of what would eventually become a major literary myth.

Jakob ten Brinken comes from the novel *Alraune* (in
English *The Mandrake*) by German novelist Hanns Heinz Ew-
ers (1911), about the mad doctor's experiment impregnating a
prostitute with the semen of a hanged murderer. The hapless
woman conceives a female child, Alraune, whom ten Brinken
raises. She has no concept of love, and suffers from obsessive
sexuality. After she learns of her unnatural origins, she aveng-
es herself against the scientist.

There have been a number of films based on the novel
including the classic silent film *Unholy Love* (1928), directed
by Henrik Galeen, starring Brigitte Helm as Alraune and Paul
Wegener as ten Brinken, remade two years later with sound as
The Daughter of Evil, directed by Richard Oswald and again
starring Brigitte Helm.

Nanon Zanzi comes from the American silent horror film
The Unknown (1927), directed by Tod Browning and starring
Lon Chaney as carnival knife-thrower Alonzo the Armless (in
one of his best ever performances) and Joan Crawford as the
scantily-clad Nanon Zanzi, the carnival girl he hopes to marry.

Finally, *Giphantie* (1760) by Charles-François Tiphaigne de La Roche (1729-1774)[4] (Giphantie is an anagram of Tiphaigne) is perhaps its author's best-known book. The imaginary landscape it presents is a map of the author's ideas at a time when the distinction between "fiction" and "non-fiction" was not as clear as it is today, and "science fiction" simply did not exist yet.

In *Giphantie*, a group of characters discover the secret land of Giphantie located deep in Africa, where a race of secret supermen lives in majestic isolation. Although *Giphantie* uses the literary device of "Elementary Sprits," it contains another important device which brings it closer to the tradition of scientific romance, the foundations of which it helped to lay. Requiring a synoptic view of human history, in order that the author can comment on its broad shape—in a vein closer to lamentation than satire—Tiphaigne hit on the idea of presenting a series of *tableaux* [pictures] "painted" by light itself, offering a detailed description of a liquid substance that can be used to coat a mirror, so that if it is placed in a dark room to dry out, it will preserve the last image that formed on its illuminated surface: an "invention" that won him a place of honor in modern histories of photography.

Tiphaigne was a proto-scientist, a physician by profession, whose "serious" books were endeavors in natural philosophy and agricultural science, and who imported a considerable amount of that work into his criticisms of contemporary French society. He had undoubtedly read Voltaire's Swiftian satire *Micromégas* (1752), which can be recognized in hindsight as the founding text of French scientific romance, and disapproved of it thoroughly.

Jean-Marc Lofficier

---

[4] Included in *Amilec*, Black Coat Press, ISBN 978-1-61227-033-3.